CW00517750

ONE

OF OUR ELVES IS

MISSING

CHRISTIAN WARREN FREED

Excerpt from *From Whence It Came* 2023 Christian Warren Freed
Cover design by Warren Design
Author Photograph by Anicie Freed

Warfighter Books
Holly Springs, North Carolina 27540
https://www.christianwfreed.com

First Edition: April 2023

Library of Congress Cataloging-in-Publication Data
Name: Freed, Christian Warren, 1973- author.
Title: One of Our Elves is Missing/ Christian Warren Freed
Description: First Edition | Holly Springs, NC: Warfighter Books, 2021. Identifiers: LCCN 2022916396 | ISBN 9781957326290 (trade paperback) | ISBN 9781957326320 (hardcover) | ISBN 9781957326313 (Ebook)
Subjects: Urban Fantasy | Paranormal

Printed in the United States of America

10 9 8 7 6 5 4 3 2 1

DREAMS OF WINTER
A FORGOTTEN GODS TALE #1

'Dreams of Winter is a strong introduction to a new fantasy series that follows slightly in the footsteps of George R.R. Martin in scope.' Entrada Publishing

"Steven Erickson meets George R.R. Martin!"

"THIS IS IT. If you like fantasy and sci-fi, you must read this series."

Law of the Heretic
Immortality Shattered Book I

'If you're looking for a fun and exciting fantasy adventure, spend a few hours in the Free Lands with the Law of the Heretic.'

Where Have All the Elves Gone?

'Sometimes funny and other times a little dark, Where Have The Elves Gone? brings something fresh and new to fantasy mysteries. Whether you want to curl up with a mystery or read more about elves this book has something for everyone. Spend a few hours solving a mystery with a human and a couple of dwarves - you'll be glad you did.'- Entrada Publishing

Other Books by Christian Warren Freed

The Northern Crusade
Hammers in the Wind
Tides of Blood and Steel
A Whisper After Midnight
Empire of Bones
The Madness of Gods and Kings
Even Gods Must Fall

The Histories of Malweir
Armies of the Silver Mage
The Dragon Hunters
Beyond the Edge of Dawn

Forgotten Gods
Dreams of Winter
The Madman on the Rocks
Anguish Once Possessed
Through Darkness Besieged
Under Tattered Banners
A Time for Tyrants*

Where Have All the Elves Gone?
One of Our Elves is Missing
Tomorrow's Demise: The Extinction Campaign
Tomorrow's Demise: Salvation
Coward's Truth
The Lazarus Men
Repercussions: A Lazarus Men Agenda

A Long Way From Home+

Immortality Shattered
Law of the Heretic
The Bitter War of Always
Land of Wicked Shadows

Storm Upon the Dawn

<u>War Priests of Andrak Saga</u>
The Children of Never

SO, You Want to Write a Book? +
SO, You Wrote a Book. Now What? +

*Forthcoming   + Nonfiction

ONE

Israel McFadden hated the creatures he was assigned to ward over. Their very existence haunted him, mocking all he once believed and stood for. To Israel, they belonged in cages. Why he accepted the position in the first place eluded him. Never a great thinker, he was a typical upstate New Yorker trying to make a living. Lacking the splendor and opportunity of the big city, the quiet city of Newburgh left him looking for more.

That "more" came after reading the paper one day. The employment section promised menial work, but one caught Israel's attention. Digging out his best, and only, suit, he headed across the Newburgh-Beacon Bridge and to a nondescript building perched along the Hudson River. After a perfunctory interview, he was hired— immediately then escorted down river to be fitted for uniforms and given a sidearm.

Israel never imagined being a security guard, but the pay and benefits were more than anything he was going to make elsewhere, and, despite his distaste of his current life, he enjoyed where he lived. He was close enough to head down to the City to make some noise but far enough away to live quietly. What more could a man ask for?

Once in processing finished, he was herded into a black van with tinted windows. They sped down Breakneck Rd, aptly named for those unsuspecting travelers who'd met their ends over the past few centuries and pulled into a gravel driveway.

Looking around, Israel was unsure of what needed guarded at the small cottage on the banks of the Hudson.

Confused, they led him inside and down to the basement. His nerves threatened to get the best of him then as his imagination ran wild. Israel wanted to bolt and would have if not for the pair of armed guards following him. A woman in a dark suit, long blonde hair tied back in a tight bun and bearing a severe look, waited in the small room below. She nodded at him before pushing a button beside the fireplace—Israel's eyes widened. The wall shifted, revealing another passage.

He followed the woman down a small flight of stairs that deposited them in the mouth of a tunnel. An elongated golf cart sat, waiting.

Three years later and he had decided he hated his job.

***

Lunch clutched in an old school pail at his side, Israel stepped out of the cart after it pulled to a stop. He nodded to his counterparts on the nightshift as they stumbled past, yawning. Never the sort to make friends easy, Israel decided long ago to keep his head down and do his job. Hurrying to his locker to change, he stowed his lunch and slipped his military issue utility belt on, checking the charge on his stun gun. One last glance at the clock and he was off to start his shift.

The fact that Israel worked on Pollepel Island, or rather under the abandoned Bannerman Castle, no longer phased him. The former military surplus warehouse changed hands from the late Francis Bannerman to the state of New York over a century ago. Why the federal government bought it was a secret no one was willing to divulge. And Israel didn't care. He never cared much for history: let the past stay there was his motto. His only concern was with the prisoners housed in the depths of the maximum security penitentiary nicknamed the "Grinder" by its employees.

Veteran wardens assured him the worst offenders in history were kept locked in their cells, far below the sun's warm kiss. Israel found no reason for doubt. Every day he made the rounds, all occupants eager to beak free and, if promises were to be believed, wring his neck before ripping his spine out through his ass. Visuals more than enough, Israel vowed to do his best to prevent that from happening.

An alarm buzzed as the three foot thick door slid open. Israel stepped into the main passage and avoiding eye contact with any cells. Forcefields accented the steel bars securing the prisoners. Forcefields ... Growing up reading campy science fiction magazines awakened an active imagination but he never supposed the government was developing such far-out technologies. Of which he could never speak a word of, lest he share the same fate as the miserable creatures arrayed before him.

"You haven't been fired yet?"

Israel flinched at the rumbling voice as he passed the cell of a particularly nasty ogre responsible for slaughtering several herds of cattle, most of a poultry farm, and three innocent hikers in the Idaho reaches of the Rocky Mountains.

"I'll get fired the day they release you, Ogden," Israel retorted back.

Taunting became a daily ritual. With little else to occupy their time, these immortal creatures attempted to make the most of their incarceration by picking apart the guards. No harm in words, Israel's mother always told him. Laughter followed him down the hall, each foul note digging into his skin. A panoply of threats trailed after him before Israel gained the presumed safety of the central guard hub. Closing the door behind him, he leaned back and exhaled.

"You still let them get to you?"

3

Not this again. "You can't tell me you're immune to it, Dawes."

"Doesn't matter if I am or not. I get a kick out of watching you squirm." Grinning, the man turned away. "Sign in and make your first rounds."

Israel was no fan of Sergeant Dawes. The sergeant was just as mean as some of the prisoners, with his leering grin and single gold tooth. Tattoos on the back of his hands offered the dichotomy of heaven and hell yet for all his bluster, Israel doubted Dawes had ever been in a real scrape. Still, the disturbed man was his superior and until word of promotion or reassignment came down through channels, the one person Israel needed to listen to.

Clipping the pen on the clipboard, he headed out the door wondering why they continued using archaic items like stun guns and bullets when they had forcefields. The constant hum of generators deep beneath the Hudson River was a boon companion these days. Winter was approaching and soon, if it got nasty enough, the river would freeze over enough it could be walked across. He'd never tried that, but he heard rumors of cadets from the United States Military Academy, located less than a mile down river, being so bold. And they were the future leaders of the nation—Israel scoffed, feeling the first bead of sweat form on his brow.

The time for bemusement ended as he entered the next section on his rounds. Israel clutched the grip of his baton. Raw power emanated from the darkest cells. He never managed a glimpse of either occupant for impenetrable darkness swathed the adjoining cells. The longer he worked at the Grinder the less inclined he was to discover whatever hid in the darkness.

Israel walked faster, ignoring the subtle whispers in the cobwebbed corners of his mind, and was soon past their corrupting influence.

Rocks walls flanked him as he plunged deeper into the prison. An odd assortment of dwarves, elves, gnomes, and trolls spit at him, flipped him off, and offered curses. A gnome threw his customary handful of scat and snarled. The small man never spoke, prompting Israel to wonder what crimes he was accused of. He wasn't foolish enough to ask.

Of the one thousand and seventy-two souls incarcerated in the Grinder, only two treated him with any respect.

The first was a toothless old goblin with more lines on his face than a contour map and a penchant for playing chess. Hobbling with a crooked cane, the wizened creature was forty-seven wins into an unbeaten streak against Israel. Acknowledging chess wasn't a strength, the security guard felt he improved with each defeat, humiliating as it was. The board was set up in the hall, Israel moving towards the goblin that waited.

"Good morning, Edrich," he said.

The goblin's eyes, dulled from centuries of use, lit up at the sound of his voice. "Young McFadden, morning already is it?"

"Same time every day," Israel replied, smiling. "Get anything new to read overnight?"

The goblin shook his head. "Still dissecting your Bible. Fascinating book, though I don't recall many of the actual events happening the way they are described. Perhaps one day I can finally put this to rest and start easier reading. I've had my eye on the *Silmarillion* for quite some time now."

Israel didn't know what that was and wasn't interested to find out. A look down confirmed the chess board was reset. Time to begin his quest to end the losing streak.

Israel pushed the queen's pawn forward two spaces.

"Have a nice day, Edrich," Israel called over his shoulder as he continued down the hall a short time later.

"Mind yourself, young man. There's a fell tide on the wind," the goblin called after him.

Not understanding what any of that meant, Israel kept walking. He paused to return the glares of a trio of particularly angry dwarves, though his experience suggested every dwarf was angry. Perhaps it had to do with their height. Staring past their bulging muscles, Israel was reminded of old prison movies where the neo-Nazis lifted weights all day and stood around looking menacing. It wasn't a stretch to imagine the dwarves as part of that crowd.

"Keep smiling, pretty boy. I'll knock those fucking teeth down your throat," one growled. "All you got to do is open the door."

"Still don't have stupid written on my forehead, Lars," Israel replied. "Maybe tomorrow."

"Fuck you."

Petty words aside, Israel was terrified of the dwarves. They promised violence on an impressive level. Should they ever get free …

The rock face gave way to reinforced titanium, signifying the start to the most dangerous inmates in the prison. He never enjoyed coming down here, so far from help should anything go wrong. Of course the thought was infantile. They were deep underground in one of the most secure locations run by the Department of Extra Species Affairs, DESA for short. The entire prison was trouble.

Israel reached the end of the hall where a single occupied cell faced him. There, sitting cross legged on his bed, was a slender elf warrior. His eyes were closed, with the backs of his hands on his knees, open palms facing up. Long, raven black hair draped over his shoulders. Sinewy and lightly muscled, he was everything Israel wasn't. There was a quiet lethality about the elf, one inspiring fear deep within Israel's soul. If ever a being should be called an apex predator, it was this man.

An ear rose, the pointed tip moving his hair as Israel approached. He was one of the newer prisoners. Some high-profile case with a sealed file. That alone gave Israel pause. Creatures like this weren't meant to be entertained by mere guards. Yet whereas the other inmates offered death threats and thoroughly unrealistic sexual opportunities with his mother, this one man treated him with kindness.

Today, something felt off and Israel didn't know why.

"Good morning, Agent McFadden," the elf said without opening his eyes.

Israel swallowed the unexpected lump in his throat. "Good morning, Xander."

TWO

Prison life had not been kind to Xander. The now infamous accomplice to the murder of the High Elf king, he took the blame for all that had happened in North Carolina five years earlier. Regardless that he had been helping Gwen, the would-be heir to the throne, in her coup attempt. Xander kept his mouth shut during their clandestine trial and Gwen was only too happy to let him bear the brunt of the scrutiny. Their long game might have ended in failure, but the king was dead, and the queen left toothless.

For his part, Xander cared little for the politics of it. He was a loyal soldier to the High Elf throne and the betrothed to the heir apparent, well, former heir. Watching from his cell, Xander saw Gwen stripped of her crown, titles, and lands, leaving her bereft and little more than a commoner. A quick guilty verdict later and she was being carted off to another secure location far from him. Elven authorities, at the behest of DESA lawyers, decided they were too volatile to remain together.

Rumors reached him of a power vacuum filling the void. Smaller clans and families broke away from the light and dark factions, turning the quest for the throne into a muddled arena from which no clear winner would ever be decided. While not their plan, Xander couldn't help but feel bemused at the pettiness of his people. His sister was dead, he was a convicted criminal, and the prospect of living several millennia more left a foul taste in his mouth. The only factor making it worse was the testimony of the inept human Daniel Thomas.

Whatever his appeal was with Xander's sister was lost on him. The man made a living off writing nonsensical stories based on his people. The insult alone was worthy of execution, but the elven communities embraced the man, making him a bestselling author for over a decade. A never-ending joke on a cosmic level. Xander hated the man more than anyone in centuries and vowed to get his revenge.

"Today promises to be extraordinary, Israel," he said, eyes squeezed shut.

"What makes today so special? It's another Monday morning. The Jets lost and I'm out fifty bucks."

"Tsk, tsk, Israel. When are you going to learn to stop wasting money on that team? They're not terribly accomplished for all the talent they've had through the years," Xander chided.

Israel shrugged. "Namath's curse. One of these days I'll be right. You'll see. The Big Green are going to take the trophy and shut the world up."

Admiring the man's pointless optimism, Xander repressed a smile. He liked the down on his luck security guard, making what had to come next more difficult.

"I had hoped you were taking the day off."

"Why is that?"

"Because I like you, Israel. I truly do," Xander said. "And I'm sorry."

Israel's eyes partially closed, suddenly wary. He took a half step back, hand falling to his stun gun. "For wha—"

The forcefield flickered before fizzling out with an exaggerated groan of melting electronics.

The cage was open.

Freedom beckoned.

Israel was struggling to comprehend what was happening, taking too long. Xander was on his feet, crossing the space between them in three strides and slamming a ridge hand into the side of Israel's neck before the man had a chance.

Checking that he still had a pulse, Xander patted him on the chest. "I truly am sorry. None of the other guards intrigue me like you. Perhaps you will find a healthier job after this."

Straightening, Xander checked the long corridor stretching back to the command room. Time was of the essence and, true to promises that had been recently made, no alarms sounded after the forcefield's collapse. No additional guards were scheduled to make their rounds this way for another four hours, giving him time to collect his thoughts and cycle through the plan, again.

Pacing ten steps up the corridor, Xander found the false panel in the wall and pressed. A click and the whirl of gears later revealed the hidden passageway.

Expecting a trap, he, once a champion of the light, ducked into the beckoning darkness. The panel slide shut behind, leaving him with but one way—forward. His natural night vision kicked in quickly and he was moving. The passage was barely wide enough for him and, in several places, he was forced to turn sideways or duck to avoid striking his head on questing roots or exposed rocks. The earth smelled damp, almost moldy. He imagined the sound of rushing water, frowning at the thought of gallons of dirty water overhead. Freedom beckoned but had only become possible in the last months.

Turning one of the guards hadn't been overly difficult. Xander took advantage of their loose morale code and empty wallets to make the promise of vast riches and a lifetime of contentment to gain access to the outside world and his freedom. There was still plenty of time for something to go wrong, to be the victim of betrayal, or worse, but Xander refused to spend another miserable day trapped in isolation. He was a creature eternal, a knight of the realm of fairy, not some dirt chewing dwarf content to sniff his own shit in the forgotten confines of the twilight world.

He picked up the pace, unused muscles burning.

He was going uphill, out from under the watery prison, but to where? Xander finished counting to one thousand and reached out to touch the damp mud wall blocking his path.

Nothing happened.

It took little imagination to envision a host of leering guards filing up the tunnel behind him with more than stun guns. It was then Xander realized immortality was the cruelest joke of all. He might live forever but could still be killed by any manner of ways. The irony mocked him.

Pushing harder, hands fumbling, Xander was at last rewarded with finding the lever to open the door. Blinding light flooded in, forcing him to throw a hand in front of his face as he turned away. The pain burned as he was blessed by the sun's sweet kiss for the first time in years. Blinking to regain his vision, Xander stepped out into the world as freedom wrapped welcoming arms around him.

Stumbling the first few steps, Xander leaned against a thin maple. Black spots danced across his eyes, fading with each passing second before he was afforded the opportunity to take in his surroundings. The ruins of an old castle stretched high above him. Ivy and vines crept across the façade suggesting the absence of any physical presence for a long time. Flowing water was on either side.

An island. He was on an island.

Clever bastards. Xander appreciated the efforts the government went through to establish their tiny hell.

Looking downstream he spied a series of buildings on the bend in the river. Another government facility? Or the quiet sweep of a university? He knew not and turned his gaze north. A large bridge stretched across the river. To the left sat a small marina filled with boats. Getting there, with the distance and current working against him, would prove a challenge and, in his weakened condition, was not possible.

The hoot of a train horn bellowed. Xander's head snapped to the sound, and he was rewarded by witnessing the barreling monstrosity emerge from the mouth of a tunnel to his right. Faces dotted every window, suggesting he was nearby a major population center. Then he spied them. A pair of men dressed as 1800s whalers sitting in a small dingy nearby. Dark skin and filthy clothing, the smaller one caught his attention and beckoned him.

Xander closed the tunnel door and hurried over. A reek settled over the boat. The fetid stench of men who lacked a relationship with cleanliness surrounded him. Unable to contain his disdain, he halted on the shoreline. Brackish water sloshed against the rocks and onto his shoes.

"Hurry, man! We don't have all day!" hissed the beckoner.

The second added, "Hurry! We can't get paid until you get delivered!"

Mercenaries. Xander scowled. Worse, they were gnomes. Oh how he despised these money hungry creatures. "Where are you taking me?"

"We got our orders."

The beckoner smirked. "Don't you worry about that."

"I'm not going anywhere until you tell me where we are going," Xander snapped.

The gnomes exchanged worried looks.

"Listen to this one! Free ten seconds and the convict thinks he's a prince."

The beckoner shrugged. "Snooty, isn't he? Maybe your highness will like it better back in your cell?"

Xander snatched the man by the throat, ignoring the host of insects crawling through the gnome's mangy beard. The second gnome squawked, oar splashing as he leaned away.

"Perhaps I did not make myself clear. My name is Xander, and I wish to know where you are taking me."

The snarl in his voice produced the scent of warm urine trickling in the boat. Xander's scowl deepened as he shoved the gnome back. Like it or not, they were his only means off the island.

"Xander! We're sorry!"

"Yeah, didn't mean no harm by it. Orders is orders, you know?"

"They said wait here at this time and escort a prisoner across the river," the urine-soaked gnome added, and the other bobbed his head.

"Answer my question or I'll kill you both," Xander growled.

Years of pent-up frustration threatened to break free. Never the one for words games, Xander was a straightforward man. He lacked the subtly of speaking around the point, preferring to remain direct to a fault. Such was expected of true champions. Such had been expected of him once.

"Okay, okay. There's a van waiting for you on the other side of the river."

"Said if we didn't deliver they was going to kill our families."

The beckoner grimaced. "You got some nasty friends, Xander."

Friends? He didn't think he had any left after the botched coup attempt. Resigned, Xander stepped into the boat, throwing his hands out for balance as it rocked beneath him. The dingy groaned under his additional weight and he was convinced they were going to sink well before the gnomes rowed across to the rendezvous point.

Friends ... The nature of his escape, complicated enough, grew more so as his mind raced through the possibilities awaiting him. Committed, he settled in for what promised to be an uncomfortable trip. No one had told him anything other than he was to escape on this day. The rest, it was promised, would be explained once he was free.

One of the gnomes thrust a dusty brown jacket at him. "Put this on. Can't have you going about in your prison clothes."

"No. Won't do at all."

Xander became aware of his state of dress then. The bright orange jumpsuit shouted "convict" and was perhaps the most recognized uniform in the western world. It took great effort, and more than a little convincing, to slip his arms into the garment. Xander gagged at the stench, silently cursing his "friend" for procuring the resources of a pair of gnomes to make his escape. A hat, filled with holes, strands of hair, and other items he lacked the desire to learn more about, dropped into his lap.

It wasn't much of a disguise, but it would do.

The dingy rowed out into the mighty Hudson River and a pair of gnomes began their battle with the current. *Stupid fools. They couldn't have brought a boat with a motor?* Xander closed his eyes and attempted to recenter himself, ever thankful his passage went unnoticed by those who knew him.

Or so he thought.

THREE

Wind blowing, water sloshing, Xander couldn't recall ever feeling seasick … until now. His stomach heaved, threatening to rush up through his throat to deposit in the Hudson. Why the gnomes, he hadn't bothered learning their names, were taking him to the distant shore instead of the one close at hand was lost on him. Trusting others proved difficult under normal circumstances yet he was forced to rely on a pair of dimwits to get him to safety. He prayed they knew what they were doing.

Or else.

Inch by inch the dingy drew nearer to shore. Focusing on his surroundings rather than his rebellious stomach, Xander took in the scenery.

A marina now sat off to his right. The small boats rocking with the waves. Nestled between mountains, he spied houses dotting the landscape, hidden amongst the myriad of red, yellow, and orange leaves. Fall was here and with it the crisp chill of winter's promise. Never one for the cold, he longed for days of gentler climates, before humans overtook the world and began their reign of pollution. Of course there were no humans during the last great ice age, and the world froze. Perhaps it would again one day again.

"Can't you row faster?" he asked through clenched teeth.

"Can't."

"Nope. The river is too strong. Never you worry. We'll get you where you need going."

Marveling at their, he supposed, feigned idiocy, Xander gripped the gunwales tighter.

15

The dingy eventually pushed onto shore, not beside one of the inviting wooden piers of the marina, Xander noted with dismay, but the wild, untamed shoreline of uninhabited wilderness. The distant drone of engines told him he was far from being alone however, forcing him to reevaluate his situation.

He no longer expected pursuit. Israel should have awakened by now and would be running back to his superiors, but his story would fall upon deaf ears until supervisors were forced to examine the unsavory character of one Sergeant Dawes. No riches and retirement for him, Xander chuckled. How easily mortals were led astray by shiny objects.

Rising on shaky legs, he stepped onto free soil for the first time in years and gave the gnomes a cursory glance, noticing how neither moved to follow. "Still not going to tell me where I am?"

One shrugged. "Not our place. Boss will be here soon to get you."

"Nope. Not our place at all. Take care."

And with that they shoved back off, as if desperate to get as far away from him.

Frustrated, Xander watched until they were back in the channel and the current took them downriver. He exhaled a deep breath, jammed his hands in the foul jacket pockets, and turned around.

A railroad was behind him, matching the one on the opposite shore. Deciding he'd done enough waiting, Xander began strolling west, away from the river. He came upon a road not long after and looked north and south. No cars. No foot traffic. He refused to believe he was alone. Luck was never so easygoing.

Then he spied it. The dull red glow of taillights from a car wedged among the brush. A thin plume of smoke pumped from the exhaust pipe beneath a New York state license plate.

Xander headed for the car. Regardless of whether it was here for him, he planned on taking the vehicle and making good his escape. Both front doors opened when he was within five meters. He halted, longing for a weapon. Two figures emerged. Both were dressed similar, wearing dark clothing with heavy sweaters barely concealing the bulge of holsters. One was a man. The other an elf.

"It's about time those damned gnomes delivered you," the man growled.

Sending a frown at his companion, the elf turned to Xander. "We've been sent to escort you away from here and to a secure location."

Sent by whom? Why won't anyone give me the straight information? I'm tired of being marginalized. Has so much changed since my incarceration?

The human made a show of checking his watch, a cheap brand on a plastic band. "Time's wasting. We don't have long."

Filled with questions and growing increasingly frustrated, Xander shed the filthy jacket and hat, orange jumpsuit be damned, and got in the back seat. The time for subterfuge was over. He was tired of playing by the rules of others. Opening his mouth to bark at his rescuers, a thought came to him. What if the balance of power had shifted so much during the years of his imprisonment he was no longer considered relevant?

The thought proved sobering. Xander had been at the top of the food chain for centuries. But was it him or his acquaintance with the princess that kept him there? Closing his mouth, he sat back in the faux leather seat to think.

The king was dead, though Alvin's time ended long before he was stabbed in the back by his beloved daughter. Xander and Gwen took the fall for the assassination but their quest to overthrow the monarchy failed. Gwen's mother remained and the queen of the dark elves was a spiteful woman. No doubt Morgen remained in her lofty lair high above the city, plotting and planning. He was beginning to think he and Gwen had been played from the start.

Was their, presumed, carefully cultivated plan to usurp the light elf clans all a ruse instigated by Morgen? Since splitting with her husband and taking half the clans with her, the queen had been on a crusade more vindictive than any in history. She alone plunged their kind into an endless series of wars from which there seemed no escape. The thought of being a dupe, set up and sacrificed awakened both terror and anger in him. They should have killed her when they had the chance, instead the queen continued playing out the long game in safety.

Xander glanced at the small brick bar as they drove by it. No lights, no vehicles in the parking lot. "The Old Castaways" said the sign, but the name meant nothing to him. He guessed, from the size of the river and the car's license plate he was somewhere in New York, most likely along the Hudson since it was the only major river flowing north and south in the state. *But where? How far north?* Neither man in the front seemed inclined to discuss anything with him, leaving Xander simmering in a foul mood.

The car drove on and soon they merged onto a larger highway, heading north. 9W was lightly trafficked at this time of day. And instead of staying on the main road, they took a right and headed downhill. Xander spied flashes of the Hudson peeking through trees. A short trip later they emerged in a quaint waterfront area filled with shops and restaurants.

Were circumstances different he might have enjoyed a summer afternoon here, watching the gulls swoop in and families playing in the small park under the ever watchful gaze of the massive bridge high above. They hit a pothole and Xander felt something bump against his leg, a duffle bag.

"You have a change of clothes, shoes, and a jacket in there," the elf commented, holding out the bag. "It would be best if you changed before your meeting with the boss."

Boss? Scowling, Xander unzipped his jumpsuit.

The car pulled to a stop not long after he finished changing. He was certain they drove around the block once to give him time to become presentable for whoever his mystery benefactor was.

Finishing tying the last shoe, Xander felt decent for the first time in years. The clothes, while far from being fashion forward, were the perfect fit and lent him an air of respectability. At someone understood his importance. The prospect of being led to the slaughter though remained in the back of his mind. It didn't take much self-awareness to recognize he was not the man he once was.

The elf exited the car and hurried to open Xander's door. Without a word exchanged, Xander climbed out and followed the elf's pointing hand.

A small park was before him. He spied a lone man on the far side of a statue ringed with plants and an iron fence. A few civilians milled about. There were power walkers out for their morning exercise. Some teens skipping school and trying to figure out where to go for the rest of the day. A pair of mothers entered the park, pushing strollers, their faces were blank behind the dark of their sunglasses.

It was just another day along the Hudson. No one paid much attention to anyone else. One of society's great downfalls was the trend toward self-obsession through contrived conveniences like social media and the false feeling of being important to strangers. Xander never understood it but used those same networks to manipulate his way to within a step of the throne. Some games were worth being played.

Pulling his light jacket's collar closer to his neck to keep out the lusting gusts of wind, Xander gave the elf a final look. "What clan are you from? I don't recognize you."

The elf shrugged, the corner of his mouth ticking up. "Doesn't matter. We're all here for the same cause." He nodded in the direction he had pointed. "The boss doesn't like to be kept waiting."

"No one does," Xander retorted in a heated tone. "One last thing," he looked back at the car and distracted driver behind the wheel, "why are you working with a human? When did they become our allies?"

"These are desperate times, Champion. You'll soon find out ... You should go. I like my job and prefer keeping my head attached to my shoulders."

Unsatisfied with the answers, Xander scrunched his face and headed toward the lone man. Back to him, there was nothing about the man to indicate who or what he was. A long, black trench coat draped down to midcalf, leading to a pair of impeccably shined leather shoes. His hands were in his pockets.

A waft of cologne weighed the air the closer Xander got. The smell was almost alien after so many days locked away in the Grinder. The man's hair was streaked through with grey and impeccably maintained.

Xander was unable to make out any other distinguishing characteristics. He could have been one of a million men.

Xander halted a few steps away, keeping the man's back to him.

"I trust your journey here was without peril." The man's soft yet stern voice carried on the wind.

Xander stiffened. He recognized it but failed to put a name to it. "Enough. Who are you and why am I here?"

"You have always been impetuous. Ever since I first met you you've provided more than your share of opportunity for me to shake my head. Yet here we are."

"Answer my questions or I walk," Xander snapped.

Grunting, the man slowly turned, giving Xander his first look at a face he hadn't seen in a thousand years.

"Shit."

FOUR

"Shit indeed, Xander." The man smiled. "Welcome back. It has been far too long."

Face pale, Xander swallowed the nervous spittle choking him. *Not long enough for me. Not by a longshot.*

A trio of gulls swooped down, landing on the statue's outstretched arm. They cocked their heads, as if interested in the fateful meeting. The slop of the tide rivaled their strangled cries, threatening to distract him. So many clashing sights and sounds after years of isolation left him disoriented, but not enough to ignore the threat standing before him.

"I seem to recall our last meeting on less than favorable terms," Xander said.

Basil Kadis broke into a predatory grin. The pointed tips of his teeth showing. "For you perhaps. Those events worked out splendidly for me."

The prime minister of the high elf clans, Basil was, in Xander's opinion, the worst of them. Not a royal or a soldier, the man was a professional bureaucrat. Their history stretched back to the schism ripping so many families apart. Xander, ever the loyal soldier, found himself at odds with the man from the start.

"I assume I have you to thank for this morning," Xander said.

"You do," Basil replied. He lifted his gaze to the statue of Christopher Columbus, arm pointed out over the river. "Fascinating how mankind is determined to immortalize legacies for trivial matters. Do you remember when the Europeans first came to these shores, believing themselves to be discoverers? Arrogance is ever a flaw."

"What do you want, Basil?" Xander, growing impatient, demanded.

"I'm sorry. I didn't realize you had somewhere else to be," the prime minister snapped. "I freed you for one purpose only, regardless of whatever ideations you may have." At his wince, Basil tsked. "Oh yes, I know of your petty quest for revenge in the hopes of reuniting with your beloved Gwen. Would it sadden you to learn the princess is scheduled to be married to a more suitable heir?"

The man must be mistaken. Theirs was a love capable of withstanding eternity. For this information to be true Gwen must have been in extreme distress. *Or manipulated by her mother. Yet again.*

"Did you break me out just to gloat? If so, you can put me back in my cell and schedule a regular visitation," Xander said, tone dry.

Basil sniffed at the threat but waved him off. "We have more important matters facing us, Xander. A war is coming. One I am afraid neither side is ready for."

Placing personal desires on the backburner, Xander waited for him to continue.

"Alvin's … death has left a power vacuum among the clans. Morgen has gone into seclusion. If she has interest in retaining the throne she has yet to show it. The clans are splitting. Factions emerge to contest for succession. The old battle lines are fragmented, threatening to unravel all we have worked so hard to achieve. A new order rises, and I am in need of allies. Even ones who are old enemies."

Xander barked a laugh. "You expect me to help you? A few years ago you would have had my head but now, when the world seems lost, you come begging for me, the champion. Ha! The irony soothes me, Basil. What if I say no?"

Basil slightly tilted his head, eyes shifting. Xander followed his gaze and was not surprised to find the long, dark barrel of a rifle poking over the lip of a nearby restaurant's roof. Some questions didn't need asking.

"Fair enough. What are you asking?"

A smug look on Basil's face. "Simple. I need you to eliminate several key members of the opposition forces. These insurgents are much too dangerous to be allowed to live. Should they succeed, we will lose everything."

"I'm not an assassin. There are others for that." The thought of gunning down unsuspecting men and women went against all he was taught and trained to believe. Xander prided himself on a strict set of morals rising above the petty squabbles of the clans and family rivalries. As Champion, it was his role to defend the throne from all threats. That understanding threatened the careful balance he created in his mind, opening doors of thought where none should have been.

"Indeed, but none with your intimate knowledge of the clans," Basil replied. "Making you indispensable for this task." The prime minister leaned closer. "Xander, we have our differences and I admit I will never embrace you as a brother, but this could be the end of us. If the throne is destroyed, the royal bloodline extinguished, we will become little more than an abandoned footnote in history. Tens of thousands of years of struggle lost in the blink of an eye. Are you willing to accept that?"

Once again, Xander felt all choice was robbed from him. He was being thrust back into the realm of political intrigue, complete with the requisite backstabbing, plotting, and viciousness he and Gwen once vowed to eliminate.

"When was the last time our race proved worthy of remembrance?"

Basil stiffened. "Proud words considering you were convicted of regicide."

"I didn't kill hi—"

"I thought as much. Thank you for that, Champion."

Basil's leer was a monstrous sight to behold and Xander flinched.

"There. You see. You can be reasonable. I've long believed it was the loving daughter who plunged the blade in her father's back, despite your testimony and willingness to play the dupe. She will be dealt with later.

"Of course, should you agree to assist me in this matter I might find a way to keep the princess from the center of scrutiny. Provided you successful complete your assigned tasks," Basil grinned.

A sinking feeling plunged through Xander's core. He was trapped, with no logical escape. He was faced with the prospect of owing the monster before him, an elf who spent decades plotting to ruin him, for the sake of a woman's love. Xander was forced into an enviable position. He must abandon his quest for revenge and, potentially lose the woman he loved to sate the prime minister's needs or face summary execution.

"How long do I have to decide?" His voice projected defeat, a feeling he was unaccustomed to.

"I need to know now." Basil's dark grey eyes swept back and forth over Xander's face, studying for facial tics, the rise and fall of muscles as the internal debate played out. It was a game he played innumerable times, always ending the victor—Xander would know. Basil Kadis was a man used to winning. During those rare occasions where he didn't get his way his opponents were quietly disposed of.

Xander's shoulders dropped in defeat. "Fine. I'll do it."

"Smart man," Basil remarked. "My men will take you to a nearby hotel so you can clean up. You reek of prison. Once there you will be provided with dossiers on each target. The mission shouldn't take too long to complete. Do this for me, for the clans, and your debt will be cleared."

"If I fail?" Xander asked.

Basil Kadis walked away without answering.

***

Standing beneath the torrent of hot water, Xander placed his hands on the shower wall and lowered his head. It was good to feel normal again, even if it was through the simplicity of a shower. Water poured through his hair, covering his face and forcing his eyes closed. The strange sensation of pressure on his eyelids reminded him of those first dark moments after the trial. How his freedom was systemically stripped away, debasing every ounce of individuality he once enjoyed.

Clothes were taken and burned. He was forced into the unflattering orange jumpsuit, a uniform he maintained for years with coiled frustration. Colognes and perfumes were replaced by the natural stench of body odor. His skin took a mottle hue without exposure to sunlight. Abject misery threatened to rob him of sanity, forcing him to the edges of a realm he was loath to explore. The travesty of having his world reduced to a ten by ten cell, when once he roamed the world at whim, proved the most damaging to his psyche.

Xander opened his mouth, luxuriating at the water flowing over his lips. Steam clung to the ceiling in thick clouds. The sensation so enthralling he considered draining the hotel of its hot water, or at least give it his best effort.

He felt the filth of the Grinder washing away. Leaving him with a far greater conundrum: Basil Kadis and his proposal.

After drying off and wrapping a towel around his waist, Xander strolled through the room, opening the shades to reveal the greyish-blue hue of the autumn sky. *They couldn't have freed me in the middle of summer ...* Muted sunlight flooded the room. It would have to do.

Xander clicked on the television, scrolling through the channels until he found the news. Mortal affairs seldom interested him, but there were morsels to be gleaned between the lines of several stories. One only needed to know how to read them. Not finding a story worthy of his attention, he blew out the breath lingering deep within since leaving the Grinder and looked down.

A pile of manilla folders sat on the small desk beside the television. The dossiers. Blowing out his frustration, Xander decided to dress first. He looked to the new suit laid out on the end of the bed, complete with belt and polished shoes.

Say what you will about Basil's pomposity, the man knew quality. Slipping into black slacks and a loose-fitting white shirt, Xander buckled the belt and ran a hand over the flat of his stomach. It felt good to be alive again, if slightly malnourished and stifled from lack of exercise or sunlight.

The growl trolling through his stomach reminded him he hadn't eaten since last night. Already late morning, Xander called down for the only meal that felt fitting and was prevalent on the limited menu.

Waiting for his cheeseburger, Xander made a cup of coffee. It was the one human vice he enjoyed without complaint. Soon the rich aroma filled the room. Luxuriating as it was, he could no longer ignore the files demanding his attention. Frowning, he snatched the first one and flipped it open.

"Albus Turin," he muttered.

The name meant nothing. He didn't recognize the man. Nor would he any of the others, he supposed. Basil was ruthless with a clear agenda. Xander imagined each target in the packet was either a rival or a threat. Eliminating them, if Basil's word was true, would preserve the hierarchy, but would also leave the prime minister at the top of the food chain. With the king dead and no strong competition remaining, Basil Kadis was poised to reign for many years. Xander felt that familiar bad taste in his mouth and the first inkling of a plan to ensure Basil remained in his station formed.

"What have I gotten myself into?" he asked, closing the file and tossing it back on the stack. Rubbing his face, he reached for another.

Twenty names.

Twenty victims.

He did not doubt their guilt in what they planned, only the manner in which were to be dealt with. Prison life gave Xander plenty of time to reflect upon his own deeds, offering suggestions for a better way to live. Admitting he was a victim to his own desires was the first step. The marriage to Gwen, now unbalanced if what Basil said was true, drove him to acts of what could only be termed as despair. In those moments of plotting, he abandoned the principles that made him the elves' Champion and became a monster bent on self-service.

He'd do what Basil asked, clear his name and resume his place among the clans but he'd do it his way. The world was vast and filled with places to evade inquisitive eyes. If escape was not possible, given the prime minister's global influence, there were other ways to disappear.

The road to redemption was a long one and he had just taken his first steps. The day promised to be bright after all.

FIVE

"Thanks for coming out and thank you for being a loyal reader."

Daniel Thomas scrawled his name on the title page of his latest novel, *Plight of the Dark Elf*, and slid the book across the table to the young lady. He absorbed the giddy look etched upon her face as she picked the book up and cradled it like a newborn.

The look of raw joy filled him with vigor. Once down and out, thrust aside by the torrent waves of sparkly vampires and teenage nonsense, okay perhaps not nonsense but certainly nothing he found enthralling or enjoyable, Daniel's literary career found new life and he was maximizing it while he could.

Spending the last two hours signing who knows how many copies of his new book to fans, some new and some old, awakened feelings he once took for granted during his hay day. It wasn't always such. There were several years of floundering thrown between patches of success. The book industry was ruthless, downright brutal on occasion and, as a former soldier, he was often the victim of his own frustrations and hardheadedness.

No one ever told him how to be a normal person again and he was a man too proud to admit when he wasn't doing something right. Most of the time. Having been a few years since he last donned a uniform, Daniel made every mistake possible during his trek to become a bestselling author. Then came the Raleigh incident a few years ago. Not only did he learn all those fantastical creatures he wrote about existed, but they walked among us in plain sight, and no one was the wiser.

It took months to get used to the idea and, despite his harrowing adventure ending at the North Carolina Zoo resulting in the murder of the king of the light elves, Daniel found himself slowly being pulled into that world. Discovering he was famous among the elves, dwarves, and what have you's was an added bonus, even though they viewed his work as comedy rather than the action/adventure it was meant to be.

A cramp in his signing hand forced him to set the pen down as the lady walked away. She presented the autographed copy to her waiting friends standing outside and began a babbling conversation he couldn't make out—Daniel finally remembered what being an author was supposed to be.

The store manager approached him. Pushing her glasses up her nose, she said, "That was incredible! I can't believe we had so many people show up."

Daniel shrugged. "What can I say?"

The truth was, he hadn't been expecting anyone. Signings were hit or miss. His first one, at a quiet bookstore on the North Carolina coast, resulted in no one showing up for two hours and a lonely hundred mile trip home into the setting sun. Tonight, at the premier store in the heart of Raleigh's Village District, he not only sold out, but was left with the promise of returning as soon as his next book was released.

Life was good.

"I want to thank you for stopping by. You were a hit today."

"Thanks for having me. I admit, I wasn't expecting much. This blew me away," he replied. "When's the next one?"

She laughed. "Write the book first and we'll talk. Have a great day, Daniel."

"You too."

Daniel started collecting the remaining bookmarks and stickers on the table. He had another event in a few weeks down the road in Fayetteville and these things costed money. By no means struggling, he wasn't drowning in wealth either. He liked to think he was comfortable and that was enough. Slipping his pen in his bag, Daniel stretched his shoulders and rose. That's when he spied the lanky man looking in through the window.

Shit.

"Thank you again. I appreciate the opportunity," he called to the staff, shouldering his bag, and heading for the inevitable meeting outside.

The sun was bright and shining. The product of living in the south. October was in full swing, and it was still in the mid-70s with just a hint of rain lingering on the horizon. Daniel couldn't have picked a better place, at least not in the continental United States, to retire.

Exiting the bookstore, he took a sharp right in the pointless attempt at avoiding the man.

"Aren't you a little old for that, Daniel?"

He made it three strides before stopping. "You people know how to ruin a day."

"I just do what I'm told. I see you're doing well for yourself. Back on the top of the charts."

Daniel spun. "You're a long way from Washington, Blackmere."

Agent Thaddeus Blackmere, sharply dressed in a bureaucrat's dark suit and wearing a deadpan look, gestured with open hands. "We go where we're told. Speaking of which, I have need of your unique talents."

"Forget it."

"I wish I could, but you signed the contract. You and your wife both."

Daniel's anger rose. Threatening him was one matter, going after his wife was another. Jabbing a quivering finger at the agent, he snapped, "Stay away from her. She's got nothing to do with whatever nonsense you are trying to drag me into, Blackmere. I'm warning you."

If Blackmere was impressed, he failed to show it. The disinterested look scrawled across his face was akin to feigning excitement watching paint dry.

"Xander has escaped."

Daniel froze. The name inspired a range of emotions, each vying for supremacy. Xander was, by all means, the most dangerous man in either camp of elves and he vowed revenge against those who put him behind bars ...specifically one Daniel and Sara Thomas."

"How is this possible? I thought your prison was ultra-secure?" Daniel accused.

"It is." Blackmere pulled his collar closer to his neck. "He had help. One of the security guards, it turns out. Some men are easily bought. The point is Xander is now loose, and we have no idea where he went."

"And you want to take me away from my family with that maniac on the prowl?"

Blackmere shook his head. "I want you to help us track him down and put him back in a cage where he belongs."

"I'm supposed to do that how? My time in uniform ended years ago. I'm done playing soldier."

A handful of onlookers peering out the bookstore's windows caught Daniel's attention. Her jerked his head, Blackmere following him to stand out of view.

"You know as well as I do that our time in uniform dictates who we are for the rest of our lives," Blackmere reminded. "As much as you'd like to retreat into the

33

privacy of the civilian world there is still that bug reminding you of what once was and could be again. Warriors don't stop, Daniel."

The last endeavor through Raleigh was filled with violence on levels parallel to his combat experiences. He hadn't expected a running gunfight across the state, each moment more harrowing than the last. That elf bodies disappeared in a puff of black ash and smoke upon death did little to rob the psyche of knowing dead was dead. A possible repeat performance sent his stomach churning.

"You do recall what happened the last time," Daniel said.

"This time will be different," Blackmere assured.

"How so?"

"I've assembled a team for you to assist in hunting down Xander and remanding him to custody," Blackmere said. "You will have operational command, though the term means little to many of your teammates, being what they are and all."

That made Daniel suspicious. "What they are?"

Blackmere reached out to slap Daniel on the shoulder. "Wouldn't want to spoil the surprise for you. Rest assured they are among the best in the business. Bounty hunters, trackers, and mercenaries who have all worked together at one point over the last hundred years or so."

So creatures. "What do you need me for? Sounds like you have it all figured out."

"Look at this another way, Daniel. Xander wants revenge against you for helping spoil his plot to take the throne. You're his primary target. By getting you away from here and back in the field you're not only seizing advantage of the situation, you're also taking pressure away from your family. Sara will be safe."

"You can't guarantee that."

34

"No, but I can stack the deck to make it happen."

Daniel stepped back. "I don't see how."

"I believe I can persuade Norman Guilt to resume his watch over her. Daniel, they will be safe. We need you. There is no telling what Xander can accomplish with a hate filled heart and plenty of vendettas."

Daniel paced, frowning. A train of thoughts barreled through his mind, all leading to the inevitable conclusion that agreeing to terms with the federal government was the worst mistake of his life. He signed his life away once before, and it damn near killed him. But at least then it was part of the job, at the time. This took things to a whole new level.

It had sounded like a good idea to sign at the time. After all, how often would he be dragged back into the subversive world of elves, dwarves, and shady government agencies? The actual answer to that question wasn't to his liking. Seeing Blackmere again reopened old wounds he wasn't ready to visit.

Yet here he was being dragged back into that hidden world and thrown to the wolves.

He stopped and faced Blackmere. "Fine. When do I leave?"

"That's the spirit! Go home, get some dinner. I'll send a car for you in the morning. There'll be a private plane flying out of RDU for you at zero eight."

At least I get to sleep in. "Are you coming with me?"

"To an extent," Blackmere hedged. "I am a Washington man, after all. You'll be placed in good hands, Daniel. You have my word."

Right. Daniel headed for his car. Sometimes life was downright unfair.

***

No one noticed the quiet young woman sitting on a bench three stores down the sidewalk. Earbuds in, she bobbed her head to an unknown beat. Loose strands of purple hair bounced over her shoulders. She looked like every other college girl in town: eager to meet the world and oblivious to those strange goings on under her nose. But behind those reflective shades were watchful eyes devouring everything Daniel Thomas and the government agent discussed. Instead of headphones her earbuds were listening devices.

Viviana Cal had been outside through the entire book signing, her interest in the matter far from personal. Surprise at Blackmere himself arriving almost forced her to give away her cover. She concluded the rumors were true. This news was urgent, superseding all other parameters of her mission.

Blowing a bubble with her gum, Viviana struggled to maintain a elusive expression as she collected the small bag beside her, drained the last few sips of coffee, and headed off.

Wheels were in motion, and she was unsure of the direction. With Xander loose, their world was about to get much smaller.

SIX

Pulling into his driveway, Daniel was reluctant to shut the engine off. The temptation to drive off, to disappear from the questing eyes of DESA, had strengthened during his ride home. Any joy he felt from the signing's success had been washed away as vivid memories of his introduction to the world of elves played out. Yet as much as he wanted to forget those terse moments, to hide, Daniel felt that old itch awakening.

There was no denying he missed certain aspects of being in the fight. Most warriors did. There was ever the random moment while perusing the grocery store isles or at a crowded restaurant where sharpened instincts took over. The occasional lament of becoming mundane after years of living on the edge. The dichotomy proved frightening to many, himself included. It was a winless war.

No point in delaying, Daniel cut the engine and got out, popping open his Volkswagen door while slinging his pack over one shoulder. Sara would have seen the headlights and was no doubt eager to have him discuss his day—if for no other reason than to shut him up. They learned long ago to keep business and home lives separate. He didn't want to hear about her work anymore than she did his. *How am I going to explain this to her?*

"Hey hun, how did it go?" Sara called from the kitchen as he opened the door and stepped inside.

If you only knew. Clearing his throat, Daniel said, "Oh, it had its ups and downs. I sold out."

She poked her head around the corner. "Look at you! I knew you'd do it."

"Yeah. What have you been up to?"

She ran through a litany of chores and simple tasks occupying her day. More of the usual. The kids went to school. She vacuumed after the dogs. Went to lunch with her work friend Amanda, and so on. Normally Daniel would have taken comfort from that, but with recent circumstances changing his approach to life, it took little imagination to see prying eyes lurking just around the corner, following her throughout the day in anticipation of the right moment to strike.

He cleared his throat to get her attention. "Is dinner almost ready? I'm going to take a quick shower."

"We're not going out to celebrate?"

"I'd like to enjoy my win for a while longer before we need to spend it." He'd fallen for that before, in the beginning, and always wound up spending more than he earned.

"Lucky for you I felt like cooking. Chicken has another ten minutes. Go get the stink off," Sara laughed.

Dropping his bag off in his office, Daniel headed upstairs to clean up and take a little more time trying to figure out what to tell her.

He was drying off when a thought struck him. *What if Blackmere had already been here?*

He got dressed and hurried downstairs: Dinner was plated and ready to eat. She handed him his plate and they settled down to what promised to be the most awkward meal of his life.

"I got a visit today," Daniel said after swallowing a mouthful of rice. As usual, her chicken fricassee was delicious.

"From who?"

"Whom."

"What?"

"It's from whom," he corrected.

She pointed her knife at him. "Okay, literary genius, save it for your characters. Who did you see?"

"Blackmere." There. He said it. The name was out in the open. No turning back now.

She nearly choked on a bite of chicken she had just taken before setting her fork down. "What did Thaddeus want?"

Thaddeus? What the f— "When did we get on a first name basis with the government?"

"He's an old man, Daniel."

"Doesn't make him any less lethal."

"You're dissembling," she chided.

You know me too well. "Xander escaped. They think he might be coming after us."

"Us? You're the one who screwed him over. I had nothing to do with it," she protested.

"That's how we're playing this? Damn it, Sara, this is serious. Our whole family is in jeopardy." He paused, only then noticing the silence. "Speaking of which, where are the kids?"

"Sleeping over at my sister's," she said. A fire awakened in her eyes. One he hadn't seen in years.

"Anyway, Blackmere wants me to lead some kind of team to hunt Xander down and put him back behind bars."

"What did you tell him?"

His eyes widened. "What do you think? I said yes. It's the only way to ensure you're safe and DESA stays off our backs."

"I knew we should have never signed those contracts," she growled. "Fine. You're hunting down a man who can disappear at will and has more contacts established than we can dream of. How hard could it be? When do you leave?"

"In the morning," he replied. "Blackmere has a plane waiting for me."

"That is … fast."

"It has to be. Every minute this guy is loose increases the threat to us," Daniel said.

Sara hummed. "Are you going to kill him?"

Daniel admired her brave face. Suspecting she put on a façade for his peace of mind didn't exactly calm him, but it put him in a better place. That and knowing they spent much of the past few years bringing her up to speed with self-defense and handgun training. Sara proved a better shot than him. Slightly insulting but comforting.

"I don't want to kill anyone, Sara. You know that."

"We don't always get what we want," she fired back. At his flinch, she sighed. "Sorry, that was uncalled for."

"I get it. We're stuck in a nasty place. Hopefully this team Blackmere is putting together can get the job done and get me back here pronto."

"You and I both know nothing ever goes according to plan," she said.

He broke into a grin. "Doesn't mean I won't try."

"Really hard?"

"Extra really hard." He leaned over the table to give her a kiss. "There is a bit of good news in all this."

"Per diem?"

"I wish," he said. "Since Xander is a decided threat, Blackmere is assigning an old friend to watch over the house while I'm gone."

Her eyes brightened. "Norman?"

He nodded. The gargoyle, once a staunch enemy, became their friend after the assassination. Stalwart and unflinching, Norman Guilt was the only other man in her life she enjoyed conversations with, or so she'd told Daniel. And apparently he played a mean game of chess.

"He might already be outside," Daniel commented. "You know how gargoyles are."

Conversation dwindled.

Dinner finished and the pair cleaned the kitchen together. They settled on the coach to watch a few episodes of their newest favorite comedy but neither focused. Once again their world was changing, and they were powerless to stop it.

***

Storm clouds rolled in, blanketing the Raleigh skyline with unnatural darkness, as if the very weather itself understood the immensity of the moment. Blinking lights atop the downtown high rises turned the clouds haunting shades of red and green. Taking it in from atop her private lair, Morgen stood before the large bay windows with her hands clasped before her. Her face was locked in consternation.

The queen of the dark elves was a shadow of her former self. Ideations of power had fled when her estranged husband was murdered. Though they had differences, she never stopped loving him. Millennia of shared history wasn't easily cast aside.

A flash of lightning reflected across her face. The sternness of her high cheekbones a skeletal visage where beauty once reigned. Natural grace flowed through her, yet Morgen felt drained. Hollowed out by the betrayal of her own daughter.

Now Xander was loose and assuredly coming for her. It was only natural. He could no more refuse his nature than she. Precautions were emplaced to ensure he got nowhere near her. Regardless of his actions, Xander remained a man of honor. Morgen relied on that, slim as it was.

News of his escape spread through the clans with impressive rapidity. Morgen's networks drowned in information. No confirmed sightings as of yet, but it was only a matter of time before her noose closed around the man. After all, there were only so many places for an elf to go to ground—if that was his plan. If the latest information from the government was correct. One thing she learned early on was that no government agency was as forthcoming as they pretended to be. Layers upon layers.

Questioning the ease of Xander's escape, Morgen stretched deep into her memories of who had the power, or authority, to make it possible. Of course there was the convenient theory of human greed and incompetence, but no elf worth their salt trusted that. She contemplated calling a council meeting to address the situation but that was, to borrow a human expression, akin to herding cats. The absence of a king left many smaller clans vying for status, driving her insane in the process. Ever the bickering ensemble, lesser nobles and lords proved a worthy bane to her existence.

She sighed.

"Ma'am?"

Morgen tensed, momentarily forgetting her staff remained on hand while she made her nightly stalking of the upper floors of the Wells Fargo building in the heart of downtown. "Yes, Lucius?"

"A messenger has arrived from the Prime Minister's office."

Interesting. It was only a matter of time before Basil Kadis stuck his nose into her affairs. Morgen never cared for the ambitious man. He was, in her opinion, everything wrong with their kind: driven, heartless, and filled with greed. He always had a plan.

"What does our dear Prime Minister have to say for himself?" she asked without turning.

Lucius cleared his throat. "He requests a meeting with you at your earliest convenience. The messenger would say no more."

"As if I am a puppet to dance upon his strings," she commented, drily. "Remind the Prime Minister I am not a toy at his beck and call. If he wishes to speak with me, it will be on my terms. I am still queen of the dark elves and will be treated accordingly."

"He's not going to like that, ma'am." Lucius bowed his head and stepped back.

"No. I suspect not," she agreed with a small smile. "Send the message anyway, Lucius. I have much to consider on this dark night."

She heard the door close behind him, leaving her alone with the muted city of Raleigh as her company.

SEVEN

They landed at Stewart Air Force Base in New Windsor, New York shortly after eleven. Daniel marveled at the ease with which DESA escaped federal flight restrictions and was able to override base command to land their covert plane.

Nerves roiling from being the only man on board, he stepped onto the tarmac and was instantly ushered into a black SUV. The driver was more than happy to make conversation with him, a pleasant change from the flight up.

"This was the place all of them hostages flew home from Iran back in the 70s."

"I didn't know that," Daniel replied.

"Most folks don't. This area got a lot of rich history." Every time the driver opened his mouth Daniel caught more of a thick New York accent.

"How far from New York City are we?" Daniel asked, eager to shift the conversation.

"Bout an hour, give or take. Gotta cross the Hudson and it's a straight shot down river. Looking for a vacation?"

"Just wondering is all."

They soon pulled into an empty parking lot facing a rundown building that looked as if should have been demolished years ago. Daniel snorted. The government was quick to spend people's money but never seemed in a hurry to fix military instillations properly. "Nothing ever changes."

"What's that?"

He shook his head. "Just musing to myself. What are we doing here?"

"This is it," the driver said. "You're supposed to head inside. Someone will meet you to debrief."

"Thanks." Daniel grabbed his travel bag and popped open the door.

"Name's Louie," the driver offered. "You ever need anything, call."

The door slammed shut and the truck drove off, leaving a confused Daniel alone in the parking lot. Not having Louie's phone number notwithstanding, he couldn't think of any plausible scenario where they would reunite.

Chagrined, Daniel headed up the short flight of stairs.

Opening with a groan from decades of misuse before he managed to knock, the door swung to reveal Thaddeus Blackmere smiling at him. *Of course.*

"Daniel, good. We've not time to delay. Are you rested?" Blackmere asked, ushering him inside and down the lengthy hall.

Their footsteps echoed with sharp clips.

"How do you expect me to be rested?" Daniel countered. "Send me to the beach and maybe we can talk."

"No beaches here. Hell, they don't even have any good seafood." Blackmere shook his head. "The pizza's good, in most places, and there's a diner on just about every corner around here. Give it a few more weeks and the hills will be crawling with red, yellow, and orange from the leaves. Not a bad sight at all."

"You're dissembling, Blackmere."

Blackmere shrugged. "We have reason to believe Xander is still in the area, but our window of opportunity is closing—we need to stop him now and end this."

"I didn't see any prisons when flying in. Where was he being kept?"

"That's need to know and you—" Blackmere started before changing his mind. "You're not supposed to know this but there's a secret facility under the Hudson. Its where we keep the worst of the worst."

Daniel should have been surprised, but when it came to the government nothing was off the table. He marveled at the internal mechanisms developed to adapt to living among the elf clans, briefly wondering what it must have been like for that first person to discover the truth. He took his thoughts a step further by imaging how difficult it was to convince those in power that elves existed, enough to form a government agency devoted to maintaining good relations and, apparently, policing those miscreants who refused to blend in.

"Why not in a regular prison? They look like us, after all."

Blackmere shook his head. "True, but we can't risk exposing them to the rest of the world. Can you imagine what would happen if everyone knew the truth?" He scoffed. "Poor Timmy has always been told about the pot of gold at the end of the rainbow and then poof, one day he finds a leprechaun and makes him talk. Chaos would ensue."

Wait. "Leprechauns exist?"

Blackmere halted, turning back to face him. "Why shouldn't they?"

Unsure if his leg was being pulled, Daniel held up his hands. "Next you're going to tell me Bigfoot and the Loch Ness monster are real too."

A curious look passed through Blackmere's eyes before the agent resumed his march.

"Aliens?" Daniel pushed.

All his childhood dreams and fantasies were coming true. No answer was the same as a quiet admission in his book. A new realm of possibilities sprang to life, leaving him out of breath. If all these creatures were real, the world suddenly became a much larger and more dangerous place.

"Ghosts and vampires?"

"Not the sparkly kinds," Blackmere joked and opened the door to the stairwell. He gestured down. "What you are about to see remains private. That goes without saying. This is a secure facility, and we don't need prying eyes taking an interest."

"Why have it on an Air Force base then? Seems to me there are plenty of better spots to put a government site."

"I don't make the rules, Daniel. You will be required to sign a standard nondisclosure agreement, however. I trust you, just not enough to put my job on the line."

"I thought Sara and I were quasi-agents."

In truth, both were approached years ago to assist with DESA activities in Raleigh. Their newfound knowledge of the clans and certain ranking members of many families put them in the perfect position to maintain relations and liaison back to Washington. Somewhere along the way they made friends. The Schneider brothers were abrasive and annoying, reminding him of his days in the barracks before marriage saved him. And Daniel never imagined he'd come to call a troll named Bert a friend, but here they were. The only one he stayed away from was Morgen. That woman was more trouble than she was worth and, if Xander's latest escapade was any indication, more than likely plotting on him as well.

"In theory," Blackmere confirmed. "Daniel, you have to understand none of this is orthodox. We are in difficult times. Look at it this way. If this was the military, you would be considered inactive reserves."

"I saw a lot of those guys in Iraq and Afghanistan, Blackmere."

"Needs of the nation, Daniel. My point is you are only to be used in times of great duress or, in this instance, because of your intimate knowledge and history of the situation."

"You mean because Xander wants to kill me."

"Precisely."

The pause before answering awakened Daniel's suspicions. Blackmere wasn't being totally honest with him. *What am I missing?*

Three flights down they arrived at a small, standard office. Blackmere shoved a handful of documents across the table for Daniel to sign. All standard according to the agent. Rules within rules. Daniel wasn't allowed to speak of what he saw, did, or witnessed to anyone under penalty of imprisonment. *Blah, blah, blah.* He remembered signing something similar when his buddy took him to tour the small prison on Bagram Air Force Base when he was deployed there. Same situation, same threats. But some stories are too good to keep private. Thankfully no one ever came after him.

Collecting the signed paperwork with a government perfected smile, Blackmere tucked them into a manilla folder. "Daniel, what you are about to see goes beyond anything you've witnessed to date."

"I highly doubt that," he replied with a chuckle.

"This isn't about the elf clans. No kings or queens here. This is all DESA. While we maintain relations with the leadership to ensure there are no incidents and the clans remain secret, that is but the surface of our operations. Like any sentient species, there are good guys and bad. To control the bad we have gone to great lengths to cultivate a combat field force. They have the best weapons and training and are not on any book."

Daniel folded his arms. "Meaning they don't exist."

"Meaning they are one hundred percent loyal to DESA. We don't select for quality of character. These men and women are violent, decisive, and act without hesitation when the call is made. They are an eclectic bunch and, in some instances, should be behind bars themselves. In different times they would be the ones sent behind enemy lines to prepare for the invasion."

"How do you control a bunch like that?" Limited experience with operators who officially didn't exist was enough to convince Daniel he was better off not knowing.

Blackmere's thin smile was disturbing. "We have our methods. Suffice it to say, I am in no position to accept failure on this one."

"Sounds like neither am I," Daniel countered. The seriousness of it hollowed him.

"My hands are tied," Blackmere's apologetic tone did little to assuage the helpless feeling knotting Daniel's innards.

Daniel questioned who ran DESA and just how far up the food chain Blackmere was. He'd seen plenty of men like this during his career. Ladder climbers willing to sacrifice everything for the chance to outshine competition and gain another rung. Cutthroat and ruthless, they were apex predators circling the tank. All it took was the subtle reminder to put Daniel in his place and on the defensive.

Slipping back into his NCO persona, he asked, "Are we going to stand around here gawking at each other or do we get the show started?"

"I like your attitude, Daniel."

The relief was evident on the agent's face. "This way, please."

Blackmere opened the far door and opened a new world. Brightly lit and filled with armored vehicles, squads of operatives conducting hand to hand combat training, weapons testing, and more, the chamber stretched for at least three football fields. Daniel's mouth dropped open at the sight. *No wonder everything the government buys costs so much.*

"How is this possible?"

"Best not ask questions you aren't prepared to have answered. Follow me. Your team is assembled and waiting for you."

The spit of a flamethrower heated the surrounding area as they walked through. A grease covered mechanic with a gruff beard cursed and spat after banging his knuckles on the undercarriage of an MRAP. Daniel felt like he was trapped in a bizarre combination of reality and fiction. None of this should have been possible. Yet even as he stood in muted wonder, his writerly mind already worked through scenarios for his next book. Some things were too good to pass up.

Blackmere led him into a briefing room where an odd assortment of men and women awaited. If this was his crack team, Daniel wondered how bad the situation truly was, for not one of those assembled inspired fear or confidence.

"Ladies and gentlemen, this is Daniel Thomas. He is being given operational command of the team," Blackmere announced once the door closed.

"Whoopie-fucking-do," a slender elf snorted.

The others laughed.

Daniel felt his heart clutch. *Great, just like being in charge of my first squad. This is going to be fun.*

***

Blackmere knew this could have gone either way. There was no contractual obligation for Daniel to fulfill. The agent watched as Daniel took in the scene before him. He had tugged on raw emotions to coerce the man to assist. Self-preservation provided the perfect wake up call.

He didn't care for Daniel, noting how the man stiffened after sweeping the room. The man was an accident. Happenstance had allowed him to stumble upon the secret world and fate determined to keep him around as a player. A soldier turned writer turned solider again … In the long game, Daniel and his wife wouldn't be allowed to participate, but this was different. This was personal.

EIGHT

Uncomfortable silence settled over them as Daniel took in the ragtag assortment of people facing him. The elf bore a menacing look and was almost as pale as a sheet of paper, with stringy hair hanging down to his shoulders. The piece of hay strategically placed in the corner of his mouth, would have been comical if it hadn't showed Daniel the elf wasn't putting on an act. The cowboy hat was a bit much. Still, he'd seen stranger things during his association with the clans.

Beside the elf, propped up on a bowed table, sat a stolid looking dwarf. His beard was greasy and … peppered with bones. The dark gleam in his eyes suggested he was a bad man who didn't play well with others, leaving Daniel questioning Blackmere's wisdom. Matching the dwarf stare for stare, he shifted focus to the innocent looking girl to the right.

Dressed in sensible shoes, ones any elder might enjoy, and a flowery sundress, she didn't look a day over sixteen. She blew a giant bubble and waved at him behind a warm smile. He knew better than to take anything at face value with these people and wasn't about to make the error of false assumptions.

The last figure in the room was a gnome. Hoping for a similar experience like he'd had with Mort, Daniel went to shake the man's hand. His surprise as the gnome recoiled produced laughs from the room.

"No touch. No. Don't like touching," the gnome sputtered.

"He don't like being touched," the dwarf grumbled, burped, and fell silent.

Daniel fired a nasty scowl but held his tongue.

52

Recollecting himself, the gnome bowed. "I'm Hugh. Hugh Jasol. Pleasure to meet you."

"Hugh?" Daniel grew suspicious.

Bobbing his head, the gnome said, "Yes. Hugh Jasol."

"Uh, huh." Daniel gave Blackmere a queer look, but the agent only shook his head.

Sensing the meeting already devolving, Blackmere moved to the center of the room. "Since you all seem incapable of playing nice with Daniel here, I'll make the introductions. Mr. Jasol here is actually Thraken. He's an expert tracker but a bit of a wise ass. Next to him is the perpetually gloomy Klaus Grimstone. Not relation to the Schneider brothers but a handful to deal with. He's also the best shot on the team."

"I thought we were trying to capture Xander?" Daniel questioned.

"Live or dead, hummie. We don't care," Klaus grumbled.

Clearing his throat, Blackmere motioned to the slender elf. "This is Nevada Slim. Former army and demolitions expert."

"You're from Nevada?" Daniel asked.

The elf tipped his hat back, shifted the piece of straw to the other side of his mouth and said in a thick European accent, "Belarus."

Daniel's mouth dropped open. *Watch a lot of cowboy movies did we?* A million words wanted freedom, but he had no idea where to begin. Thankfully the young girl hopped in between and waved.

"Hi, I'm Jenny."

"Daniel. Nice to meet you, Jenny," he replied.

"You say that because you don't know her," Klaus muttered.

Blackmere shot him a glare. "Jenny is unique among the clans. She is … well, you'll find out after you track Xander down. The last man is Kip. One of the best drivers in the business. He'll get you where you need to be and quickly."

The door opened, interrupting the introductions, and a human male of light frame with a youthful look sidled in.

Blackmere glanced at the wall clock overhead. "Ah, Agent Murphy, you're here."

"My apologies, sir. The flight from Denver was delayed," the agent apologized. "What did I miss?"

"Nothing. We were just finishing introductions." Blackmere glanced around the room. "Good. The team is assembled. Agent Murphy will be your liaison with myself and Washington, Daniel. He's a solid field agent and one I trust implicitly. I'll show you to the prep room so you can change and get fitted for your kit. Mission briefing is in fifteen. Don't go anywhere."

"Where are we going to go? I already feel like a mushroom," Thraken replied dryly.

***

Daniel followed the agent to a small office, slammed the door shut and wheeled on Blackmere. "You expect me to put my life in the hands of a man who introduced himself as a huge asshole?"

"It's not a perfect world, Daniel."

"You think?"

"Relax, you're going to need him. He's one of the best trackers we have and your best chance to find Xander before he can do anymore damage."

More damage? What has he done? "Nothing you say inspires great confidence, Blackmere."

"This isn't a mission of choice, or pleasure. We are faced with a very real threat that must be dealt with if any of us will remain intact."

Eyes narrowing, Daniel asked, "What do you mean?"

Making a show of wringing his hands, Blackmere took a seat on the tabletop. "What do you suppose would happen if the world woke up one morning and learned that everything they ever thought was fantasy or myth was real? How many people could process those monsters do exist and they walk among us? Your fifth grade teacher was a werewolf. Your neighbor a troll."

"Werewolves are real?"

"Stay on track, Daniel," the agent admonished. "I'm serious. We cannot allow the clans to become public knowledge. There would be pandemonium. Fear and panic would ensue. It's only a matter of time before the killing begins. Camps for elves. Human nature is a brutal reality. These people have existed long before we showed up and, I hope, they remain so long after you and I are gone.

"We have an inherent duty to help preserve their anonymity and, in doing so, ensure they remain a separate and independent species. Agencies are in place around the world to help make sure the clans keep their heads down. No one wants a war. DESA exists to prevent creatures from becoming public knowledge."

Daniel folded his arms. "Which is why you have a secret prison under the freaking Hudson River?"

"As with humans, there are bad actors, Daniel. Xander fit the category nicely and now he is loose. Find him, bring him back, and let us take care of the rest."

"You talk a good game, but I need you to understand I'm not doing any of this for the government or the clans. My only concern is the safety of my family.

That's it. Save the rah-rah speeches for people like Murphy. I do this and we're square."

Blackmere nodded. "Fair enough. You've been more than accommodating. Bring me Xander and I'll ensure you never hear from us again."

His words lacked sincerity, but Daniel filed that away for later. Glancing around the almost empty room, Daniel felt lost. A cockeyed motivation poster proclaiming 'Meetings, because none of us are as dumb as all of us' hung on the far wall. A small desk with an old green topped banker's lamp was pushed against the same wall. A thin layer of dust coated the surface.

"Where do I change?"

"There are utilities and boots in your locker in the dressing room on the far end of the hall. They should be your size. Weapons draw will be in an hour. Anything else you need see the quartermaster. He's easy to find. Just look for an angry sylph cursing for no reason," Blackmere said. "Don't forget the inbrief."

Daniel popped open the locker, taking in the black fatigues hanging before him. An unsettling feeling settled over him. The last time he saw a uniform so dark was at the tank museum in Danville, Virginia. Then it had come with a red arm band with a swastika inside.

***

"While we cannot anticipate Xander's movement, we have narrowed down his travel routes to the major arteries lacing this part of the state. We believe he will head west, avoiding the major population centers before working his way back south to North Carolina and Morgen."

Daniel interrupted. "Why west? There are plenty of ways to avoid detection. What makes west so special?"

Exchanging cautious looks, Blackmere gave Murphy a clipped nod who answered, "There is a secondary facility in Elmira where the princess is being kept."

"Wait a second. You put both of these maniacs in the same state? Close together?" Daniel barked.

"Makes you wonder how humanity made it to the top of the food chain, huh?" Klaus commented, elbowing him in the ribs.

Daniel swore he heard the crack right before pain lanced through his side.

"Gwen is being kept in a place befitting her station. She is well taken care of, at her mother's behest," Blackmere explained.

"This keeps getting better," Daniel muttered.

Nevada Slim snorted. "Welcome to my life."

Jenny slipped beside him and whispered, "It's all right, Daniel. I'll keep you safe."

Questions bloomed, but he knew better than to open pandora's box. Not yet at least. Daniel offered an uneasy smile.

"The fastest, most direct route to where Gwen is being kept is along interstate 86, formerly route 17. It's a three to four hour trip from here to Elmira, depending on time of day and traffic."

"Meaning he could already be there," Klaus injected.

"Wait a second, how do we know he knows where Gwen is being kept?" Daniel asked.

Blackmere stiffened and Daniel barely managed not to scoff. Secrets within secrets.

"We have confirmed this from a pair of sources."

"What sources, Blackmere?" Daniel pressed. "You're putting all of us in jeopardy by withholding information. Secrets get people killed."

Flashbacks of his first tour in Afghanistan awakened. They'd lost four men in one day because of faulty intel and miscommunication between commands. Among them was Pham, one of his best friends in the platoon. Having no feelings for any of the people around him now, Daniel didn't want to see the same play out again if unlikely friendships did develop.

"We have a pair of security guards in custody. We believe they were complicit in helping Xander escape. Interrogations are already underway."

The reluctance in Blackmere's voice told Daniel everything he needed to know. As designated team lead, he needed to be there to hear for himself. "Can you get me in there?" he asked. "I want to hear what they have to say for myself."

"That is highly unlikely. You cannot—" Murphy started.

"Wasn't talking to you, kid," Daniel interrupted. "Blackmere, you put me in charge of these people. It's my decisions that decide who lives or dies in the field. Don't send me out with secondhand intel and half facts. I know you people have private viewing rooms. These guards don't even need to know I exist."

After a brief pause, Blackmere nodded. "Very well but say nothing while we are there. My job is on the line with this."

"So are our lives."

Blackmere motioned for him to follow and Daniel got to his feet. He caught one of the others mumbling, "I might like this guy already. Leastwise enough not to knife him in the back."

"Yet," a second voice agreed as Daniel shut the door.

NINE

The fidgety man handcuffed to the table looked without hope. Daniel found him inherently sad, as if life did nothing but dump on him day after day. He'd once been told that the world needed ditchdiggers too. At the time, Daniel had no idea what the man meant, but time and temperance showed him the truth. Not everyone was destined to be a winner. Life took it's due on everyone along the way.

"This is Israel McFadden. A minor guard who's been with the prison for almost three years. No marks on his record and a solid performer. He was found unconscious in Xander's cell yesterday morning. We believe he was the one who deactivated the wards and showed Xander a maintenance access passage topside before being knocked out."

Daniel studied Israel, noting the sweaty hands, the raw confusion in his eyes, and the lack of any confidence whatsoever. "He didn't do it. This man was a dupe. You're wasting your time."

"How do you know?"

"Look at him. He has no idea what he's doing here or why he's being made to take the fall," Daniel said. "This is the decoy. Wrong place, wrong time. What about the other one?"

"Sergeant Deacon Dawes. A more garrulous individual who is full of himself. The good sergeant's stun gun was missing, and he was conspicuously absent when the power blacked out."

"You're messing with me then, right? Why are you wasting time with this guy?" Daniel jerked his thumb at Israel.

"Assurances are hard to come by, Daniel. We need to make sure he's what he says he is. Dawes is the traitor, though we don't know why."

Exasperated, Daniel made a show of pointing at the two-way mirror. "Has it ever occurred to any of you that your scheming and intent on keeping secrets caused this mess? I know what you said about word spreading, but that doesn't lessen the impact of your decisions since Alvin was killed."

Rage twisting his face, Blackmere snapped, "You act like this is all my call. I'm not very high on the food chain, Daniel. I do what I'm told, like any good soldier. You should know that."

"Damn the consequences, right?"

"For the greater good," Blackmere countered. "We can stand here and debate ethics and politics all day, but it gets us no closer to solving the problem."

"Perhaps the problem is in Washington," Daniel suggested. *Just like everything else.* "How certain are you in your chain of command? Any chance one or more of them have been compromised?"

Blackmere froze like the possibility had occurred to him, but he loathed to accept it. Daniel could understand the agent's hesitation. One glance down that rabbit hole and his career would be finished.

"That's above my pay grade," Blackmere replied slowly. "I have a task to complete. You are the tool to make it happen. That's all I, and you, need to know."

"Can I go? Someone, please?"

Israel's voice cracked over the intercom, worry evident in every syllable. Sweat beaded across his brow. Daniel noticed a slight tremor in his arms. The unceasing tapping of the left foot, confirming his suspicions. This was a man who did nothing wrong, but thought he had and was worried for his life. He'd seen plenty like that during his time in the army, usually when they were being brought up on disciplinary charges for whatever infractions against the uniform code of military justice. Justice. The very word remained subjective, for it always fell down on those doing the accusing and their relationship with the chain of command.

A pair of agents, one male and the other female, entered on swift feet and took seats opposite him. They began their interrogation before Israel had the opportunity to open his mouth.

Israel answered in short sentences: "Yes, sirs," and "No, ma'ams." His "I did what?" had Daniel shaking his head. He felt bad for Israel.

"I've seen enough of this one, Blackmere," he said at seeing Israel bordering on sobbing. "What's behind door number two?"

Satisfied as well, Blackmere ushered them down the hall to the second room. "This man is Deacon Dawes. He's been working at the Grinder for almost a decade. Impeccable service record. Not even so much as late to a shift once. Spotless in every regard. Until we dug into his financials."

Daniel snorted. "Funny how money is the root of all evil."

"Indeed. Dawes has been living paycheck to paycheck for many years. We were able to trace his spending to the racetrack down in Yonkers. He is a most unfortunate man."

"You're thinking he owed someone a lot of money?"

"Something like that. A large deposit landed in his account the day before Xander escaped. The sort of money one could buy an island with."

"He was bought," Daniel concluded.

As with Israel, the same agents moved into the room and began their routine. Dawes, far too confident for a man in his situation, leaned back in the metal framed chair and grinned. Light sparkled off his gold tooth.

"Look, I already told you, I got nothing to say," he said with a clipped southern accent.

The agents exchanged a look before the woman said, "Good. I don't ever have to let you see the light of day again, Sergeant Dawes. You'll be placed in your own little cell in the Grinder and left to rot in front of all those prisoners you oversaw. How many of them do you suppose will feel sorry for you?"

The man leaned over the desk and whispered, "How many do you think want a piece of your hide?"

"I'm due a fair trial," Dawes protested. His voice was strained, as if gut punched. Much of that annoying confidence shattered.

"Under normal circumstances you would be, but, as I'm sure you are aware, we don't fall under the traditional government. As a separate, unofficial entity, we are given leeway to handle problems as we see fit," the woman said with a smile. "And the way I see it, I can have your body dumped in the Hudson and no one will question it."

Swallowing hard, Dawes clasped his hands. "Fine. I'll tell you. This old dude came up to me at the bar and ..."

"Got him," Blackmere crowed.

Daniel scoffed. "We already knew this. How much more does he know? I'm betting nothing beyond who bought him out."

"Putting us no closer to pinpointing Xander's location."

Nodding, Daniel headed for the door. Time was running out and they were already too far behind. The last time he felt like this Daniel found himself in the depths of an ambush firefight with the Taliban. "We should get back to the others. No doubt they're dripping with excitement for my return."

They engaged in small talk revolving around the mission on their way back to the team. Daniel expressed his concerns, again. His primary concern lay in trustworthiness. The times where unit leaders were fragged by their soldiers blistered memories in the minds of veterans. Daniel had no desire to recreate the experience after having a few memories himself.

"They're not bad people, Daniel," Blackmere insisted. "Well, most of them. Nevada Slim is, obviously, a dark elf. He'd be the one to watch out of any of them. Oh, and try not to get Jenny mad. She is … unpredictable."

"What is she?"

Blackmere quickened his step. "Best if I let her explain once you are on the road. Suffice it to say she is your most valuable asset."

"She's just a girl," Daniel protested.

"Who happens to be over a thousand years old. Trust me. Don't get her mad. The whole damned world could implode."

Daniel turned away to look out over the main training floor. A squad practiced combatives on filthy mats. Daniel's stomach soured at the thought of ringworm running wild. Mechanics and armorers worked on vehicles and weapons, all going through the motions like nothing was out of the ordinary. He was confused and unsure if the man was pulling his leg. Being the new guy sucked.

They made it back to the assembly area a few minutes later. After departing the plane, a young woman rushed toward them. A document was crumbled in her right hand, and she spoke in an excited tone.

"Agent Blackmere! We have him!" she blurted.

"Quietly please. This is a top secret operation," he scolded. Casting a look around, he ordered then, "Show me."

Handing him the paper, she hurried away.

"What does it say?"

Wordlessly Blackmere shifted so Daniel could read the document as well.

"Hey, what's going on?" a man asked.

"Having a meeting without us?" another man deadpanned.

Daniel glanced up to see the team scurrying toward them looking suspicious. Not that he blamed them. Going into an operation blind wasn't sound tactics. When they avoided his eye and looked to Blackmere, Daniel stepped away to allow the agent to take the point. Daniel hadn't earned their trust and he had guessed already as to why. Time would prove him right or wrong.

Blackmere led them to the briefing table and, making a show of tossing the paper down, clapped his hands and smiled. "One of our spies has spotted Xander at a hotel not far from here. He's at a Holiday Inn Express off Interstate 84 and route 208. That's twenty minutes from here." He lowered his voice. "Suit up and get him. This is our chance."

"What if he moves before we get there? Do we still have eyes on him?" Daniel asked.

"Unconfirmed. Regardless, we can't afford to mess this up. Daniel, take your people and hunt him down. There is a vehicle waiting outside." Blackmere stood firm, looking him deep in the eyes.

Frowning, Daniel said, "Air support would be quicker."

"We can't risk it. This has to be quiet. The smaller footprint you leave the better. No air assets, no direct support other than my communications team. You have the latest tech and gear and all the data necessary to complete your task. On the surface you will appear no more than a strange group of individuals on a road trip."

No one would ever confuse our team as friends. "What do we do when we bag him?"

"Call me. I'll have assets diverted to your location immediately."

"You just said we were alone on this."

Blackmere winced before presenting his best government smile. "You are, until you have the target secured. With any luck this will be over before dinner, and we can all go back to our lives."

Dinner. Right. Nothing goes according to plan. Nothing. I have a feeling this is going to be a long one. Daniel reached for the automatic rifle on the table and, checking the magazine for ammo, headed to the table filled with weapons and more. After all, the clock was ticking.

He snatched enough magazines to keep him in the fight and, judging from his previous experiences, grabbed a few more just in case. The Schneider brothers taught him nothing was off the table when dealing with elves. Body armor and stuff pack later, he led the team to a waiting dark SUV.

"Shotgun!" Thraken shouted and jumped in before anyone spoke.

One by one they filed in until only Daniel remained. He stared at Blackmere, wondering if this was a trap and how they were going to fare.

Blackmere extended his hand. "I know this isn't what you wanted when we first met, but neither of us have a choice. Stop Xander and save your family. It's that simple."

"If it was that simple he never would have escaped," Daniel retorted. "I can't help but feel like we're walking into a trap."

"Watch your back. These are crack assets but none of them have any love for you. After all, you're the one who exposed them to the world."

"Funny. I was under the impression they found my books pure comedy."

"Good luck."

Shaking Blackmere's hand, Daniel hurried around to the passenger side and shouted for Thraken to move. There was no way he was sitting in the back for this.

Disgruntled, and to the snickers of the rest of them, the gnome did as he was told.

Daniel climbed in and gestured for the driver to go. The SUV tore off down the empty street in a race to destiny. Whatever happened next, at least the team would meet it with the fury and gusto of people intent on vengeance.

TEN

The unmarked plane touched down on the lip of a private runway outside of Binghamton and rolled to a stop. The side door popped open, and stairs were lowered, Viviana sweeping down before it touched the tarmac. Concealed behind dark sunglasses, she wore a pleated skirt drooping to her knees and a knit sweater. Living in the south, she was unused to the autumn chill of upstate New York. The click of her heels as she strode purposefully to the waiting car was lost beneath the drowning whine of the plane's engines shutting down.

Her driver awaited her, opening the door so she could slide into the backseat. Without a word he gently closed the door and got behind the wheel.

Viviana took in the fall foliage as the car hurried down the country road. She knew everything she needed to complete her mission was in the trunk but hoped it wouldn't come to that. There'd been a time when she and Gwen were best of friends. Those days far behind them, Viviana dreaded their upcoming reunion and what she must do to preserve the sanctity of the clans.

Life seldom cared what its players wanted, however.

***

The click-clack of Nevada Slim opening and closing his knife quickly annoyed Daniel. He knew from experience every soldier had some sort of ritual or idiosyncrasy before heading into a fight. That didn't mean he wasn't ready to throttle the elf. Cramped in a tight space, there was only so much a man could take.

Daniel decided to take his mind off the noise and turned to Kip at the wheel. "What's your story?"

67

"I like fast things."

Weighted down with bodies and gear, the SUV felt like it plodded more than roared down the road. "I meant where are you from? How did you get involved with this crew?"

Kip shrugged as much as he could without losing control. "I like fast things. This is a fast thing. What more do you want from me?"

Leaning over the back of the seat, Agent Murphy explained, "Kip is a goblin. We found him on the side of the road one night. He was covered in bruises and suffering from amnesia. All it took was a stray episode of one of those drag racing shows in the hospital room and he developed this persona."

"Not gonna tell him about the track marks on his arms?" Klaus barked from the third row.

"Not my story to tell."

"Imagine that," the dwarf grumbled and fell silent.

Frustrated by the back and forth, Daniel returned his attention to the goblin. "Once we get there roll up to the front doors and keep the engine running. Hopefully we won't be in there long."

"There is one small problem," Thraken said. The squeak in his voice had that nails dragging on the chalkboard effect.

"What's that?" Daniel asked.

Heads swiveled and the gnome's face reddened. "Well, we're supposed to be doing this in secret. How are we going to do that if we go through the front door?"

Shit.

The SUV roared on.

They were almost on target.

Jerking to a squealing halt, Daniel turned to his team. "Listen up, this is how we do it. Klaus I want you to …"

"Save it, author boy. We know what to do. You sit your pretty ass here in the car. I don't need any hummie telling me what to do," the dwarf snapped, color staining his cheeks.

Grabbing the light machinegun favored by squad and fireteams, Klaus hurried off to claim the prize. The others followed, each dispersing without communication or coordination. As individuals, Daniel knew they didn't stand a chance.

Impotent with frustration, he slammed a gloved fist into the dashboard. "Murphy, follow the dwarf," he ordered to the agent milling by the car.

"Why me?" The whites of Murphy's eyes looked like small moons.

"Because I'm going to kill the son of a bitch if I see him now," Daniel growled. "I'm going after the others. Hopefully we can stop them before this all goes to shit."

Kip turned to give him a deadpanned look. "I'll wait here."

"Yeah, you do that."

Slamming the door, Daniel hurried around the side of the hotel where Jenny and Thraken disappeared. He found the gnome climbing up the façade, already several stories up. Of Jenny there was no sign—she had disappeared. Faced with an impossible situation, Daniel kept moving to secure the far end of the building and the only other access control point.

The distinctive report of a handgun firing reached him—he moved faster.

***

Xander dropped the last file on the stack and blew out a pensive breath. The list of names was a hefty collection of some of the most influential members in both clans. He saw why Basil needed them gone. If they succeeded and formed an alliance it would unravel every power base he and the monarchy spent millennia establishing. Their history was riddled with insurrections and failed coup attempts. Most failed before gaining momentum, the conspirators incarcerated. His experiences in such matters left him conflicted. There was no denying the seriousness of the matter, but he remained uncertain whether it called for summary executions.

"A job's a job," he muttered and finished the last of a now cold coffee.

Rancid aftertaste puckering his mouth, Xander glanced at his watch. He had just over forty-eight hours to prepare and complete his assignment. Two days before he earned his pardon and reunited with the love of his life: if Basil was to be believed. Expecting the double-cross, he entertained thoughts of contingencies.

His network had dried up with his conviction and Xander was never that active in this part of the country. Those precious retainers awaiting his return were cloistered around the United States in covert cells yet to be activated. Had he succeeded in becoming the new king they would have become his army of enforcers, ready to ensure the peaceful transition of power. Ironic, considering he now played that role for Basil.

A knock at the door interrupted him.

It was time to go.

Slipping into his jacket, Xander swept the files into the provided briefcase. The phone rang before he reached the door. Irritated, the elf stormed to the small table by the window, shouting "hold on" to the door when another knock sounded.

"What?" he demanded upon answering the phone.

"Sir, we have trouble."

Xander listened intently as the caller explained their situation. Combat instincts awakened, the sensations pleasing after so many years of languishing in a cell. Unable to deny he longed for the days of clashing swords and leading armies, Xander settled for his current situation.

He hung up and answered the door with far different intent from a moment ago. "I need a gun."

"Sir?"

"Get me a gun. Now," he said, peering into the hallway. "What assets do we have in the area?" Thoughts raced ahead of his tongue. "Quickly, damnit."

"T-there is a squad of dark elf commandos on the lobby floor."

"That's it?"

"We weren't expecting trouble … What's going on?"

Rubbing his chin in frustration, Xander scowled. "We've been discovered. Now get me a gun and alert the squad."

Confused, the elf asked, "What of the humans? Are we going to risk an open firefight in broad daylight?"

"Only if there's no other choice," Xander snapped. "Now, move. I need to get to the ground floor."

Following the elf to the elevator, he pushed the down button. His leg started bouncing; a nervous habit he developed in prison, despite dedicating hours of each day to finding inner peace through meditation. He frowned. Now was not the time for the jitters.

Annoying music filtered through weak speakers feigning ambiance. Amusing as it was, he had no time for the forced pleasantry. The elevator jarred as it halted. A chime announced their floor and the doors stuttered as they jerked open. Grimy light flooded the car.

The elf who had come to fetch him got one foot into the hallway before stumbling back with a grunt. He slammed into Xander, knocking them both backward. Blood blossomed on the front of his shirt. He gave Xander a confused look, hand clutching at the wound above his heart, before bursting apart in a cloud of ash and black dust.

Swearing, Xander hit the button to close the elevator door.

A second round pinged off the mirror on the back wall. Sparks singing the hair on his neck. A third struck the door as it sealed shut.

Naught but ash and a sidearm remaining of his companion, Xander snatched the weapon and checked the magazine—nine rounds. It should have held more. Why was the man not carrying a full load?

Nine rounds and an unknown number of enemy forces: a tender situation that just grew perilous, and he was trapped on the third floor of a strange location, cut off from communication with his minders.

This wasn't a fight he was looking forward to.

Xander took cover beside the doors, poking the barrel of the Glock 17 out to draw any unwanted attention. Foreign noises bounced back to him. The sounds of humanity going about their business. He smirked at the thought of forcing a fight in their midst. Unless there had been witnesses, no one would ever know of the dead elf, assuming his ashes to be naught but the product of a poor cleaning job. The indignity infuriated him. Convinced the way back to his room was clear, Xander stepped into the hall where he found a small girl with long blond hair in pigtails standing before his door. She waved and smiled at him.

"Hi, you must be Xander," she said, her voice a golden laugh over the strained atmosphere. "I've been looking for you."

He squinted. There was an odd quality about the girl. One he was vaguely familiar with. Instincts screaming, Xander clutched his weapon tighter. It was her eyes that drew his attention, sparking his ire. Pinpointed and glowing red, they seethed menace: Xander recognized death when he saw it. Retreating to the elevator wasn't an option, nor was going back to his room. His one option, limited at best, was the rear staircase at his back. He checked over his shoulder. It was a fair distance, but he had a chance. Even if was a slim one.

Praying the commandos were aware of his location, he raised his pistol and emptied the magazine into the girl. She flew back, striking the wall with a fleshy thud. The metallic click announced the gun was dry. Xander stared at the body, hoping against hope he killed her. He noticed there was no blood, instead a dark miasma oozed from the bullet holes. The last time he encountered such a creature ...

Xander threw the empty pistol down and ran for the stairwell behind him.

A growl came from behind him, accompanied by the words, "Oh, you shouldn't have done that."

A glance over his shoulder confirmed his suspicions. Dark clouds seeped from the girl's body, absorbing her until naught but a mass of darkness filled the hall. Flesh and bone disintegrated, transformed into something else. Something wild from when the world was young. With a torrid scream, the creature flew towards him.

She was hungry.

ELEVEN

Bounding down the stairs, Xander was afraid. Felt genuine fear for the first time in centuries. The eldritch creatures posing as a young girl shouldn't exist. Far older than any elf, it was a nightmare thought to be extinct.

Weaponless and lacking support, Xander knew death when it stalked him. He also knew there was little chance of it being here alone. No time for a plan, he hurried to meet his fate, hoping against hope at least one exit was clear.

Xander opted for speed and surprise over secrecy as he lowered his shoulder and barreled through the door leading to the ground floor. The clang of metal slamming against the wall echoed, announcing his position to any listening. *Tick-tock.* Xander took a split second to ensure the hall was clear and make a decision. Daylight beckoned down the lonely corridor and with it the temptation of freedom. No fool, he knew the front would be heavily guarded. But where was his support? The thunder of running boots wrested his focus; time was up.

Abandoning his initial tactic, Xander hurried down the hall to the rear entrance. Get outside and away from his assailants, then he'd figure out where to go next. He needed weapons and a vehicle. It was a little more than an hour to reach the meeting location and he still had time to develop a strategy. If only he might escape the hotel.

Xander hit the door, executing a combat roll upon exit in the event those awaiting him proved trigger happy.

"Don't move."

Still on hands and knees, Xander's heart leapt. He recognized the voice but couldn't place it. He slowly raised an empty hand. "I'm unarmed."

"I'm not," the man replied. "On your feet, Xander."

The hint of an accent. A mortal smell. Xander broke into a grin. "Daniel, I hadn't expected them to send you. After all, I was coming for you in due course."

"And here I was hoping to never see your face again."

"Is that any way to talk to an old friend?" Xander tsked.

A scoff. "When were we ever friends? You used me from the moment you saw me in Ariel's office."

"My sister never did have good judgment of character. I would have killed you but needed you to escape with the box," Xander explained. "It was a friendship of convenience."

"Says you. I actually liked your sister," Daniel snarled. "Enough talking. We can do this one of two ways. Either let me put these cuffs on you or I drill you between the eyes."

Xander rose, turning to face his captor while hoping the nightmare he'd awoken in the hallway didn't arrive. "Do you think you have it in you, Daniel? Still pretending to be the warrior, I see. The hero of the battle out to save the world." He hummed. "You're nothing but a pale comparison to what you once were. A shadow of greatness, washed up and out of shape and I know you lack the stones to kill me."

Fingers twitching on the rifle; the slightest pressure on the trigger, Daniel blinked. Twice. "Try me and find out. I'll scatter your ashes on the wind, Xander."

Xander's hands clenched into fists. His eyes narrowed, calculating. The chill midmorning air

75

produced a thin plume of mist with each breath. One. Two.

He launched at Daniel, coming low to catch him beneath the rifle. A shot fired, going wild into the trees behind him. Bodies collided. Xander crushed Daniel to the ground, knocking his rifle away and hammering a fist into the man's exposed temple. Daniel grunted and went unconscious.

Climbing to his feet, Xander reached for the rifle and was driven to the ground. Tiny fists began pummeling him from behind, striking his head and upper back. Angered, he pushed up to his knees, reached over his shoulder to snatch his assailant by the collar and threw him into the hotel wall. The satisfying sound of bone snapping reverberated back.

"I have just about had enough," Xander growled, reaching for the rifle again.

"Aw, but you haven't had a piece of me yet," a man threatened as he stepped around the corner, machine gun leveled at the him. He spat a wad of tobacco juice at Xander's feet. "I never liked elves. You talk too much and think you're better than the rest of us."

"Oh shut up and shoot me already, dwarf. Your insolence bores me."

"My pleasure." The dwarf raised his weapon, finger slipping into the trigger well.

A flight of arrows sped through the air, striking the bole of the small maple tree to their right. Others flew past them. The dwarf, realizing the ambush, turned and leapt to the side with a curse as a second flight tore through where he just stood.

Xander breathed a sigh of relief. At last. Abandoning his quest for a weapon, he ran toward the commando squad that was approaching. Six dark elves, arrows nocked to hold the dwarf at bay, were arrayed in a line, three kneeling, three standing. Arrows against machine guns wasn't ideal, but each was dipped in fast acting poison capable of being manipulated to either kill or maim.

Xander was halfway to them and the safety they represented when he saw the dark object land at their feet. His eyes widened right before he flattened himself to the cold ground. A blinding flash followed the hollow metallic bang as the munition detonated destroyed the squad. The shock wave roiled over Xander, pummeling him with unrepressed fury. His ears threatened to burst. His teeth rattled.

When he managed to pull himself off the ground Xander was alone. No sign of the dark elves remained. Whoever was foolish enough to use a bomb in a public setting like this wouldn't be deterred by any talk or misdirection. Knees wobbling, Xander stumbled away from the scene before any other surprises popped up.

He made it to the front parking lot without further incident, still weaponless but he had more options out in the open. He scanned the area for the car that brought him here, hoping against hope at least one of them was alive. Events thus far proved less than enthusing, leaving him at a disadvantage. Xander spied the van parked haphazardly by the doors. Exhaust funneled from the rear and a goblin stood beside the driver's door smoking a cigarette. How he was unaware of recent events was beyond Xander, but he used it to his advantage.

Xander stuffed his hands into his trouser pockets and slowed to a stroll as he approached the driver. That warm smile he used to ease into tense situations and charm his foes through the ages slid into place. He drew out a hand and waved. "Got an extra one of those?"

The goblin bobbed his head, reaching for the pack—he never made it. A ridge hand slammed across his throat, crushing his windpipe and dropping him to his knees. Xander struck twice more, ensuring the goblin was crippled and beyond saving. No one else around, he stepped over the writhing body and readied to jump into the vehicle. A second car screeched to a halt behind him, the driver frantically waving him forward.

"Come on, man! We need to move," the driver called. "Police have been alerted and are on the way."

It was the human. Of course he survived.

Xander jumped into the car and buckled up. They roared off, leaving the debacle in their rearview mirror.

"Where's Crispin? What happened to the others?"

Xander shook his head. "Dead."

"What? All of them?"

"I didn't stutter," Xander snarled.

"Shit!" the driver slammed his palm on the steering wheel several times. "Shit! What are we going to do now? I didn't sign up for this."

Xander's eyes narrowed. *Oh, I have plenty of ideas on what to do with you, annoying creature.* Instead of acting on impulse, he slowed his breath and said, "Calm down. We still have a task to perform, and I need you to get me there. Now, what's your name?"

"My name? Who cares about that, man?"

"I said calm down and tell me your name. This won't work otherwise."

Fingers up and spread, thumbs guiding the wheel, the driver exhaled and nodded. "Okay. All right. I'm Dale."

"There, see? Not so hard. Dale, I'm Xander. Can I count on you to get me where I need to be? This is very important."

"Yeah. Sure. It's not far, but once that's done I want to be far away from here, man. The boss didn't say anything about being hunted."

No, I don't suppose he did, but then again Basil always plays his cards close to the chest. What else have I gotten into; I wonder?

***

Daniel awoke to raw pain, everywhere. His head thundered from Xander's punch. Vision blinking in and out of darkness, he groaned and rolled over. What happened? He remembered getting the drop on Xander, then ... Daniel blinked rapidly, hoping to clear his sight, and scanned his surroundings. A crumpled figure lay nearby. He squinted before recognizing Thraken. The gnome lived but looked to have taken a worse beating than himself.

Ashes flitted across his face. The familiar tang suggesting much worse had happened while he was out. Heavy footfalls announced Klaus. The dwarf appeared fine, making Daniel want to kill him.

"Bastard got away," Klaus said upon seeing him awake. His baritone rumbled like an avalanche down cold, lonely mountains.

Daniel glared. "This is all your fault! If you would have waited while we made a plan Xander would be in custody already."

"Easy, hummie. I did what I thought was best. You're the one in charge."

"That means you do what the hell I say! This isn't a democracy." Daniel trembled with rage. Spittle flew from his mouth. The index finger pointed at the door bouncing with each syllable.

"Will you two shut up!" Thraken whimpered. His pulled himself closer to the hotel wall, unwilling to meet their gazes. "This is all of our faults."

Klaus shrugged. "He's got a point. None of us did any good, did we?"

"We could have," Daniel reiterated.

"Not a chance. They had a commando kill squad here," Nevada Slim said with an awkward drawl as he strolled up to them. "I took them out with a homemade special, but Xander still got away." He paused, frowning. "Anyone see Jenny?"

As if on cue, she skipped out from the backdoor, that perpetual childish smile etched on her face. "I'm here. That was fun!"

Genuine excitement filled her voice, leaving Daniel stymied in confusion. Nothing in his experience suggested anything fun about what had just happened. They'd had their butts kicked and were once again falling behind. The game became more perilous.

Brushing some of the leaves and debris, Daniel snatched his rifle off the ground. "Come on. There's still a chance we can catch him."

"Not without knowing where he's headed," Thraken pointed out. "Face it, Daniel. We lost."

As much as he hated to admit it, Daniel knew the gnome was right. He dreaded the inevitable call back to Blackmere. Doing a quick headcount, he asked, "Hey, where's Murphy? Anyone see him during the confusion?"

They looked about but found no trace of the DESA agent. *How am I going to explain this?* Suspicions of betrayal awakened, leaving Daniel stumbling. *Hey Blackmere, it's me. We lost Xander and I think your agent is a baddie.*

The handheld radios on their belts cackled at once. "You guys need to get up here. I think I found something."

Daniel blew a sigh of relief.

Murphy.

TWELVE

The battered team, blanketed in the shame of failure, huddled in what had been Xander's room. Heads down, they were quiet for the most part. The only member not engulfed in self-deprecation was Nevada Slim. If the dark elf felt bad for killing his own kind he didn't show it.

Daniel looked at the handful of files spread out across the bed. Faces and names of people who meant nothing to him but were obviously important. His thoughts bounced between the ineffectiveness of his team, a position he had yet to fully embrace, and his brief confrontation with the man who wanted him dead. *I had him.*

"Who are these people?" he asked after shaking off the negativity infesting his mind.

Murphy flipped through a file. "Businessmen, low level politicians, millionaires. All important in their own right."

Rubbing a sore shoulder, Daniel asked, "Do you think Xander's staging a coup?"

"After spending years in prison? How?"

"He was always the best of us," Klaus piped in. "A good man we looked up to. I don't remember a cross word said about him."

Daniel glanced at the dwarf, biting his tongue. There would be a time and place for airing grievances. Picking up Xander's trail before it went cold took priority. A seemingly impossible task further complicated by the team's inability to work together. He understood why he was being ostracized, but Blackmere's assurances of the rest having worked together fell short of his expectations. The real question became how was Daniel going to get them to gel together to complete their mission?

"Regardless, there must be a connection between his previous attempt at stealing the crown and these people," Murphy interjected.

Reaching down, Nevada Slim snatched up a file and stared hard at the photo clipped to the cover. His index finger trembled.

"What is it?" Daniel asked, spying the movement.

"This is my father," he whispered. "A terrible man bent on accumulating wealth and power. He runs one of the world's largest black market munitions enterprises."

Stunned silence dominated them, all save for a quiet gasp then giggle by Jenny.

"I don't suppose you want to give him a call?" Daniel asked. The significance of the moment was lost on him. Whatever history Slim had with his father was convoluted, perhaps strained, but unless the elf was more forthcoming there seemed little point in prolonging a redacted conversation. No one else offered any information, making this the only lead.

"About what?"

"Right. Murphy, could it be possible Xander is after something else? We know he wanted to shift the balance of power by removing Alvin and Morgen and placing Gwen on the throne. These files suggest either an underground cabal pulling strings, or it could be a hit list."

Murphy blinked, realization dawning. "You think he's out to kill them?"

"I've seen enough movies to think it. The question is why."

Clearing his throat, Thraken waited until all eyes were fixed on him before speaking. "What about who he's working for? I mean the guy was in prison for how many years? There's no way he could put together these dossiers in a just a few hours."

Son of a bitch. Xander has a boss. Daniel turned to Murphy with eyes wide. "We have a new problem."

"I need to call Agent Blackmere."

Daniel nodded. "Yeah, you do."

Once Murphy left the room to make his call, Daniel moved so his back was to the window. It had been too long since he last addressed a squad or platoon. Rust coated his instincts, but like every good soldier, the right way to yell at people never truly left.

"Look, I don't know what happened earlier, but we all failed miserably," he began. "Xander should be in handcuffs and on his way back to the prison by now. The only way we are going to catch him is by working together, as a *team*. Not this individual John Wayne nonsense."

"John who?" Jenny asked.

Klaus snorted. "You're supposed to be our leader."

Daniel's fists clenched. "I was trying to do just that, but someone had to jump out the truck and go rushing in without a plan."

"That's the problem with you humans. Too much time wasted talking about it instead of doing it," the dwarf snarled. "I had him until you and the gnome got in the way."

"Seems to me like you didn't have anything except a bunch of new holes in your chest if I hadn't dropped that grenade," Nevada Slim commented. One boot was propped against the wall, lending him a look straight out of a cigarette commercial.

"What's your beef with me, Klaus?" Daniel decided to get to the source of the issue. "You've been giving me grief from the moment we met. Let's clear the air, because I'm not moving forward with you until we do. I have too much on the line to play games with a dwarf with a bad attitude."

Arm muscles bulging, the dwarf stepped closer. "Fine. You want to know my problem? It's you. You've been profiting off our people for how many years now? Turning us in caricatures and jokes for the rest of the world to laugh at. I'm not a joke. He's not a joke. She's … well, she's not someone I want to get mad."

Daniel sensed the issue went much deeper, but being no psychiatrist, he wasn't willing to poke the bear. "You do realize I had no idea any of this existed, right? No one does. For most of the world you are creatures of imagination. That's why it's called fantasy."

"Do I look like a fantasy to you, hummie?" Klaus snapped.

"Maybe with a little lipstick," Thraken suggested.

The dwarf spun, pointing a finger at the gnome. "You keep your gums together. This is between me and him."

"What do you want me to tell you, Klaus? I'm just one of a million other authors who grew up reading and watching movies about you. Never once did I assume any of you were real, not until I stumbled on Ariel dying. Do you need an apology? Will an 'I'm sorry' assuage any ill feelings keeping you from playing nice?"

"You're getting real close to losing a tooth."

Daniel stiffened. "I'm not trying to be friends. All we need to do is get along until Xander is back in custody. After that you can come try and knock it out. There's nothing but air and opportunity for you, Klaus."

Huffing, the dwarf stepped back. "Fair enough. I look forward to rearranging your face."

"This is tense!" Jenny squeaked suddenly.

Her childlike admission dispelled the tension just enough. Daniel relaxed his fists and tossed the file he'd been holding back on the pile. They remained locked in silence until Murphy returned. All eyes expectantly fell on the DESA agent. Daniel studied the man and concluded he was still green. That made him a liability.

"What's the word?" he asked.

Murphy cleared his throat. "Blackmere is making a few calls. He is … concerned with this new development and has a few ideas but doesn't want to make a guess until we learn more."

"Unless we're ordering room service we need to get back on the road," Klaus suggested. "Staying here solves nothing and it won't be long before the police arrive."

"We don't know where Xander is heading," Nevada Slim countered.

"West. We need to assume he is still heading west," Daniel said. "I agree with Klaus. Let's get back in the truck and prepare to move. Blackmere has our number."

"I don't think …"

"You don't need to," Daniel cut the elf off. "Let's roll. I'm sure Kip is wondering where we are."

"Damn it!" Klaus opened and slammed the truck door.

They'd found Kip, what was left of him anyway, scattered through the front seat and on the ground in little piles. Yet another victim in Xander's campaign of terror. Daniel frowned at the loss, despite not knowing the man at all, and wondered what could drive a man to abandon all his principles and become the villain. None of it made sense to his writer mind. It was a story pulled from dark mysteries. A more damning question arose from the jumble of thoughts. What was Xander's endgame?

"Now what?" Murphy fretted. It was clear he hadn't expected any casualties and now there were at least eight dead, who knew how many witnesses, and a potential firestorm of blowback should this make the local news.

"We keep moving. There'll be time to mourn Kip when the mission is finished," Daniel said. "Anybody want to drive?"

"I'll do it," Nevada Slim offered. "But we need to clean him out first. I'm not sitting on remains."

***

Basil Kadis settled into the cushions of chair and gazed out the small window to his right. The private plane was preparing to takeoff, carrying him far from mayhem he had unleashed in upstate New York. For the first time in centuries his heart was light. Setting Xander free and turning him to the cause presented the best opportunity for Basil to assert control over the clans and cleanse the upper echelons of those resisters to change who stagnated the clans.

The very real possibility of Xander failing remained high but it was a gamble Basil willingly took. The only true opposition to his plan came from Morgen. The isolated queen was trapped in a world that no longer needed nor wanted her. Removing her might prove problematic, but Basil was a man used to solving impossible situations. The prime minister considered himself a practical man of exceptional intelligence. So long as he remained ahead of the others, unwilling participants in a game they didn't know was begun, he remained the sole best chance of shifting the balance and returning the clans back to their rightful place as the dominant species.

"We are set for takeoff, Prime Minister. It is a two hour flight time to Raleigh," the steward announced. "Can I get you anything?"

"Yes, Hampton. I believe an old fashioned is in store," Basil said. Bourbon was the one human contribution he enjoyed, and it was time to celebrate.

The wait was finally over.

**

Viviana read through the email report with a frown. Whatever violence occurred in Newburgh was swift and decisive, directing her train of thought down roads she had once thought impossible. Until recently the clans operated at night and as far from prying eyes as they could to preserve the secrecy of their kind. Now the debacle outside of a hotel threatened to undo all they had worked so hard to secure. *A firefight in broad daylight, with witnesses?* It was in direct violation of the clans' agreement with the Department of Extra Species Affairs and longstanding treaties signed by all major parties.

Exposure became a real possibility, leaving Viviana reeling. How easily it could all come crashing down due to the ignorant acts of vengeance sparked by a single man. Yet why now? What game did Xander play and who was responsible for releasing him upon the unsuspecting world? Until she had those answers, Viviana remained a step behind.

Her phone rang, disrupting her thoughts which, she admitted, was for the best. Viviana read the caller id before answering. This might just prove the answer to her questions.

"Why hello," she said. "I wasn't expecting you to call."

She fell silent and listened as the man on the other end filled in many of the blanks.

Given a new target, Viviana ended the call and slipped her phone back into the jacket pocket. First thing first, she needed to have that conversation with Gwen. Then she would deal with Xander.

THIRTEEN

"No more hotels."

Dale rolled his eyes but the car kept rolling past a string of hotels and fast food joints announcing their arrival into Middletown. Only a few miles from their engagement with DESA's strike force, Xander knew they were far from being secure. But without the firepower and support of the dark elf commandos he was in desperate need of security.

The twin factors of being under-armed and hunted left him cagey. Ever a pragmatic man, Xander decided acquiring weapons came first then, with so much time remaining before the meeting, he needed to find a place to lay low. Time in which his enemies would assuredly use to zero in on his position and do their best to stop him. Frustrated, the elf placed a hand over his rumbling stomach.

"Sure you're not hungry?" Dale asked.

Xander shook his head. "I need more than this pistol before I can eat."

"Relax. We lost them. It should be smooth sailing from here to Roscoe."

"You have no idea who we are facing," Xander scolded. "These people won't stop until we are both dead. I need time and the ability to defend myself if we are to have any chance."

"Why would they kill me? I'm just the driver!"

Xander offered a feigned look of sympathy. "You think that matters? Our friends back there were uninterested in getting to know us before they attacked. You have one factor going in your favor, however."

Fingers tapping the steering wheel, Dale asked, "Yeah? What's that?"

"You're human. Disposing your body takes time and effort."

Far from comforted, Dale blinked. Xander almost felt a twinge of pity for the man. Almost.

"Y-you need weapons. I know a place. Mr. Kadis suggested we might need it."

Of course he did. "How far?"

"A mile, maybe less. It's one of the special areas Mr. Kadis has established across the state. He says you never know when an emergency will happen."

Xander fought the wry grin from breaking through. Basil Kadis was a man of impeccable taste and the deep thinking of a chess grand master. Never leaving anything to chance, he meticulously worked through each problem, anticipating trouble and establishing contingencies to prevent controversy from sticking to him. It took centuries to master, a fact made more difficult by the invent of the technology age, but Basil always came out on top. By every regard, the man was a villain.

Dale pulled the car off the interstate and into the heart of Middletown. Cutting north up Dolson Avenue, he mouthed the building address repeatedly until his eyes caught the gleam of the neon sign advertising a gun and pawn shop.

Xander's eyebrow arched, unimpressed but amused at the audacity. "This is Basil's secret location?"

Dale shrugged, dropping the car into park and cutting the engine. "Mr. Kadis says sometimes the best place to hide things is in plain sight."

Xander got out and headed for the front doors before noticing Dale was gesturing at him to move to the side. "Not the front. The shop owner doesn't know about this. We were told to use the side entrance to keep a low profile."

"A low profile in the middle of the day?" Xander gestured to the nearly full parking lot. "You do realize there are at least a hundred people who can see us right now."

Another shrug. This was becoming infuriating.

"I just do what I'm told."

Wonderful. Yet another stooge in an increasingly lengthy line. "Who is our contact?"

"He's an acquired taste. Goes by the name Sweeny."

Xander suppressed a groan. He knew the name and Dale's description more than fit.

"Tell me why I shouldn't turn you in for the reward right now?"

Oily skin shining under the luminescent lights, Sweeny stalked out from behind a makeshift counter of weapon's crates. He pulled up the back of his falling pants, farting in the process. Nose curling, Sweeny glared at Xander with the enmity of centuries. Pimples covered his cheeks, turning his face a rosy complexion. Filth encrusted fingernails accented sinewy arms lacking definition. Nothing about the man suggested anything worthy of remembrance. Well, leastwise not kindly.

"Sweeny, always a pleasure," Xander answered.

An aroma wafted off the man, lending authority to the grime impossibly stained in his clothing. The choker necklace with a hollowed out .50 cal round on it seemed a bit much, but Sweeny prided himself on his knowledge of weapons, and who to sell them to.

Holding up his right hand, Sweeny displayed the nubs of two fingers. "I still owe you, you bastard."

"That was three hundred years ago. Surely enough time has passed to let bygones be," Xander retorted.

"When's the last time you tried picking anything up with half a hand?"

Already exasperated, Xander no longer felt like playing. Sweeny was a notorious arms dealer with a nasty temper, even for a lich. Xander supposed being undead did that to you. Their one meeting, resulting in the elf taking half the lich's hand, was during a minor skirmish in Canada. He didn't recall why they were fighting, only that they were employed on opposite sides of the conflict.

"Those were different times and, as I recall, you were trying to kill me and turn me into one of your minions," Xander snapped. "I didn't come to remember the past. I need weapons, enough for a large job."

Nonplussed, the lich hoped up on the counter, each swing of the legs cracking the aged boxes. "Guess that puts me in the driver's seat, don't it?"

"I'm sure Basil will compensate you handsomely for your assistance."

Sweeny recoiled.

Throwing the prime minister's name around produced the desired result and the lich lost some of his fervor, Xander suppressed a chuckle.

"You working for Kadis now? I never thought I'd see the day."

"Times change."

Unconvinced, Sweeny rubbed his scruff. "Uh huh. What do you need?"

"Dale, tell the man. I'll be waiting outside."

Dale emerged a short time later dragging a large plastic storage container. The wheels bowed under the weight. His cheeks were red, and his breathing labored.

Xander watched, not feeling inclined to help, as the man continued across the parking lot to their car. He grinned upon catching Dale cursing under his breath. The frailty of humankind continued amusing him, causing the elf to wonder how they became the dominant species. He only moved once Dale finished loading the weapons and kit.

"Thanks for the help," Dale snarled once they were both in the car.

"You seem a capable man. Far be it for me to impede your progress."

Turning the key, Dale threw the car into gear and roared off.

They gained the interstate and headed west, out of the flat lands and closer to the lower peaks of the Catskill Mountains. Perhaps not the most idyllic trip, though the accents of changing leaves brightened much of the dull. Xander caught numerous sidelong glances directed at him, accompanied by the tap of Dale's left foot.

"What was all that back there with Sweeny?" Dale asked.

"Has this been bothering you?"

The man nodded causing Xander to hum before answering, "Sweeny and I have a sordid history. We've never been friendly, especially not after he tried killing me during the French and Indian War."

"When was that?"

"Not a student of history I see: We crossed paths in 1757."

Dale's eyes bulged. "Holy shit! Man, you're that old?"

"Far older. That was merely when we found ourselves on opposite sides of a war neither of us belonged in," Xander replied. "I have walked this planet for almost a thousand years."

He could see the wheels working overtime in Dale's mind. Xander knew humans found difficulty seeing beyond the scope of their limited lifespans. That any creature was capable of living centuries proved beyond the subtle range of rationalization in the human mind. He considered letting the man stew in his ignorance for a time.

Xander never cared for working with mortals. They proved too needy, clingy with their infantile behaviors. Seldom did one show any sense of higher achievements deserving of his time or patience. The wealth of the human mind proved dangerously low, in his opinion. Dale certainly fell down the food chain, but the man had his uses. Primarily ensuring he arrived at the target location on time.

"Where are we heading to? The mission isn't until tomorrow night."

"Monticello Raceway," Dale supplied, his tone hesitant. "There's a horse track and casino up in the mountains. Plenty of folks coming and going. We should be able to disappear for the night and head to Roscoe in the morning. Shouldn't be more than a half hour drive."

Xander frowned. There was too much time between now and the meeting. Far too long for anything to go wrong. He knew from past experience the DESA teams could be ruthless, often hounding their prey into submission without firing a shot. That they actively attempted to kill him at the hotel was proof enough he needed to go deep enough underground to stay alive.

DESA too had a nasty habit of selecting the worst to their hunter teams. Men and women with sordid pasts capable of unprecedented aggression with points to prove. Others sought redemption for past wrongs, making them both dangerous and unpredictable. Xander had run across the dwarf before and there was no love lost. The

94

monster in the hallway was a different story. She shouldn't exist. He once led a campaign to eradicate them from the New World. A campaign thought to be successful ... Clearly it wasn't.

Shaking off the growing sensation of impending doom, Xander focused on the task at hand. Reach the meeting site and eliminate those seeking to destabilize the hierarchy. Straightforward, if unpleasant. He'd never considered himself a mercenary for hire. Now he was trapped in a spiral of self-destruction that only reuniting with his beloved Gwen and escaping overseas might address.

The car sped on. His ears popped, announcing their ascent into one of the premier mountain ranges in the northeast. Not that it mattered. Xander was a man focused on the mission. Scenery be damned.

FOURTEEN

Why the royal family chose the heart of North Carolina to be their home base confounded Basil for centuries. Far from idyllic, the terrain was uninspiring, the weather too temperamental for his tastes, and the lack of anything of importance nearby stifling.

Born to a wealthy family in what would become Vienna, Basil Kadis used his generational wealth and family's influence to parlay himself into an indispensable position among the clans. Winning the coveted position of Prime Minister allowed him to right old wrongs and develop and enact policy designed to keep him in power for generations to come. Yet despite all his achievements, he continued to find himself in the heart of the American south.

The elevator rumbled to the top floor before depositing him into a warm lobby where he was greeted by an elderly woman with a suspicious gleam in her eye. Once pointed in the right direction, Basil directed his adjutant to get a drink at the bar and wait. He didn't anticipate a long meeting.

Climbing the circling grand staircase a few minutes later, he found his way to one of the private meeting rooms, drink in hand. He entered without knocking.

Morgen awaited him with that condescending look he'd endured for far too long. *So much for the element of surprise.*

"Basil, how good it is to see you again. You should have announced your arrival so I might have planned a proper welcome."

Charming and political, she dripped venom with every word. There was no love lost between them, forcing Basil to reevaluate how far he could push her before the wheels came off.

"Your majesty," he offered a curt bow, "it appears my coming did not go unnoticed."

"Foolish of you to believe any matter of significance escapes my attention. Why are you here?"

"You have never been fond of the standard pleasantries."

Morgen pursed her lips, eyes narrowing. "Leave the games to the children. You and I have been far to entwined over the years to beat around the bush, as the humans say. Why are you here? I will not ask a third time."

His left eye danced; a twitch developed over too many meetings with king and queen. Puffing out his chest, Basil calmed his nerves. There was no turning back. "Very well. I have come to inform you of Xander's escape. As a result, the Forum has been called to decide whether you have lost the ability to rule. It brings me no pleasure to tell you this, but there will be a vote of confidence within the fortnight."

Out of the myriad reactions he envisioned, laughter wasn't one. Morgen's golden laugh spread through the room, reverberating off the soundproof walls to strike his ears as tiny bolts of focused hatred. His left eye twitched again, unstoppable as Basil succumbed to annoyance. "I don't recall saying anything humorous," he ground through gritted teeth.

"You honestly expect me to believe you managed to organize a coup without my knowing? You are many things, Basil, unintelligent not one," she chided. "I've been waiting for this since Alvin died. Ever you seek to elevate your station in life, at the expense of others mind you, but you forget one fact."

Bitch. "That being?"

"Your ambition makes you transparent. Or did you believe I would think Xander escaped from the Grinder on his own? With no help or support from the outside? The former champion is a resourceful man, but even he lacks the name power to gather allies to his cause," Morgen explained. The delight in her voice ground upon him, mocking his carefully laid plans and dreams of ascension.

"I've had people watching you since that first night. Every move you have made was witnessed and reported on by my network. I am the queen of the dark elves, Basil, not a commoner with limited resources."

Arrogance shone in her tone, forcing him to shrink back. Yet he still replied with, "Perhaps that is true. Perhaps not. Do not be so foolish as to think I have not prepared for this, however. The vote will be held, and you will be found in no confidence by the ruling houses. The stain of your leadership will soon be washed away, and a new day will dawn for our people."

Morgen folded her arms, an angry finger tapping against her forearm. "Just like that Basil Kadis will sweep in and unite the clans so that we may prosper and return the world to our dominion. All shall be as it once was. Is that correct?"

"Enough," he conceded.

She stepped forward, swift and lethal. A crimson fingernail jabbed into the bottom of his double chin. "Dear Basil, even should your ploy succeed, I will remove you from the equation. Try me and I will eliminate every trace of your bloodline until only you remain. And then, alone and forgotten, I will spend an eternity tormenting you to the point you can dream of nothing but taking your own life. Such pitiful existence is your future, Basil. But I leave that choice to you."

Humiliated, reeling in confusion, he trembled from head to toe. "You will rue this day, Morgen. If it is war you want, war you shall have."

"Shall I escort you out?"

The nail jabbed deeper, piercing flesh. A warm trickle dripped down her finger to splat on the multicolored carpet.

"I can find my own way," he growled, leaning forward and applying more pressure to the wound. "I won't forget this, Morgen. You shouldn't either."

He stepped back, hand grasping the handle. Before leaving, Basil said, "The funny part is I came here to convince you to join my side. It was the only chance you had of saving face. I feel sorry for you, Morgen. I truly do. How low fall the heroes before they are devoured by the abyss."

The door closed behind him as he seethed with impotence. All his carefully wrought plans torn to shreds by a cunning player.

***

Thaddeus Blackmere sat behind a small desk in his appropriated office far from the comforts he was used to. Washington deemed it necessary for him to remain in the field until the matter with Xander was resolved, much to his chagrin. He once hoped his field time was ended, earning a lofty position in the agency after the assassination debacle a few years ago. Instead of leading from behind a desk, Blackmere found himself being sent on wild goose chases and life altering missions. Penance for his failure in North Carolina? He didn't know.

Skimming through reports and real time information, Blackmere flipped through the downloaded files confiscated by his team. The failure at the hotel infuriated him, but he was impotent in the matter. Agent Murphy and Daniel directed the flow of events and his confidence in their combined abilities remained high despite the setback. A thin smile creeping across his face, Blackmere knew Daniel's acceptance to the team was far from guaranteed. His fame among the clans was legendary, if but for the wrong reasons.

Half accepted him as a quiet champion, alleviating their problems through the driving fiction of his books. The humor in his characters and tales brightened many days, even if Daniel never intended for his books to provide comedic value. The other half reviled him for making a mockery of their traditions and history. They vowed to do nasty things should they ever get hold of him. Empty rhetoric as far as Blackmere was concerned. The same voiceless noise humans presented when disturbed and knowing there was nothing they could do about it.

The odd collection of miscreants he saddled Daniel with were a mixed bunch. Most had no qualms with following the human's lead, but it was the dwarf who threatened to upend the mission should his temper become unleashed—it had been a risk worth taking. That and Klaus was one of the few available to respond.

Blackmere pinched the bridge of his nose. His eyes burned from endless scanning and scrolling. *What am I missing?*

That these names were captains of their industry and influential took moments to confirm. Elfkind was well documented by DESA and, thanks to the cooperation with the throne, each dossier provided a wealth of information filling in the empty puzzle. The one piece eluding him thus far was why were they gathering in an obscure location just hours after Xander was freed?

Blackmere found it worth considering that this powerful group played a major role in Xander's plans. With so much power behind him, claiming the throne and finishing what he started would be within his grasp. Not only would this produce a swift transfer of power, it also provided Xander with the resources to fundamentally change the clans for the foreseeable future. All Alvin and Morgen once thought to accomplish would be washed away in a cascade of failure. *Perhaps it was time?*

Their enmity produced the schism, reducing the clans to groveling shades of their former dominance. With each side constantly at the other's throats, there was little room for improvement or advances. Humanity pushed ahead while elfkind mired into an unprecedented staleness. This might prove their one opportunity to correct their course and right old wrongs.

King Xander. Blackmere groaned. He was missing something. No doubt the most important factor of all.

But what?

Frustrated, he decided to get some fresh air.

The bustle of agents and trainees filled the hall with militaristic sounds, reminding him of those days when he had to deliver paperwork to the SEAL training compound during his stint in the Navy. That raw testosterone fueled atmosphere was charged with excitement and terror. He felt similar among the teams here as they prepared for every contingency. The only real difference was the acceptance of women into the ranks.

Stepping outside, Blackmere cleared his mind and pushed the scents of sweat and gunpowder away. The sun was dropping over the western mountains, promising a chill night. He stuffed a hand into his pocket and produced a cigarette. When he resumed his smoking habit was a mystery, for he didn't remember.

Inhaling the bitter tang of nicotine, Blackmere stiffened as a thought, unbidden, crawled through his brain, permeating those quiet chambers of reason delivering him to repeated success throughout his careers.

What if ... Xander had been freed and set loose to kill the people in the dossiers? The repercussions would ripple through the clans, toppling the current powerbase until chaos reigned. From the ashes a new order would be born and, if Blackmere's guess was correct, woe be unto humanity should that beast become uncaged.

The cigarette fell from his mouth. A shower of sparks striking the concrete.

What if.

FIFTEEN

"Are you certain? I understand." Agent Murphy hung up the cellphone, a flustered look twisting his face enough to produce a giggle from Jenny. Ignoring her, Murphy cleared his throat. "That was Agent Blackmere," he began. "He said the dossiers belong to the most influential members of the ruling families and are either accomplices or targets."

"Meaning we need to get moving to stop Xander from finding them." Daniel ran through a host of scenarios. None of them ended well. "Did Blackmere say anything about where we can find these people or when?"

"Agent Blackmere was unsure."

Daniel twisted around as much as his gear and seatbelt allowed. "Why do insist on calling him that? He's just Blackmere."

Murphy's eyes bulged. "You can't be serious. He is a legend in DESA. New agents are taught of his exploits during initial training. If I can become half as good as he—"

"Uh huh." Unimpressed, Daniel ignored the fumbling, starstruck agent. Idolizing a superior was a dangerous game. "So what you do you say, Slim, care to reach out to your father now?"

"Nope."

Daniel bit back the curse threatening to leap off the tip of his tongue. "Whatever daddy issues you have need to be set aside, for the mission."

Another mile went by with Daniel stewing before Nevada Slim pursed his lips, muttering, "Okay."

Daniel should have felt relief but found only consternation. "You're a pretty verbose guy, huh?"

"I didn't know he was German," Thrakus whispered to Klaus.

The dwarf snorted and said, "Idiot."

Daniel rolled his eyes. "Pull over at the next spot and give him a call. We need all the ammo we can get for this and given we have no idea where Xander is heading or why, I need a way forward."

"Okay." Nevada Slim pulled the truck off to the widened side of the road at the bottom of a hill. "Let me call."

He jumped out, slamming the door so their conversation remained familial.

"We know Xander is going for the princess," Murphy said to fill the silence.

Watching Nevada Slim become animated, almost shouting into his phone amused Daniel for reasons he failed to understand. He glanced at Murphy. "We assume that is his target. That intel remains unconfirmed. I need tangible evidence to stop Xander for good."

"Wouldn't it be prudent to head to the facility she's being kept in to cut him off?"

Daniel suspected this was the agent's first assignment, and what a hell of a situation he had been thrown into. *Poor kid. He didn't even know he was handed to the wolves, ripe for chewing.* "Not with this new information. We can make a better plan once Slim gets back in."

Turning, he watched as Nevada Slim slipped his phone back into his breast pocket and, placing both hands on his head, tilted his face back and closed his eyes. *Not good.* Daniel's impatience urged him to go to the man. Time was wasting and his family's life was at stake. Parlor tricks and theatrics could wait until Xander was back behind bars where he belonged. Precious seconds ticked by.

Nevada Slim walked away, leaving the team in suspense. Deciding he needed to clear the air, Daniel got out and beckoned Murphy to join him. They huddled on the opposite side of the truck, closest to the busy road. The mechanical screams of passing vehicles followed by the whip and rustle of clothes snapping against their skin provided a welcome distraction from the tension building.

"How long have you been an agent?" Daniel got straight to the point.

"A few years," Murphy replied, blinking several times. "Why is that impor—"

Daniel silenced him with a hand. "I spent three years fighting in two different wars. I was part of the group that hunted down Xander the first time he turned rogue and assassinated the king. This isn't a game. We don't have time for you to express your puppy love for Blackmere. I need you to get your head in the game, follow my lead, and provide me with backup whenever I need it."

"I know what I'm doing."

"Not saying you don't, kid, but this isn't a training assignment. People are going to get killed. We've already lost one member of the team. I can't afford to lose any more. That means you keep your head on a swivel, remember your training, and start acting like a government agent who doesn't officially exist."

Flustered, Murphy's cheeks reddened. "I can do my job, Daniel. Don't worry about that, but when this is finished you and I are going to have a conversation on etiquette in the field."

"You're fucking with me, right?" His mouth went dry as the urge to punch Murphy in the mouth surged. Every bit of this mission reminded him why he never wanted to be in charge of people again. Too many personalities. Too many issues. They needed a win, and fast, if he had any chance of pulling them together.

In reply, Murphy climbed back in the truck.

"So much for adult time," Daniel muttered. Spying Slim back in the driver's seat, he hurried to join him.

"My father gave me a location to meet him," Nevada Slim said once he shut the door, each word dominated by that thick Slavic accent. "It is not far."

"Why is your father in upstate New York?" Daniel asked. "I thought you were from Belarus?"

"There is meeting nearby."

"I got twenty on the other names in those files being part of that meeting," Klaus rumbled from the backseat.

"Oh, I like games!" Jenny exclaimed. "Can I play too? Twenty-five!"

"Fifty!" Thraken shouted, caught up in the spirit of things. "Fifty what though?" He huffed when Klaus' elbow punched his ribs.

Daniel bit his lower lip before asking Nevada Slim, "Did your father say who this meeting was with?"

"Da. This will be fun."

***

Viviana stared up at the old Civil War prison dominating the far side of the street. Fog and low-lying clouds hid the upper floors of the red brick building. An eerie sensation crawled down her spine, as if she could hear the distant screams of those Confederate soldiers who lost their lives within the drab brick walls, far from home and scared. Tragic, though far worse had been done to her people through the centuries. Why anyone thought to keep one of elfkind, royalty no less, in such deplorable conditions was beyond her. Yet another reason to despise what humanity had become.

The click of her heels was muted in the autumn morning. She pulled the collar of her jacket around her tighter and walked with deliberate intent to the former prison. Undergoing renovations and, to modest extent, rebuilding, the historic value of the building was a far cry from the larger, dominating Elmira Corrections Facility occupying most of the hillside farther up the road. Neither location enthused her, but Viviana settled for the obscurity of the past to conduct her business.

Some deeds demanded to remain unwitnessed.

A burly construction worker in a florescent yellow vest, hard hat, and half smoked cigarette dropping from the corner of his mouth moved to intercept her. To the average human he was a middle aged, overweight man trying to make a living. She knew him to be much more. He was one of the elite. The Old Guards once assigned to ensure the safety of the royal bloodlines.

"Lady Cal," he said in greeting. "We were not expecting you so soon. I trust your flight went well."

"Coming here is never a joyful experience, but the journey was at least pleasant. Thank you," Viviana replied. "Where is she?"

"Come, I will guide you."

Following his lead, she entered the building forgotten by time. They headed down into the basement, where she expected to find a spider infested cell containing the disgraced heir to the throne. To her surprise, the Old Guard opened an iron cased door nestled behind a fireplace unused since the 1860s and ushered her into the well-lit tunnel leading down. An appreciative glimmer danced in her eyes.

Eventually they found themselves before a lone cell at the end of an interminably long tunnel. There, curled up in an easy chair watching television, was the princess. Viviana questioned the luxury of her confinement. A large bed with plush mattresses, privacy bathroom, kitchenet and a living space to enjoy the latest shows was accompanied by a full bookcase. Perhaps the most unsettling item in the cell was the black and white family photo standing before the castle at the entrance to the Magic Kingdom. The audacity.

"Good morning, Princess," Viviana began.

Gwen refused to look, intent on Lucy and Ethel's current hijinks. "Viviana Cal. My mother's favorite toy. What do you want?"

"An even exchange." Viviana pulled off her leather gloves, making a show of slapping them in an empty palm.

"I have nothing you need. You may return to Mother and tell her I am quite content with where I am. She need not worry."

Gwen's insolence was infuriating and a far cry from their days of friendship, forcing Viviana to swallow her pride. Too much was at risk to give in to base temptations. "Cute, but there is more going on than you have been privileged to."

"You don't say."

Snooty bitch. "Perhaps it would interest you to learn your beloved is on the loose with a mission to kill?"

Gwen leapt to her feet, rushing to the bars. Electricity shimmered as she got too close. "Xander is free?"

"By nefarious hands. He has been turned into a tool of assassination. Does it bother you to know the love of your life is little more than an unpaid murderer for hire? How low the lofty have fallen."

"He would never do that. Xander is a man of ideals and moral integrity," Gwen protested.

"He is also a man in desperate need to remain alive."

"I don't believe you." The words were weak, almost faint. Fire bled from Gwen's eyes, leaving her diminished. Close to breaking.

Good. This was easier than I suspected. "There is still a chance to save him. Death need not claim him this day, but I need your help."

"What can I do?" Any pretense of Xander's innocence was gone. Gwen's desperation was clear.

Viviana stepped close to the bars, feeling the tingling sensation ripple up her chest. She laid out a bare plan that would ensure Xander's survival and remove them both from the interests of the hierarchy and DESA. It was an implausible scenario, but the only viable option open to her.

She smiled.

SIXTEEN

The truck pulled off the main road and onto the overgrown driveway leading to the abandoned and forgotten building nestled deep in the forbidding woods. A home of unrealized grandeur, there was a dark air surrounding it. Daniel felt his chest tighten as he took in the ivy-covered walls. Weeds and vines crept up from the ground, green tendrils of inviting decay. The building was massive and one he remembered reading about. A ruin stretching back to the late 1800s when dreams yet ran free in this part of the world.

Craig-E-Claire was originally a summer lodge meant as loving tribute to the builder's wife. But life seldom goes the way we want. Unfortunately, Bradford Gilbert passed away before their dreams were realized. His wife sold the property, and it eventually made its way into the hands of one Ralph Wurts-Dundas. Not one to be content with the status quo, Dundas began construction on a massive castle. He died before it was completed, and the curse kept growing from there. One tragedy after another befell Dundas Castle until it was abandoned.

It was the perfect place for a clandestine meeting.

"Would you look at this place," Daniel whistled. "I don't think I've made enough in my life for something like this."

"It is small compared to where I am from," Nevada Slim replied.

Likely growing up in the splendor and history of Europe robbed him of any shared enthusiasm. This thought prompted Daniel to imagine the sights each of his team had born witness to through the centuries. He itched to know more, to hear their thoughts and memories as they recounted days long gone. Too bad he couldn't find a one of them to sit down and discuss the past with.

Six armed men in dark suits and sunglasses emerged from a vine covered arch. Assault rifles raised; the leader held up his hand. The truck ground to a halt and Daniel rolled his window down as the man approached.

"Trolls," Klaus muttered. "Nasty bastards always did think they were better than us."

"Stow it. The last thing we need is you starting a war," Daniel whispered.

The troll halted beside the truck and, after scanning the interior and setting eyes on each, spat a wad of phlegm. "Looks like you guys are lost."

"We're here on invitation," Daniel countered, presenting a false smile. He glanced at Nevada Slim and noticed he was keeping his eyes averted.

The troll shook his head. "Don't remember seeing you on the list."

"I haven't given my name yet."

Click. The rifle slipped off safe. "Turn around and go back where you came from. We don't need you here." He scanned the interior again. "Leave. Now."

Nevada Slim leaned forward so the guard saw his face. "My father expects us."

Demeanor shifted and the guard stiffened. "Of course. I will let him know you have arrived. Pull your vehicle around the back. One of the staff will escort you to him."

A clipped nod and the truck pulled off; Nevada Slim turned to Daniel. "See? Not so hard."

Daniel didn't know whether to shoot or thank the man. Forcing himself to focus on the task at hand, he went over the list of names: Dark and light elves. Dwarves. Goblins. Trolls. The pantheon of races gathered together and working in concert for the first time in generations.

111

Given what he knew of their complicated politics, this alone was sufficient to frighten him.

A chamberlain awaited them as they crawled around the expansive castle. His face was long, withered with lines and scars. The pain of an endless life was on display in his eyes and in the way he comported himself. Wiry, the man bore the mark of a lifetime of violence. His suit was ill cut, baggy in the wrong places, tight in others. The pencil thin moustache on his upper lip looked painted on. He was anything but a butler.

"Welcome to Dundas. My name is Chamberlain. I am to escort you to Baron Visilias. You may not bring your weapons in, alas."

"I'm not going into this snake pit unarmed," Klaus warned.

Chamberlain offered a grin. "Then it appears our interaction is at an end. Good day all. You may see yourselves out."

"Hold on," Daniel blurted. "We need to speak with Slim's father immediately."

"Rules must be obeyed. These are troubled times after all."

Patience worn thin; Daniel agreed. "Fine. No weapons. Murphy, you and Slim are with me. Everyone else wait here." Hurrying to avoid further confrontation, he unclipped his sidearm, left the rifle in the seat, and followed Chamberlain—choosing to ignore the fact the man used his title as a name.

"Wait here please."

Chamberlain deposited them in what was once a servant's quarters built off the main kitchen and disappeared into the castle proper. Daniel folded his arms and leaned against the wall as he struggled to process the influx of information Blackmere fed them. Complicated twists and turns were all part of the game when it came to the elves. The subterfuge placed Daniel in a constant state of catch-up, much to his disgruntlement. How the others fell into the flow of things went beyond him—an infuriating complication he did not need.

"What sort of man is your father?" Daniel asked, unable to handle the outlandish direction his thoughts were being carried to.

"Stern. Good. I was fortunate to have him for my father."

Daniel eyebrow arched. "Those are the most words I've heard you say at one time."

"Now is not the time for silence."

Chamberlain rejoined them, his gaunt and ghoulish demeanor was made creepier in the false light and permeating gloom of the castle. "The Baron will meet with you now, provided you are ready of course."

"What about our companions?" Murphy asked.

"They will be seen to. Guests here are accorded the finest treatment. Food and drink for every species is available," Chamberlain said dismissively.

Smirking, Daniel's views on the man changed. *I guess Murphy is an acquired taste.*

***

"We ought to go in there and bust a few heads, make them talk to us," Klaus said, his tone one of a man determined to start a war, Daniel be damned.

"No, no, no. You heard Daniel. We need to sit and wait," Thraken chided. His face twisted, beads of sweat spreading across the gnome's face. "This is a fell place. Spirits watch everything. The shades of the dead surround us."

"I don't mind," Jenny said. "We can all be friends."

113

Klaus' hostile gaze softened. Unlike Xander, he did not know what Jenny was, only a vague idea of the terrible kind of power she contained. Why she'd been chosen for this mission remained a mystery. One he unwillingly admitted he was terrified to discover.

Thraken, eyes wide, shouted, "Friends with spirits? Oh no. No, that won't work. We belong in different worlds."

"There are paths between worlds, silly goose," Jenny replied.

Her deadpan delivery chilled the air between them. Before Klaus could reply a thin film of frost spread across the crackled leather seats. Jenny's eyes glazed over a chalky white as she raised a hand and began swirling her index finger. The air shimmered as a vortex formed. A hole in the veil of reality, darkness spread from the center until it grew wide enough to make out the myriad of demonic faces leering back at them with hungry intent.

"That's enough!" Klaus shouted.

"Jenny, stop! Please, before it's too late!" Thraken added. He ducked down behind the false protection of the seatback, teeth chattering.

Pouting, Jenny snapped her fingers and the vortex dissolved. "Pooh! You're no fun. I need better friends."

"Ahem."

They turned, surprised to find Chamberlain standing alongside the truck with his hands behind his back. Klaus fumbled to project his standard anti-social façade while Thraken poked his head above the seat.

"I have been instructed to provide you food, drink, and restroom facilities should you need them," Chamberlain drawled. "In the guest house of course."

Eager to be aware from their nightmare companion, Klaus hoped out. "I can eat, so long as I don't need to leave my guns behind."

"No need for dramatics. I know you, Klaus," Chamberlain replied.

The dwarf squinted, peering closer at the elf. His eyes widening with recognition. "Is that you Ca—"

"Chamberlain if you please," the elf cut in. "Now, food and drink await. Collect your friends and we can get out of this dreadful damp."

***

They found themselves ensconced in a massive room that was clearly a former library. Cobweb strewn bookcases filled three walls; a wooden wall of stained oak broken only by large windows streaked with a century of grime. It took little imagination to see them filled with the best volumes of human history, warm lights illuminating author and title. An empty fireplace nestled between two red chairs inspired visions of pipe smoke and deep conversational debates. Daniel felt at home.

Dark clouds rolled in, bringing the promise of a late autumn storm. Time was working against them. The patter of rain on the windows evoked dark thoughts.

"Is your father always this paranoid?" he asked.

Nevada Slim tossed away the chewed straw he'd been working on. "He does as he must."

"Well, the prodigal son returns." The booming voice of Baron Visilias filled the room as he swept in. His immense frame dominated the doorway.

Daniel turned to take in the man: A custom suit worth more than a year's wages accented by Italian shoes and a half smoke cigar hanging from his mouth completed his well-manicured visage. Overweight and domineering, Visilias had large cheeks and a pinched nose. Wisps of grey hair stretched across his balding pate. His eyes smoldered with intensity.

"Come to beg for money? Or perhaps you need help getting out of yet another mess?"

Nevada Slim stayed silent and gestured to Daniel.

"Baron Visilias, he comes because he has to. What can you tell me about Xander?" Daniel asked, thrust into the most uncomfortable situation he envisioned.

"You are?"

"Unimportant. All you need to know is I'm in charge of this team and we're against the clock," Daniel replied.

"Father, what are your dealings with Xander?" Nevada asked when the Baron stayed silent.

"Xander?" he gave them a quizzical look. "Locked safely away in a human containment facility. No worry to me or anyone else."

Daniel stepped forward. "You're not working with him?"

"Working with him? Are all humans this slow? I told you he is in prison."

"Then it would surprise you to learn he has escaped and has a pile of files on you and, I'm assuming a handful of others gathered here, is no doubt on his way to change your mind."

Fists clenched, the Baron glared first at him then at his son. "What have you brought down on me?"

"He did nothing, but Xander is coming, and we believe he aims to eliminate you all tonight or tomorrow," Daniel pressed. Fancy titles and blustery attitudes meant nothing in the face of impending doom. He had seen plenty of mid-level commanders stumble through bad presentations to desk ridden leaders and politicians.

Visilias wilted, like they all did.

"Good news for you is we're here to stop him. If you agree to let us do our jobs."

Disoriented, Visilias stumbled to the chairs, a cloud of dust billowing as he sat. "Why ... Why is he coming here? No one knows of this meeting. Or so we thought."

"That is what we were hoping you would tell us," Daniel replied.

SEVENTEEN

Rain lashed against the window as the sun continued its slow descent over the mountains. Muddied darkness swelled in as the light retreated. A wave of darkness promising a long night. For the small group assembled in the dilapidated library, it was the awakening of apprehensions and fears. An inspiring fright of things yet to come. Daniel shook off the eerie sensation whispering from the shadows to focus on Baron Visilias as he began a detailed and traumatized past few, if any, humans had been privileged to learn.

"Before the schism, when the clans were yet whole, a quiet discontent was born. It began as a whisper. The voice of unhappiness with the crown. Never uttered aloud, mind you, but spreading from one great house to the next. I paid little attention to it, being half the world away." The Baron's face turned into a sneer. "Why that fool chose to come here, to an uncivilized land, was beyond me. In Europe we had an infrastructure. An established way of life. What was here? Tribes and endless leagues of wilderness stretching from coast to coast. There were no historic cities. No interwoven kingdoms dependent upon one another.

"It was a wild time filled with adventure and, for some, terror. No different from the ruling families in feudal England. Always scrambling for greater positions and the constant quest for power. Who learned from whom I wonder?" Shaking his head, Visilias wrung his meaty hands.

"At any rate, many of us found ourselves trapped. We were unwilling to commit lest our actions tipped the balance irrevocably to one side or the other. Our leadership system had worked since long before the dawn of man, stretching back to an age of dinosaurs and ice ages. Yet here we stood on the broken edge of a fragile world. Perhaps human influences drove some to sedition. Perhaps not. What I do know is it was a precipice from which we would never recover."

"Which side did you fall on?" Daniel asked.

The sneer deepened. "My loyalties were never in question. Nor those of my compatriots even now assembled in this ruin. We continue serving the crown, even if I disapprove of our current rulers. You mortals have a saying about death and divorce. Too bad we did not adhere to it. Even in death Alvin's decision to remain married after the schism continues haunting us." The rumble of distant thunder reached the walls, stealing Visilias' gaze.

"How does Xander fit into any of this?"

A change came over the elf. "He was created to cleanse the ranks, so to speak. A weapon of implacable virtue, unwavering in his dedication. Alvin and Morgen sent him into the trenches to root out heresy. The slaughter was impressive; Xander was a machine. His sword struck where directed. It was in those dire moments, when all teetered on the verge of light and darkness, that we made up our minds. For any monarch to willingly sanction the slaughter of his people was an affront to all we stood for. I could no longer stand by in support of the festering corruption made apparent."

He sighed, the heavy sound of centuries of regret and guilt. "When the schism came we moved with utter surety, thus cementing our lot in life for generations to come. It was with heavy heart I turned my back on Alvin. He was once a close friend, but I couldn't stand his blind ignorance any longer. When the wars began, we dedicated all we had to stopping the evil of sedition from growing. That Xander continues his crusade of tyranny is the sad mark of our failure."

Daniel held up a hand, eyes crossed. "Hold on. You're telling me Xander and the light elves are the bad guys here?"

"What other possible interpretation is there?" Visilias replied. Sitting in his chair under the dull lights he appeared much older now. A shade of what glory he once was or aspired to be.

Daniel studied the man, curiosity clashing with all he had been told to believe. The great lie, he assumed, was in the perception. After all, did any true villain believe themselves evil? He doubted it, though some of the more nefarious names in history must have had those inklings. "At least this explains why Xander is on his way here," he muttered. "Baron, do you have any ideas as to who might have directed him here? I've met Xander a few times and he didn't strike me as the sort to act on a whim."

"He never has. Each move is calculated. A process of conviction," Visilias replied. "I am a man of many enemies, as you can imagine. We all are. It might have been any of them."

Frowning at the dance of words, Daniel pressed, "Perhaps if you explained the purpose of this clandestine meeting we could get to the bottom of the matter."

The veins on the backs of Visilias' hands popped. "Ah, that is not open for discussion."

"You're not giving us much to work with."

"And you don't need to know more than I have told you. Events are in play that have the potential to shift the balance of power in the clans and, hopefully, restore us to one unified voice. Of that I shall speak no more." Visilias paused, eyes narrowing. "What is it you hope to achieve from this night?"

"We need to stop Xander and return him to custody," Daniel replied.

"A noble goal. You believe this is possible with the handful you have brought? My son included?"

"The one thing I've learned from dealing with your kind is anything is possible, Baron."

"So true, my boy. So very true. If you will excuse me, I shall speak to the others and discuss our next moves while figuring how to incorporate your team. We are not as defenseless as you might assume. Chamberlain will direct you to the kitchens where the rest of your people await."

"He's ducking the subject," Daniel growled as soon as Visilias departed the room.

"My father is private man."

Daniel groaned. "That's not helpful. His reticence will likely get him killed."

Shrugging, Nevada Slim said, "If he dies, he dies. That is not for me to decide."

Like father, like son. Daniel faced Murphy. Until now the agent had remained silent, neither voicing opinion nor offering helpful suggestions. "What do you think?"

"There is more going on here than we are led to believe," Murphy answered. His uncomfortableness with being forced to contribute evident by the twisted look on his face.

Daniel snorted. "No kidding. Can we trust the Baron?"

"To save his own life? Yes, but not much after that."

They were interrupted by Chamberlain entering the room. Expression perked as if he'd caught the entire conversation, he cleared his throat with a predatory grin. "Gentlemen, if you would follow me. The Baron has instructed me to ensure your needs are met, for the time being."

"What did the Baron mean when he said this place has defenses?" Daniel blurted.

If he hoped to catch the elf off guard, he failed. Chamberlain broke eye contact and motioned for them to follow. "I'm sure I don't know what you are talking about."

"My mistake."

They moved through a winding corridor that deposited them into a servant's kitchen off the main house. Once designed for the staff to feed themselves, it was secluded and away from every important aspect the building had to offer including an exit route. There Daniel found the rest of the team feasting. Chamberlain left them without a word.

The message was clear: Wait here and do not ask questions.

"Hi Daniel!" Jenny exclaimed.

"What's our move?" Klaus demanded.

"Who knows," Daniel muttered. "We're unwelcomed guests caught up in a scheme no one seems interested in explaining to us."

"Typical elf. Doesn't trust anyone."

Nevada Slim's eyes narrowed but he stayed silent.

"Least they gave us food." Klaus walked to the counter filled with a variety of cold cuts, cheeses, and bread.

Daniel wanted to say more, anything to calm their nerves or restore a sense of balance but Jenny's incessant tugging on his trousers broke his train of thought.

"Daniel, this place has powerful energy," she whispered. "The veil between realms is very thin here. Too thin."

"What do you mean?" he asked.

She shook her head and walked off.

Sometimes, I hate my job. He surveyed the room. No sense of unity, no cohesion. Each member seemed lost in private thought or rumination. Thraken eyed the food with rapacious glee, as if he hadn't eaten in years. Crumbs and droppings slipped from Klaus' mouth, covering his chest and beard in a vulgar display of barbarity. Nevada Slim retreated within himself and sat on the floor, legs crossed, and eyes closed. Only Murphy remained close. The agent devouring emails or some government nonsense on his phone. It was a combined experience Daniel never felt during his time in the Army. The question remained: How did he take them from individuals to a team?

"Any word from Blackmere?" At Murphy's glance, Daniel gestured with his chin to the phone the agent held.

"Nothing of value. All we know is Xander is coming here to kill those assembled."

"We assume he is coming to kill them," Daniel corrected.

"Given his allegiances to the king and after hearing Visilias' story I think that is a reasonable conclusion."

"What if it's not?"

Murphy cocked his head. "What do you mean?"

"What if Xander is really coming to lead them? Allegiances shift with time. You heard the Baron. Every certainty has a breaking point. Alvin is dead. Morgen presumably rules the dark clans yet and her daughter no doubt pines for her lover's return. We might be trapped here."

"Daniel, I don't think that's the case."

"And I don't want to be caught in the open with my pants around my ankles," Daniel snapped. "We can't treat Visilias and his crew with open arms only to be stabbed in the back the moment Xander arrives."

"But Blackmere never ment—"

"He didn't have to. Don't you watch television? How many times has this been the plot of a book, show, or movie? I'm not dying here tonight, not for Blackmere, not for the elves, and damned sure not because of your blind faith." Daniel's anger boiled. "The more I think about it the more I'm starting to agree with Klaus. Xander needs to be put down, for the good of all."

"Damned right he does," Klaus mumbled between mouthfuls of a sandwich a certain hungry Great Dane. "One shot right between the eyes and poof! No more Xander. No more worry."

"I do not believe my father will side with Xander."

Murphy's head bobbed. "Exactly! You heard the man. He bled with disdain for crying out loud."

"Could have been an act. We've been duped before."

"Daniel, I appreciate what you're trying to do. If I had a wife and kids, I'd do anything for them too, but that doesn't mean we jump at every shadow or chase every ghost."

"Shhh," Jenny cautioned. "They are already listening to every word we say. Don't invite them in."

"Who?" Daniel asked.

"The ghosts, silly."

Of course. Ghosts. "I need a drink."

"Beer's in the fridge but I got a flask back in the truck if you want the heavier stuff," Klaus said after a wall trembling belch.

Shaking head, if for no other reason than to clear the crazy, Daniel summarized their situation aloud: "So we are surrounded by ghosts, trying to outwit a violent mastermind intent on either turning a handful of powerful people or slaughtering them, and we have no idea when." At their nods, he added, "At least there is food and beer."

"Right-o!"

"Not helpful. People, we need a plan."

EIGHTEEN

Dawn broke with unusual grandeur. Rays of pink shaded in blue stabbed through the curtain of night, slashing it apart as the nighttime world vanished back into shadows to await the coming night. An endless cycle perpetuated by cosmic shifts. An entire underworld crawled into hiding as hues of pink soon blazed with faded gold. It was, without a doubt, Xander's favorite time of day. Trapped between realms for that briefest of moments bereft of worries, pain, or guilt. Alas it but lasted a heartbeat.

Closing his eyes in silent prayer, he turned from the windows overlooking the racetrack and a wide valley beyond. Endless miles of trees stretched away, myriads shades of fall in their dying leaves. He never cared for this time of year for it signified the ending of life, even if for only a time. To an elf, it was the reminder that even immortality was naught but slight of hand. How many friends had he lost over the years? Surely too many to count. Xander viewed the winter with quiet lament.

The incessant knocking at his door disturbed his morose reflections. Frustrated with the disturbance, he snapped the door open and stared down at Dale's drawn face. The man was holding out a cell phone.

"It's the boss. He wants to talk with you."

In no mood for games or verbal chess, Xander accepted the phone. "Basil."

Gesturing Dale off, he closed the door and returned to the window view as the Prime Minister unleashed upon him.

"I understand matters are not proceeding as planned. This is troublesome, Xander. My commandos were among the best in my arsenal." Basil's voice was heavy with projected authority. A parlor trick at best for one such as Xander.

"Grenades and ambushes don't care about their effectiveness," Xander replied. "You should have sent me more men."

"You shouldn't have squandered the resources I allowed. Where are you now?"

"At a horse track close to the target building—secure enough, for the moment, though the quality of your hirelings is in question."

"Every detail of this operation was planned and vetted, by me, long before you were sprung from your cell. How were you discovered so quickly at the hotel?"

Eyes narrowing as his thoughts warred, Xander slowed his voice down so Basil understood his intent. "My guess is an informant, or one of your people leaked information back to DESA. You didn't tell me Daniel Thomas was hunting me."

A pause. "Is he now? That changes matters."

"In what way? He is an unexpected impediment, little more."

"Driven by revenge perhaps."

Xander stiffened. "Revenge for what? I've done nothing to him."

"You are the target of his angst. Or did you forget your role in the events leading up to Alvin's death?"

He and Daniel never got along and true, Xander used the human to help return to the princess to him, thus facilitating the grim finale of events at the North Carolina Zoo. But that was certainly not enough to fuel the desire for revenge or invite any compulsory need to hunt him down … *What if it was though?*

"Basil, I need more men if I am to complete my assignment and fight off DESA."

"You were given enough men when this started," Basil countered. "I need something from you before I consider committing. An act of good faith."

Bait dangling, Xander grounded out, "So long as it is within reason." He felt the smug satisfaction pulsing from the other end of the line, as if Basil already knew what his answer would be. Men were like Basil were the ultimate predators. Never to be trusted, no matter the circumstance.

"Good. I knew I could count on you," Basil exclaimed. "I am dispatching a unit to you. They should arrive at your location before dusk. Do not squander this opportunity, Xander. Think of the horrors poor Gwen is enduring while you dither."

"If one hair on the princess's head is harmed I swear a campaign of vengeance the likes of which the clans have not witnessed since the schism. Don't push me on this, Basil."

"At least you have some fight left in you."

***

Xander spent the better part of the morning inspecting and cleaning weapons. Unwilling to trust in Basil's charity and dealing with Sweeny's desire for revenge from centuries past, there was the real possibility of one or more not working. The only way he would discover that was when he didn't need to.

He tossed the pistol down and looked at the bed in disgust. Over five hundred rounds, three pistols, a short barrel carbine, and a bow and arrow.

Never one for modern weapons, Xander preferred the comforting feel of a solid ash bow, drawstring pulled tight against his cheek. It was the old ways that prevailed through undulating waves of modernity as ages came and passed. Lethal and effective, he trusted a bow far more than any contrivance of man. He could sneak upon his foes and eliminate them without a sound; the same could not be said for the loud report of a gun.

Reaching for the bow, he appreciated the craftsmanship in the curve and the mark of runes running the length—lightweight yet powerful. Xander pulled the drawstring, testing its weight. The kiss of the string to his cheek was an old friend come to reminisce on days of glory past. He felt invincible with such a weapon in his hands. Almost as if the world was returned to what it should have been.

But like all illusions, it faded. Xander knew there was no return to the past. No dance through time capable of reversing the sweeping tides of humanity as they rampaged across the globe in quenchable greed. Ever a stain on the planet, humans personified all the wicked traits of so many of their contrived gods. Oh there were some good among them, but the path was laid bare when the first man killed his brother so very long ago. Trapped between worlds, Xander failed to envision a proper future.

Perhaps it was for the best. The endless war between the clans continued spiraling, driving them further apart until naught but animosity remained. Xander's once noble quest to reunite the clans and save his people had shattered. The best he could hope for was a smoldering ceasefire. And even that seemed out of reach.

He returned his gaze to the sun kissed trees, now resplendent in their autumn glory. The desire to rescue his beloved and escape to a distant corner of the world, at least until the current wave of hostilities abated, drove him. Basil was a man who wanted the world … He could have it as far as Xander was concerned. Nothing good came from exceeding one's reach. This current debacle was evidence enough for that.

Heart heavy, Xander began strapping on weapons. It was going to be a long night.

**

Dale's palms were sweating, making his attempts at gripping the steering wheel more difficult than it should have been. In fact, nothing was the way he envisioned since first accepting the position with Basil Kadis. He was supposed to be a driver. Nothing else. Now he was trapped in the middle of a mad campaign of lunatics and people who disappeared in a puff of smoke and ash when they died. How was that natural?

The car pulled down the winding highway, through what should have been a scenic tour of fall foliage in the lower Catskills. Even if he were a simple man into nature, Dale would have found it difficult to concentrate. Too much was happening for him to feel comfortable. That and the very real possibility of death creeping toward him stole his focus. He didn't imagine surviving the coming nightmare, and that was problematic.

He studied the elf seated beside him through casual glances out of the corner of his eye. The vibe in the car shifted the moment they left the casino. Instead of worry or fear there now was a man prepared to go into battle sitting beside him.

Dale remembered listening to his grandfather speak with his friends, always when they thought the children weren't listening, about his time in Vietnam. The stories frightened and enthralled him, but none were as real as his current situation. Envisioning marching into a foreign jungle while praying the elusive enemy didn't shoot him before he got them seemed the better end of the deal. Dale didn't know what the immediate future held, but it promised to be violent. The look in Xander's eyes alone confirmed it. *Crazy. I must be crazy.*

Cutting the lights, the car rolled to a quiet stop. The crunch of gravel under tires the only indication of intruders. Dale exhaled slowly. His heart thundered. He was unable to stop his hands from dancing on the wheel and dashboard. This wasn't right. None of it was.

Unable to keep his eyes focused on one place, Dale scanned the immediate area with the anticipation of hordes of angry elves pouring from the gathering darkness.

"Relax, Dale. This is not going to be as bad as you believe."

Fairly certain Xander lied to his face, Dale snorted. "Easy for you to say. You have all the guns."

"I'm also the one taking all the risks," the elf countered. "Sit here and wait for my return. With any luck this unfortunate business will be concluded before midnight and we can be on our merry way."

"Right. Sit in the car."

"Unless you see a horde of elves coming to kill you. Then I suggest you flee."

Dale's eyes bulged. Visions of a mob of angry elves charging at him soured his stomach.

"I'm kidding," Xander said with a smirk. "No one will be focused on you. It's me they will want to stop. Well, us." He pointed and Dale saw a vehicle camouflaged in the trees ahead of them. Gathered around the black van were six elves in dark armor and ready for a fight. *The backup Basil promised. That's a relief.*

Xander exited the car, drawing a pistol and holding it out as an offering. "This is my favorite weapon. I've had it for many years, and it has never failed me. Use it if you must, but I will need it back upon my return. Am I understood, Dale?"

Swallowing, all Dale managed was a nod. It was a subtle assurance enough to placate his rising fears. His service to Basil had proven uninspiring until tonight. Now his mind couldn't help but wander down roads he'd rather not explore. His fingers found the cold handle of his lone pistol. A sympathy weapon. Never having shot anyone, Dale didn't know how to act.

Looking satisfied, Xander closed his door and disappeared to the back of the car. Once he finished collecting his kit from the trunk, he headed to link up with the waiting commandos.

Dale watched as they met and discussed the operation before disappearing into the gloom. Soon they were lost among the trees, silent assassins stalking beneath a cascade of fallen leaves and the smell of wet timber. A quick glance at his watch reminded him nothing was granted in life and, tonight might be his last.

Alone at last, Dale became aware of every minute sound around him. Insects. Birds. The flit of bat wings dancing over the car. It was going to be a long night.

***

Deep in the bowels of Craig-E-Claire a restlessness awakened, stirred by the confluence of approaching events. It began as a quiet whisper, groaning from the bowels of the earth where dead things go to rest. Slowly it crawled up through dirt, bones, and detritus of history until it grew powerful enough to pound upon the cement subflooring. Going undisturbed for centuries, a hunger grew until it consumed the walls, brick and stone. Those inside were gripped by the overpowering sensation. Those outside discovered trepidation and the sudden desire to turn and run. Once summoned, it could not return until the promise of ancient blood oaths was fulfilled.

This night, the forgotten would feast and blood would be spilled.

A wail gripped Craig-E-Claire that echoed throughout the cosmos. At least. Freedom.

NINETEEN

"What was that?" Klaus bolted up from his chair, eyes roving the closest hall.

They'd all heard it. Each reacting by grabbing for weapons and leaping to defend themselves from the sonic scream echoing in their minds. All that is but Jenny. She remained asleep on the far countertop, wedged between a set of cabinets long bereft of the fine china they once held.

Daniel glanced at her and, for reasons he might never fully understand, was thankful that she slept on. Pressing the release button, he slid his magazine free and ensured he had a full load before slamming it back into place with a metallic click. It was an old habit developed during his time overseas. Better prepared than dead.

"That was ancient," Nevada Slim commented as he pushed his cowboy hat up to reveal narrowed eyes. "My father keeps his secrets."

"I don't like this. No. I don't like this at all," Thraken muttered, wringing his hands.

"Relax. You're Hugh Jasol, remember?" Daniel half chided. The snipe produced a timid grin.

The sudden pounding, urgent and furious, thundered through the castle. Daniel caught the hurry of boots running this way and that, all unseen from their limited vantage point. What he initially viewed as a boon quickly devolved into a limitation. There was no way he could formulate a cohesive battle plan locked away from every major entry point.

"Looks like we're about to have some fun," Klaus grinned.

Much of the day was spent going over the security situation with Chamberlain before Daniel and Murphy were taken on a quick tour of the ground and main building. What they saw left them disheartened. This particular castle was never intended to withstand any sort of assault, nor was it possible to barricade every entry point simultaneously.

Xander was going to get inside. The only question was when.

"Has the meeting started yet?" Daniel asked to break the silence among his team.

Murphy glanced at his watch. "A few minutes ago. We should get moving."

Thraken moaned. "To where? It's not safe anywhere!"

Complicating things further, Chamberlain had insisted his people were enough of a deterrent for any potential enemy, even one so esteemed as the disgraced champion of light. Daniel and his team were given impossible constraints and told to stay out of the way should matters go awry.

"Hey, do you see this?" Thraken pointed out the nearest window.

The world was reduced by a bank of fog so thick they could only see their bleak reflections staring back through the glass.

"This is a bad place," Klaus grumbled. He clutched the light machinegun he held just a little tighter. For once, Daniel didn't disagree.

Stretching with an exaggerated yawn, Jenny hopped down and hurried to the window, where she immediately drew the outline of a smiley face. She turned to face them and said, "Everyone deserves to be happy, grumpy dwarf."

"I'm not grumpy."

She giggled, eyes going wide in delight. "Ooh! The house is awake! It's beginning!"

"What is, Jenny?" Daniel asked, peering into the gloom to see if he could spy whatever got her excited.

She offered a sly wink. "You'll see. We all will. Very soon."

"Shit."

***

There are many powers at play in the universe. Some for good. Some for bad. Most just trying to stay alive long enough to be forgotten. What lurked beneath Craig-E-Claire was the worst of all. It was a power seeking revenge for perceived wrongs.

Every step Xander took was met by lancing jets of pain spiking deep through his skeleton. Never before had he encountered such mind-numbing terror.

Bow and arrow jiggling, he broke into a trot covering the brief distance from the last tree to the side of the building.

Dark but for a flickering orange light by the front door, where a pair of guards dressed in black suits and armed with Skorpion machine guns from the former Czechoslovakia stared into the night, the building loomed like a menacing shadow in the night. It was a scene from an old horror movie. The whisper of impending doom. The note so subtle murmurings of "go away or else!" Xander once thought such tropes were little more than fanciful imagination, but every story had an origin.

Pushing ahead based on his limited exposure to the building upon arriving, he shuddered upon feeling the cold stone wall press against his back, as if fingers were stretching forth to snatch his very soul. He felt, more than saw, dark energies swirl around the compound. Some vast and terrible deed was committed here, trapping countless hapless souls to an eternity of torment. The promise of joining them high, Xander hurried to the nearest door and laid a glove upon the handle.

Unlocked and unguarded. Just as promised.

Xander twisted and pushed just enough to crack the door and peer inside. A darkened room return his gaze, near impenetrable with regular sight. It was further proof of a terrible demise awaiting. The urge to turn and flee rose. None of this was part of the bargain. Desire clashed with obligation and, while understanding what twist of fate lurked in the unseen night, Xander knew failure on his part meant death for his beloved. He cursed his sense of duty and slipped inside.

Suddenly only the exhilaration of completing his assignment and reuniting with Gwen mattered, arranged marriage be damned.

Xander led the commando team inside, arrows nocked and ready to fire. Though the entry point was as promised empty he knew any manner of alarms or silent triggers might already have sounded. Time became his enemy.

They moved with the whisk of combat fatigues brushing flesh as they crossed the room and entered a small hallway leading from the servant quarters. Each dark elf, that he was forced to rely on them for security an affront to all he once stood for, took rehearsed positions, fanning into a reverse wedge with Xander on point.

The echo of footsteps halted them in place: half crouched and drew back. Poison tipped arrowheads blackened to reduce visibility aimed down the long hall. A lone elf appeared, old and hunched. In his hands was an empty serving tray. Xander released the tension and motioned the others to follow. This man was not their target.

The elf scurried into kitchens and Xander counted to ten before motioning them forward. Reaching the end of the hallway, they shied away from the soft glow of a fireplace as he leaned around the corner for a quick glance. He gestured for the nearest elf to flank him. Once in position, Xander nodded, and they stalked around the corner and fired. Two guards burst apart in a shower of ashes before either could react. As a unit they moved onward, ash and dust drifting onto their uniforms.

Soon they gained a pair of doors opposite from each other. With a hand motion, they broke into two teams, the lead pair following Xander deeper into the bowels of the angry building. Murmured voices drew his attention. His heart quickened despite countless years of marching into peril. Reinforced footsteps behind told him the others finished clearing their assigned rooms and had rejoined them. Seven against an unknown number, perhaps unsuspecting. He liked their odds. They kept slinking down the main hallway, coming to a single door at the end.

"You never could stay out of trouble."

Xander stiffened at hearing a voice from his past. One he never expected to hear again. He lowered his bow, slightly. "This is none of your business. Step aside."

"I don't think so," Chamberlain moved to the center of the door frame. The pistol in his hand pointed at Xander's chest. "I missed once. I won't miss again."

"You're making a mistake," Xander countered, a hint of sorrow in his words. "Move. I won't ask again."

Time slowed. Xander heard the arrow drawn back behind his left ear. Chamberlain's eyes widened. The arrow zipped past Xander's head, feathers kissing his cheek. The gun fired. Pain blossomed in his shoulder as he cried out. Chamberlain dove. The arrow burrowed into the oak door. Guards flooded the hall.

Pandemonium ensued as arrows and bullets flew free.

It was the worst possible situation Xander envisioned. One in which all might die, and the mission remain unfulfilled. He ducked behind cover and felt around the wound. Blood trickled down his back, suggesting an exit wound. Satisfied it wasn't life threatening, he aimed at the nearest guard, wincing as fresh waves of pain lanced through his upper body, and fired. The arrow struck the elf in the chest, and he pitched backwards.

"We need to move!" one of his commandos shouted.

Xander agreed. "Take the team and split up. Draw the guards away. I'll slip back and finish the job. Now go!"

Bodies moved. A dark elf burst apart after being shot in the back. Xander ran through his drifting ashes. Wrong. It had all gone wrong.

Somewhere deep in the house an ancient wail arose.

***

"Did you hear that?" Daniel hissed.

Klaus, machinegun pointed down the nearest hall, nodded. "Gun shot. Looks like the fun's started."

"And we're missing it," Daniel replied. He keyed the handheld radio. "Murphy, we can't sit here like this. You heard the weapon report. Xander is inside already. Every second we delay means our hosts are in increased danger. We need to converge on the assets and stop Xander now."

Silence for a fraction of a moment too long that had Daniel's suspicions rise. "You heard what the Baron said. We weren't needed. Backup only."

"I don't give a damn what he said. He doesn't sign the paychecks. You can sit in place if you want. The rest of us are moving."

Unwilling to wait, and risk losing their targets, Daniel jerked his head for the dwarf to follow. Time was running out. The frantic sounds of pitched battle faded, suggesting more than he wanted to consider.

"Everyone, collapse on my position and let's go hunt some elves."

"Daniel, don't do th—"

He cut the radio off and gave Klaus a shrug. "Rookies."

"Don't worry. I'm with you, hummie. Let's kill that son of a bitch and grab a drink."

"For once we agree."

The pair stalked off into the bowels of the castle. Somewhere up ahead a gunfight raged. Nerves jumping, the former soldier slipped back into a persona he'd tried hard to get rid of.

***

Xander checked the area a final time. Guards and commandos were gone, their efforts to slaughter each other echoing throughout the darkened halls. Of Chamberlain there was no sign. All the better. Xander had no wish to kill the man, despite their longstanding enmity. His hopes for reconciliation dashed the instant Chamberlain fired at him, but some hostilities were forgivable. Some.

Satisfied the way was clear, Xander crept back to the double doors. The murmur of voices had continued, suggesting a certain ease none of those within should feel. One of the pitfalls of immortality was the ever-rising sense of complacency. The foolish notion that nothing could kill you. Had the people in the room remembered all things die Xander's job might be harder.

Shoulder screaming from the gunshot wound, he nocked an arrow and shoved the doors open.

His surprise at there being no interior guards nearly made him stumble. The combatant in him expected trouble the instant he stepped within, yet naught but enraged faces stared back at him. Suspecting a trap, Xander drew back and took aim at the nearest elf.

"What is the meaning of this?"

"You should not be here!"

"Where are the guards?"

Endless questions streamed in an obvious delaying tactic. Instead of plunging into his task, Xander froze. None of the men and women assembled had ever done him wrong. Many were known by name only. They were the elder statesmen of their race. Killing them promised instability for generations. Was it a risk he could willingly take? Could he live with himself knowing he was the catalyst for the final destruction of elfkind? What would his bride to be think? Could she still look him in the eye and proclaim her love?

He shook his head. "I don't want this."

Baron Visilias stepped forward, open palms at his side. "Of course you don't. You're being used as a pawn, Xander. What do you suppose Kadis will do with you once you've completed his task? Or did you truly think he would let you reunite with the princess?"

That Basil meant to eliminate him the moment word was received of mission success hadn't crossed his mind until now. Infuriated, Xander clutched his bow tighter. The arrow trembled as he drew it back in impotent rage.

TWENTY

Machinegun fire stitched the wall to Xander's right. Wood chips and slivers slashed his face and hands. In the shock, he loosed his grip and the arrow sped true, striking Visilias in the chest. The older elf blinked twice before slumping to the ground. Others broke and ran, suddenly fearful for their lives. Rounds continued striking the aged wood paneling, promising to grind Xander to a pulp once they connected. He ducked aside, horrified with what he'd just done, and ran to the opposite side of the dimly lit room where a side panel slightly ajar offered escape.

The warmth of a raging fireplace kissed him as he passed. Xander pried open the panel with his foot and, cursing at the cobweb riddled stairs, hurried away before his assassins could catch up. The last thing he heard was raised voices. One in particular he never wanted to hear again. *How had they found him so quickly? Again.*

***

Daniel rushed into the room, staring at the arrow jutting from the Baron's chest. A few others crowded the fallen man, but instead of helping they were in the way. Daniel got the sense they wouldn't be upset if he died. Ignoring the strange internal power struggles of the elves, he slid his rifle around to his back and snatched the first aid kit strapped to his thigh.

"Move," he commanded and knelt beside Visilias. What little battlefield first aid he remembered didn't promise to be of much help.

Klaus spat a mouthful of red phlegm. "Where'd the bastard go?"

A trembling woman gestured to the far wall.

The dwarf took a step forward but stopped. He glanced at Daniel before he drew his handset. "We have him. Xander is trapped on the upper level. Everyone collapse on my position now. I can't take him alone."

Feeling the first inkling of a team building, Daniel cut the arrow a few inches from the chest and applied a patch of quick clot gauze to cauterize the wound. Visilias coughed a mouthful of blood, his breathing shallow and labored. Unless the man received proper medical attention soon ...

"We're losing opportunity," Klaus growled. His natural predisposition for violence surging to dominance and putting Daniel on edge. "Where are the others?"

The rush of boots was his answer.

Led by Murphy, the rest of the team stormed into the study, guns raised. Daniel saw the confused grief etched on Nevada Slim's face before he looked away. The others stood in shock. The promise of failure haunting each. Ash piles littered the area. Murmurs from the survivors drifted above the din.

"Slim, I need you to stay with your father. Keep him talking," Daniel stood, noticing he was receiving a lot of blank stares. "Someone call a damn ambulance. This man needs to go to a hospital!"

"I'm on it," Chamberlain called from behind them.

Questioning why the man chose now to arrive, Daniel decided his best interests were in not becoming entangled further. "Slim, do you got this?"

A nod was the elf's reply.

Daniel snatched Thraken and jerked him close. "Time to put those tracker skills to the test. Let's go. You're on point."

"M ... me?" the gnome exclaimed.

"It's what you do, isn't it?"

143

Klaus banged the stock of his weapon on the wooden bookcase. "Time's wasting."

Gulping, Thraken drew his pistol and hobbled to the waiting dwarf. Daniel suppressed a groan. It wasn't the best situation but a far cry from yesterday's debacle. *Least we are working together this time.*

Leaving Slim and Murphy to secure the room in the event Xander doubled back to finish the job, Daniel hurried to join the dwarf and gnome as the Thraken inched his way up the stairs. It didn't dawn on him until they were halfway up that Jenny was missing.

***

Deep in the basement, meandering a long-forgotten part of the house dating back well before the first stone was laid, were secrets no living being was ever meant to discover. The travesty of the past, a place fraught with unimaginable terror born from the collision of worlds, it was unique to the world.

Jenny crept among the spiderwebs and scurrying rats. Her footsteps naught but faint pitter-patter among the countless heartbeats reverberating through her tiny frame. Ageless, she had never felt more alive. More vibrant. Powerful.

Tracing a line through the grime of the wall on her left, Jenny beamed. "I know you're down here. All alone and frightened. You don't have to be, you know."

The house tremored in response.

"Ah, I see now. You don't want me here. I can taste your fear. It is delicious," she continued. "Tell me your names and I will take your pain away."

An old heating pipe cracked, dust and decades' worth of rust cascading down. "You must know you can't defeat me. Trying will only produce needless suffering."

A hundred spirits wailed, their chorus reaching for the emptiness in her soul; Jenny tsked.

144

"Don't be silly. You can't hurt me. I am as old as this planet. My kind existed long before your memories crawled from the water and mud. Give me your pain. Let me save what remains of your souls."

The walls buckled, threatening to bring Craig-E-Claire down on top of her. Each protest weakened the deeper she strode forward. Unlimited power clashing with unremembered power. It was a dance she hadn't been invited to in ages.

Jenny clenched her fists and the air swirled around her.

***

Crouching in the dark, Thraken felt at home. His kind thrived in being unseen; them an limited footnote as the other races pursued reckless into the future. The gnome never had aspirations beyond continuing the family business. He learned his tracking skills as a child, honing them through the years but always feeling as if something vital was missing. When DESA knocked on his door, he had leapt at the opportunity. Paired with the worst of the worst, depending on your point of view, Thraken came into his own. Nasty when necessary, incompetent to complete his guise, the gnome enjoyed his reputation of anonymity.

Until now.

He smelled Xander. The very reek of the elf champion wafting through the stairs and down a narrow corridor that hadn't been used in decades. As much as he appreciated old houses, Thraken found the prospect of being watched, targeted by one of those nasty arrows elves were prone to use, reduced the thrill of the hunt to murmured prayers.

"Do you see him?"

Daniel hovered over him. So close Thraken swore he heard his heartbeat and the drip of sweat striking the back of his neck. Gagging, the gnome pointed down the hall.

"His scent remains strong," he whispered. Why didn't anyone understand the nuances of stalking people? Lumbering about, speaking loud, and walking much too heavily to go undetected. Between the human and the dwarf, Thraken was surprised they weren't dead yet.

Daniel bumped him as he turned. "Klaus, you're up. Sent a salvo downrange and let's see what happens."

"I don't think that's a good id—"

The bark of 5.56mm rounds rushing down the hall made him flinch and cover his ears. Naturally sensitive, the gnome abhorred violence. War represented total failure to his mind. Miring him in a never-ending cycle of self-doubt.

"Here elfie, elfie," Klaus taunted. "Come on out you pointy eared bastard. I've got a score to settle."

The echo of his voice his only reply.

"Push forward. We lose him if we stop," Daniel ordered.

Concealing his discontent, Thraken rose.

***

Breathing heavily, Xander kept running as the promise of an ugly demise thundered through the hallway he'd just exited. *Damned dwarves!* Ever eager to prove their worth by shooting first.

Still, it was Daniel who bothered him the most. Unable to accept the man's utter devotion to hunting him down, Xander regretted getting the human involved in the first place. That he arrived just as Ariel lay dying was one of life's great coincidences. In a perfect world, Xander would have been there to save his sister and recover the box of Carthantos.

The world, he lamented, was far from perfect.

Alone again, the elf pushed thoughts of Basil's commandos from his head as he ran. They were of little value given his current condition. With the supposition the Prime Minister meant to kill him bouncing around in his head, Xander decided he was better off without them. The idea of linking arms with dark elves sickened him, despite it being a necessity ... for the moment.

Finding a second staircase leading down, he picked up the pace. Time was almost up. His mission devolved into an abysmal failure. No doubt Basil's fury promised to be severe.

Skipping steps, Xander knew what he needed to do. The only way to reunite with Gwen was accomplishing him mission, even if there was scant hope for success at this point. Hopefully Dale was still outside. If not ...

A second burst of rounds tore through building behind him. He caught the faint taunting of the damnable dwarf. Resisting the urge to climb back up and return fire, the champion of light inched the door open and scanned the hall, half dreading emerging into the middle of a firefight. Fortune at last smiled down upon him. The way was clear. Slinging his bow over his back, Xander pulled the snort barrel carbine forward and reentered the house. Time to fight fire with fire.

***

Baron Visilias looked up with clouded eyes; pain stretched across his face.

"Father," Nevada Slim said. His voice oddly neutral as he looked down upon the stricken man he had trouble reconciling with.

"Eh? Boy, is that you?" His father's chest gave a deep shudder. "I never treated you fairly. Not since you were a pup."

Slim reached down and grabbed his clammy hand. "Doesn't matter. We all did what we did."

"Foolish boy. You never listened. I treated you unfairly because I never wanted you. Never wanted ... a son. It is my great shame." He paused to cough. "Now I go to my demise with no resolution and naught but regret."

Slim stiffened but allowed himself to be pulled down until his father's lips were inches from his ear.

"Listen to me now. Having you was my biggest regret. You have disgraced our name and left your mother a shell of the woman she once was. Do not think that by me going to my doom I will think of you any kindlier. I will not."

"Your words mean nothing to me, old man," Slim whispered back. "Here you lay on your deathbed. The one victim in Xander's mad scheme. I will not mourn you. When you die, no one will remember your name. I promise you that."

A final gleam of fire ignited in Visilias' eyes. "Perhaps I was not as wrong as I thought. May you meet what end you deserve, Justinias."

The house groaned suddenly. A primal scream echoing the muted rage of centuries.

Nevada Slim jerked his hand free and grabbed his rifle.

Those still assembled broke and ran, the threat of being hunted be damned. Bodies everywhere, no one stopped to watch as his father took his last breath and collapsed in a pile of ash and bitter dust. A glass vase toppled and broke. Parts of the ceiling snapped free, crashing down among them. An elderly elf was crushed by a massive piece. The room emptied as the building began the slow decline to utter ruin.

"Daniel, this is Murphy. Where are you? We need to evacuate now."

No reply. Nevada Slim stared at the pile of ashes, confused, numbed.

Murphy grabbed Nevada Slim by the arm. "I'm not dying in this mess. Not for them. Come on. We can still get outside."

Giving his father's ashes a final glare, Nevada Slim adjusted his cowboy hat and sprinted to the door. Any parting words lost on his tongue as he ran. He didn't know what lurked under the forgotten castle and he didn't want to find out.

TWENTY-ONE

Daniel sank to his hands and knees and tried to vomit the lungful of dust and debris he inhaled during their frantic escape from Craig-E-Claire. Tremors continued echoing deep in the earth; raw chaos consumed the area. The castle was in ruin.

He rose on shaky legs and wiped his mouth with the back of a sleeve. Tears swelled in his eyes. "What just happened?" he managed to ask after three attempts.

Klaus, planted on his backside nearby, glared back to where the castle once stood. "We were had."

"I don't believe that," Daniel replied. "This was something else. We all felt it. That house was alive."

"Bah! How can a building have life? It's stone and wood," the dwarf sputtered.

"You should know better," Thraken chided.

Daniel glanced to see the gnome sat huddled; knees drawn with his arms wrapped around them. Disbelief in his eyes. Taking pity, for he well knew the effects of shock, he moved closer and asked, "What do you mean?"

"The world is very old. Everything growing has a spirit. The will to live." Thraken shuddered. "What was the house, but a combination of elder forces trapped within the walls?"

Unwilling to commit to sure a theory, Daniel considered the possibilities. None of them added up. If the house was alive, where did that resonating scream emanate from? Or the dark presence he felt the moment they drove onto the property? Yet now he felt a weight removed, as if the collapse freed whatever tormented entity trapped within. The real question was: Did they do it a favor or did they unwittingly unleash an element force hell bent on revenge? He didn't want to know.

"It doesn't matter. We need to find the others, assess the situation and see where to head next. I doubt we were fortunate enough for Xander to have died in the collapse," Daniel said aloud. He left his thoughts of the second part of his team private

Figures began emerging from the dark. Haggard men and women who bore the look of having seen too much. All bore cuts and scraps. That any survived was akin to a small miracle. Daniel looked into their eyes and muted reflections of failure answered back as they fled to the safety of the circular driveway.

Chamberlain arrived soon after. His drawn face pallid. Marching up to Daniel, the elf jabbed an accusatory finger at him. "None of this would have happened if not for your interference. I had security well under con—"

"Shut up," Daniel barked. "Xander was inside and moving on the meeting before you knew it. This is your failure. Not ours."

"How dare you?" the elf raged.

Klaus slipped his hand around the machinegun trigger guard, stopping the elf mid-sentence.

"Where is the Baron? He's the one I need to speak with," Daniel pressed with a fool's hope. His patience ended. Since departing the DESA training facility nothing had gone right. They remained a step behind and now it had potentially cost him half his team.

"He is dead."

Daniel's head turned as Nevada Slim and Murphy arrived. Relief washed through him as more of his team showed up, alive. The only one missing was Jenny, and he wasn't sure if that was good or bad.

"I'm sorry," Daniel said as the realization struck. Losing anyone close held devastating implications, but for a man to lose his father with whom he shared a contentious relationship in such undignified manner the results could prove disastrous.

"He was a son of bitch," Nevada said, falling back to his accent and clipped English. "Better for all. What do we do now?"

Holding his tongue, Daniel suspected there was more to the tale but was wise enough not to press. Mental health in the aftermath of trauma made for an unsteady battleground; one he was familiar enough with after surviving several bad days in combat.

"We must assume Xander is still alive. If that's the case he has two options: Either lurk around and hope to pick the survivors off one by one or book it west to snatch the princess," Daniel theorized. "We need to decide which course to follow."

"I say the princess," Klaus blurted.

"What makes you say that?"

The dwarf held out his hands. "Why, love! Xander is smitten with her, always has been. He'll go to her out of a sense of love."

Daniel narrowed his eyes. Was there another layer to the dwarf, lurking beneath the soiled, gruff outer shell?

Thraken beat him to it, asking, "What do you know about love?"

"I've been married seventeen times! Love is all we got in this shitty world. It's what keeps me going during times like this." After seeing their blank stares, he added, "What? I'm not allowed to have a soft spot?"

Nevada Slim whistled low. "That's a lot of love."

Klaus winked. "You bet it is."

One of Our Elves is Missing

Unable to take any more, Daniel stepped in the center of the group. "Ok, so we make for Elmira and stop him from getting the princess. Agreed?"

Heads bobbed. The dwarf started walking, rifle over his shoulder in the picture of a grizzled war veteran.

"We should report this to Agent Blackmere," Murphy insisted. Predictably.

Daniel spun on him. "What's your deal, Murphy? Who are you really working for? You've tried hampering us every step of the way. For a man sworn to upholding whatever it is DESA upholds, you sure aren't in a hurry to complete this assignment. Makes me think you're working for someone else."

"That's absurd. I am a loyal agent," Murphy almost shouted.

The others shifted, hostility growing. Klaus glanced at Daniel.

"I'm not buying it," Daniel said. "What's the game? I'm not asking again."

A range of conflicting thoughts sped through his face before Murphy's shoulders sagged. "Fine. I was contacted by an agent for the queen. She wanted me to ensure Xander linked up with her daughter. Something about destiny. I wasn't supposed to hurt anyone," Murphy admitted. "Honest. This was just a side job. I'm still loyal to DESA."

Daniel growled. "I'll deal with you later. Right now, we have a job to do. But if I catch you sending any messages to this contact or doing anything to jeopardize our mission, I will take a personal interest in making you suffer. Am I clear?"

A muted nod before Murphy stalked off for the SUV. Time enough to lick their wounds later.

"You should have let me put a few rounds in his head," Klaus offered as he dug through a trouser pocket to produce a cigar.

"You smoke?" Daniel asked.

He shrugged. "I'm a dwarf."

"Hi guys!"

They turned, as one, to see Jenny stalk closer. Her dress was torn and stained in soot. The pink bows in her hair missing save one. The air around her shimmered with energy.

"What happened to you?" Daniel asked.

Making a show of brushing one shoulder clean, Jenny pouted. "That house was not very nice. I changed its mind."

Daniel felt like he'd been dropped from a tall building with the admission. Lacking any coherent response, he gestured to their waiting vehicle and watched the team head that way. It was still a few hours to Gwen's prison, and they were running out of time. That and the less he knew about Jenny the better. Some powers in the world deserved to remain mysterious.

"What about the rest of us?" Chamberlain shouted as he turned for their SUV.

Daniel looked to where the others huddled together. Any pretense of being influential figures among their society was gone, replaced by the humiliation of underestimating a foe. Under other circumstances he might have enjoyed it.

"That's your problem. I don't think Xander will return. You seemed to be the means to an end, not the ultimate goal," Daniel said. "I suggest you regroup your security and get these people back to their homes as soon as possible."

"How can you be certain he is gone?"

"I'm not, but like I said, not my problem. Have a great night, huh?" Daniel resisted the urge to slap the elf on the shoulder before walking away. He'd had enough drama for one night.

Damned elves.

***

Half the state away, nestled in a small hotel room overlooking the Chemung River, Viviana Cal knew she had a problem. Events were moving rapidly now, and unexpectedly. Neither she nor the queen supposed Xander would approach his assignment with such enthusiasm. She preferred the term ruthless aggression but had no one to boast it to. Word already reached her of the debacle of Craig-E-Claire. The queen, she knew, would be furious when word reached her.

Viviana had limited time before the wayward champion found his way to the secret DESA facility here in Elmira. Woe be unto any who stepped in his path. She needed to avoid a public disaster and try to save face in the process. Then again, Xander had never been her mission. She was sent to ensure Daniel and the DESA miscreants failed in their efforts to kill him, if indeed that was the plan all along. Too much of the picture remained unclear for her liking. Viviana produced better results as a spy in Europe in 1944 than dealing with the U.S. government and their motley ship of fools.

Calling Raleigh this late at night presented unique challenges she was unprepared to handle. Morgen's rage notwithstanding, Viviana knew she needed tangible contingencies before reporting in. A matter of professionalism often lacking, she prided herself on her ability to get ahead of situations before they developed. Now Xander was loose in the countryside, and a team of no doubt restless hunters was scouring the land in search of blood.

It is a nightmare.

Her hand slid to her cell phone. Duty and sensibility clashed, leaving her stymied for the first time in decades. A thought struck. Viviana played through the details, developing a strategy that might not only see her retain her position but gain promotion from it. Forgetting her phone, the elf strode to the windows overlooking the human city, imagining she could discern the tiny, forgotten Civil War prison in the cold, dark night.

The answer to all her problems lay there. The only question was whether she had enough time to enact her plan—the future depended on it.

Packing her meager belonging, Viviana Cal prepared for the most important mission of her life. She only hoped she wasn't too late.

TWENTY-TWO

The phone rang. Its shrill whines bringing Thaddeus Blackmere awake with a start. Angry, he fumbled the buttons to shut it off. It was all part of his job of course. Every good leader of quality kept a phone by their bedside in the event they were needed during the long nights. Much as he had during his time in the Navy, Blackmere found sleep both blessing and bane. Each time he had teams in the field produced restless nights of tossing and turning, getting up at random hours to watch the news or a recorded show, but never a full night's sleep.

Blackmere rolled over, the sliver in his mind knowing he should have answered but age and tiredness conspired against him. He closed his eyes and tried to return to the blissful nothingness of sleep. The phone rang again a split second later. Cursing, Blackmere snatched the phone from the charger and took a breath to compose himself. It wouldn't do to let whoever was on the other end of the line to see him in a discomfited state.

"Blackmere."

"Sir, there has been a development you need to be aware of."

The voice was young, shaky as nerves played out. Blackmere almost smiled, fond memories of when he was that age and speaking with a high-ranking superior for the first time. *If the kid thinks I'm rough he should talk to an admiral.*

"This couldn't wait until morning?"

A pause. "No, sir. The team has made contact with Xander just west of Newburgh. It was a, uh, failure."

Blackmere's eyes narrowed. *Of course it was. Nothing had gone right from the get-go.* "Explain."

He listened as a nightmare scenario played out. The how and why wasn't important. What needed immediate attention was the mitigating the destruction of a public place with who knows how many witnesses. Blackmere felt his meticulously curated world slipping through cracks. Far more than just his job was at stake in upstate New York.

"Where is Murphy and the team now?" he growled.

A pause. "Heading west from what we have learned, sir."

Damnation. "Get my bird ready. I want clean-up crews deployed within the hour," he ordered. "The sooner we get this mess cleaned the better. Damn elves."

He hung up and considered calling his wife to tell her he wouldn't be coming home for another day at least but decided not to waste her time. She learned long ago not to get involved in his work and he was more than happy to spare her the details. Given how upset he was with being woken up in the dead of night there was no way he was willing to risk her ire. Blackmere slid from the protective warmth of the sheets and got dressed.

Twenty minutes later he was headed to the airfield.

***

Some events through the course of history have lasting memories, transcending generations until fact and fiction blur and myth turns to legend. Basil did not imagine this night was one of them. Fuming with impotent rage, the Prime Minister stalked back and forth, worrying ruts in the carpet. Plumes of cigar smoke trailed after him, hurrying to catch up. A host of emotions warred within the elf. Each led him to the singular conclusion he was loathe to accept. Xander betrayed him. A second commando team was gone, and the mission ended in total failure, the death of Baron Visilias notwithstanding.

"At least one rival is out of the way," he muttered.

Basil reached for the small glass of brandy and threw the glass against the wall. Drops of amber spilled down in a cascade of glass. Further angered by his loss of control, he clenched his fists. It had taken years to get to this point. Decades of plotting and implanting subversive thoughts among the upper class. His manipulations, secreted to a handful, resulted in that chaotic night in central North Carolina with what should have been the ultimate coup. Even that wasn't enough.

Turning the princess to his side took little effort. Ever did youth languish under the perceived restraints of their predecessors. Gwen was no different. She wanted the crown and Basil preyed upon her greed. Following her lead like a lovesick puppy came Xander. Everything had gone according to plan until that pesky author snuck his way into the situation—Daniel Thomas. Thinking the situation finished after North Carolina, he failed to consider Daniel would resurface years later, much to his regret.

Basil needed solutions. With DESA breathing down his neck and the royal family already suspicious, he grew desperate for a way out. Politics being what they were, there was no time to take his affairs to the ruling council. Many were in his pockets but not enough to influence Morgen into abdicating her throne. Basil didn't want to become king, however. He was content with being the man who pulled the strings and directed policy.

Xander. No matter how far his thoughts strayed, Basil returned to the impetuous Champion. To become the power behind the crown, he needed to remove Xander. But how? Assassination seemed out of the question; all things considered. An outright assault promised bringing undue attention to all the clans. The last thing they needed was additional government oversight. Basil chafed enough already with the liaison assigned to his office. No. What he needed was a definitive knockout punch to ensure the crown never recovered and he would be in position to elevate a new Champion.

Wheels spun. Plans formed and slipped apart. Basil chomped on the ruined end of his cigar as circles of conspiracy swirled around him. It was but an extension of the long game he mastered long ago. With Xander going dark after the botched raid there was but one course of action making any sense to Basil. The man was going for his beloved. Deciding the disgraced princess was no longer of use, the prime minister reached for his phone.

***

The crunch of tires on gravel alerted those securing the facility. The foreman strode into the parking lot to defuse the situation, trusting it was a civilian who had gotten turned around. It proved a fatal mistake. Dark clad figures emerged from the vehicle, the red lines of their tracers collapsing on his chest a moment before the spit of flame from their rifles lit the night. He died with a pained look of confusion. The attackers sped forward, ignoring the falling ash of an elf who had faithfully defended the crown for six centuries.

The lead man slapped an adhesive explosive strip on the reinforced doors and ducked back. The blast, condensed and focused, shredded the door's locking mechanism and the assault team poured inside. Small arms fire met them, killing one and wounding another. Responding with fury, the attackers slayed the remaining Old Guard in quick order. Their soldiers rushed in and secured the ground floor.

"All clear, Sergeant."

Sergeant Otero raised her visor, ignoring the mess her team had created. Muted cries from the wounded man filled the room. Her face, scarred down the right cheek, twisted in disgust. She whirled on the closest wounded elf, kneeling and grabbing him by the chinstrap.

"Shut up. Pain is your ally. If it hurts you're still alive," she ground out. "Keep whining and I'll kill you myself. Understood?"

The elf nodded submissively.

Satisfied, Otero gestured for the team medic to tend to the man, removing him from the scene lest she let rage overpower common sense. Down a man already, her shorthanded team plunged into the interior. They finished clearing the main floor, sweeping each room with the rehearsed precision of an elite unit. Growing impatient, she split them into two-man teams for the upper story.

"Sergeant, the building is empty. We're too late," a corporal informed her after all teams collapsed back on her position.

Otero gestured to the lone stairwell leading into the earth. "Not yet. Take point. You know the drill. Kill the defenders and secure the princess."

Nodding, the corporal formed ranks and led the assault into the subterranean levels. Otero's heart was thundering. The opportunity to apprehend one of the royal family, damn them all, and win glory tickled her fingertips. Impatience whispered to push aside those in front. This was the opportunity long denied her bloodline. A redemption for the past. She grinned savagely from behind her faceplate.

Reaching the bottom of the stairwell they found an iron door ajar. Her visions of the future collapsed under the real possibility their target was indeed gone. Otero gripped her weapon tighter and followed her team

161

into the empty room. Inside they discovered an abandoned cell decorated with all the comforts of home no prisoner should be allowed. There was no sign of the princess in the gloom.

Late.

They were too late.

"Get the prime minister on the horn. Tell him the situation and request new orders," she managed.

Think, damn it. Where would she go? Otero sat on the disturbed bed and tried imaging what she would do if the roles were reversed. Xander was out there, but with no guarantee of his location, searching for him was a wasted endeavor. She needed actionable intelligence if any hope of completing her mission remained. Even then …

"Sergeant Otero, the minister wishes to speak with you."

Rolling her eyes, Otero accepted the phone.

***

"How much more of this am I expected to endure?"

Morgen, queen of the dark elves and sole remaining ruler among the clans, didn't answer as she stared off into the myriad colored lights downtown Raleigh offered. To her right sat the Central Prison, conveniently placed along a main artery of railroad tracks. North Hills beckoned further right. The spires and ever growing infrastructure threatening the established skyline the Oak City boasted. A sweep left and she saw the letters of numerous banks and tech companies adorning the high rises. Vultures roosted on the tiered upper floors of her assumed throne room. Their sleeping forms akin to the gargoyles of old.

Morgen found the atmosphere exhilarating and frustrating. It should have been her people who climbed to the skies, but alas, they were never great builders nor prone to condensing into great cities. Content with remaining in small clans, elfkind eked out a meager existence on the crumbs of humanity. A travesty played out numerous times over the course of history. Ever were the hunter-gatherers forced into compliance and into a new way of life lest they be swept under the carpet, forgotten by time.

A glass of wine sat on the windowsill; half drank. Morgen was a woman of intrinsic tastes. While she enjoyed the finer things, she admitted not needing them to find happiness. There was much to be said for a simple life, even for a queen. Lurking in the upper tiers of the now empty building provided a luxury she'd come to enjoy since construction completed those many years ago. Unlike her late husband who chose the comforts of an expansive mansion in the disappearing countryside, she enjoyed this private view of the world. Even if only for a time.

"I do enjoy hearing the opinions of others," Morgen said after a moment.

Blushing, her assistant bobbed her head. "I'm sorry, Your Majesty. I thought the question rhetorical."

"Perhaps it should have been," Morgen mused. "How long have you served me, Aislinn? Two, three centuries?"

"Two hundred forty-seven years."

"Our kingdom has diminished much in that time. Who could have predicted the force with which humans have developed their world? I continue to be amazed by their eagerness to grow."

"They devour the natural world, giving no concern for the lives destroyed in the process," Aislinn said, snorting. "They will leave nothing in their wake."

"Would we be any different?"

Confused, Aislinn cocked her head. "We have lived off the earth since inception. It was never our way to destroy or devour."

"Does that make us any better than the mortals surrounding us? We war despite knowing better. We subsume our way of life in pursuit of vain glories. Political manipulations confound our ruling class, and we insist on maintaining outdated traditions. Perhaps it is best if we faded into the general population."

"What troubles you, my queen?" Aislinn asked.

"Everything. Events in New York and with Basil are most disturbing. I feel as if a great shift is approaching. One we might not survive."

As if on cue, the faint rumble of thunder echoed in the distance.

Morgen's smile was sad as she continued. "We shall see. It might just be the solitary musings of an old woman no longer useful." She glanced towards her assistant. "Go home, Aislinn. Should anything arise overnight I will summon you. There is still a little time before the storm strikes."

TWENTY-THREE

Daniel pushed the empty plate of what had been corned beef hash and eggs away and rubbed his stomach. A side of pancakes topped in blueberry sauce beckoned him. It took great effort to resist the temptation. He was tired, had eaten too much, and stewed with his inability to get ahead of Xander. The more he focused on it the further away the elf became. Or was it all an illusion conjured by thoughts of his family in peril? There were times, Daniel admitted, being a fantasy writer had its disadvantages.

"Are you going to eat those?"

He glanced at Thraken, almost surprised by the disturbance. Daniel shoved the plate toward the gnome after a moment of indecision. "Be my guest. I'll throw up if I eat anymore."

"Not good to fight on empty stomach," Nevada Slim mumbled through a mouthful of eggs.

Daniel wondered at the man. Would he be able to cope if his father was murdered in front of his eyes? Probably not. He'd witnessed terrible things during his time in combat, tonight's events not yet added to the list, and done things he was glad he never had to do again. But losing a family member was a pain too strong to ignore. How the dark elf plowed through his meal with unabashed gusto remained a mystery.

"What's our next move? The slippery bastard could be anywhere by now." Klaus drained the last of his coffee and looked around for the disinterested waitress at the far end of the counter.

Since arriving the group felt as if they were in the way, impeding the crew from closing early despite the hours posted sign on the front door. Daniel knew from past experience how the night shift crews could be, especially in small towns where the city went to sleep with the sun. He grinned at the frustration knotting the dwarf's forehead.

"I should call back to Agent Blackmere," Murphy offered.

No one acknowledged him. Daniel wiped a piece of hashbrown from the corner of his mouth instead. "We know he's after the princess. Our best bet is to get her exact location and try to intercept."

"Agent Blackmere will know where she is being kept," Murphy chimed in. His desire to feel helpful after two days of pushing their buttons and freezing during the battle of Craig-E-Claire almost too much for him to accept.

"Convenient, isn't it?" Klaus snapped.

Daniel's gaze flit between them, anticipating the growing conflict. Something about the younger agent hadn't sat right with him since Daniel first arrived in Newburgh. It might have been the arrogance, or the smug manner of Murphy's delivery. He didn't know. What he did know was Murphy was a liability instead of the asset Blackmere promised.

"I am an agent of the—"

"No one cares," Nevada Slim added.

Daniel rose, stepped out from the cramped confines of the chair, and stretched. "Enough. We've all been through a lot tonight. This bickering isn't getting us anywhere. We need to stop Xander and, presumably, whoever is holding his leash. I don't think it will be long before whoever is in charge learns most of the targets from tonight are still alive."

Nevada Slim's shoulders tensed but he remained silent.

Murphy slumped; the fire gone out. Daniel recognized the edge of defeat in his eyes and decided not to push, not yet anyway. The time for reckoning was fast approaching and he intended on being first in line. Until then patience was a virtue.

"Actually Murphy, you should call Blackmere, but I want to hear the conversation. We're too deep in this to keep messing up. Unless of course you have something to hide?"

"Oooh, secrets! I have lots of those," Jenny blurted with glee.

At Daniel's glance, the young girl shrugged with an innocent smile that stretched across her face. He suppressed a shiver.

"Ok, so dinner is over. Let's head out." Daniel waited until Jenny hopped down and skipped out the door before going up to the waitress with a wry grin. "Elves, right?"

He sauntered outside, leaving a confused young woman staring after. Things like this just didn't happen in the quiet village of Roscoe. Not until tonight at any rate.

"What do you mean he can't be reached?"

Daniel caught the words lingering on the light breeze. A sour feeling opened in his stomach, threatening to void his meal. Blackmere, while far from being trusted, was the closest thing Daniel had to a grasp on sanity since becoming embroiled in this mess. Losing contact with the agent threatened to unravel all he'd worked so hard to wind up.

Murphy's face reddened. "Tell him this is Agent Murphy. We must get in contact with him immediately. The situation is critical." After receiving some kind of response, he rolled his eyes and hung up.

"What's going on?" Daniel asked.

"Agent Blackmere is enroute as we speak."

"Here?" Thraken asked, eyes bugging.

Murphy shook his head. "No. He's heading to the princess' last known position. This is going all wrong."

Daniel rolled his eyes. No stranger to plans going to shit, he decided on a different approach by slapping Murphy on the shoulder. jarring the young man. "Cheer up, bud. We're not out of the fight yet. Blackmere presents one angle. We have others. The princess is being kept west of us, right? I say we hop in the truck and haul ass that way and pray for the best."

Murphy's jaw dropped. "Are you saying we should trust to faith to get us through?"

Daniel smiled. "If you can't trust God, who can you trust? Let's go. Time's wasting."

He slammed the door shut, wondering if he believed his own bullshit.

***

Xander stared at the ghost reflection of his face in the passenger window as endless miles of unoccupied wilderness flowed by. Red and blue lights from the dashboard glowed on the windshield, providing a flickering kaleidoscope forcing him to blink. Lost in thought, the elf ignored the quiet music playing in the background. If Dale noticed his disinterest, he remained quiet.

Aches accompanied the rash of bruises he'd suffered during the building collapse. He'd taken a strike from a large wooden beam when the ceiling fell, making it difficult to sit. Each bump aggravated him more and soured his mood. The combination of failure and cowardice speared his psyche, so long had it been since he last accepted being inadequate. Xander struggled with the quagmire he now found himself.

He never had the intentions of killing those targeted by Basil. They'd done nothing to him, but accepting the job meant continued freedom and the possibility of escape once and for all. Of course this hadn't prevented him from attempting the deed. Baron Visilias was proof of this. Xander, once resigned to his task, attempted to perform it with the professionalism expected of his position. All in the name of elfkind. The great lie.

Basil Kadis was a monster in the flesh. Working for him meant selling part of his soul, but it that's what it took to get back to Gwen, Xander had no problem with it. He forced a sneer. Xander never cared for Visilias in the first place. The man walked around with an air of authority he did not have, contributing to the fallacy of the ruling clans. Losing him was no great ordeal though Xander vaguely recalled the man having a son at some point. Should he come looking for revenge …

"So, what happened back there?" Dale asked.

Good question. Xander still wasn't sure. He knew his foes were closing in on him, pushing him into an inescapable corner where, no doubt, they weren't going to make the same mistakes as at the hotel. Right as he felt trapped, the building started collapsing. Somehow he found an exit and escaped into the night, but not without suffering minor injuries. A large sliver from the wall paneling speared his thigh, plunging down to his knee. The wound still bled despite the makeshift tourniquet he'd applied. The only certainty was a power had awakened, and it had not been happy. Yet as soon as their supernatural torment began the power faded and the world returned to what passed for normal.

"We underestimated the powers of that building."

Dale blinked, confused. "Powers? Like electricity? My uncle had this place with really bad wiring. It burned down on him one night. He al—"

"Dale, shut up."

To the mortal mind there was no way to convey the ancient forces concealed in the quiet places of the world. How can the infantile mind comprehend such impossibilities when so many struggled with the question of heaven and hell? The need to justify a higher power to quantify existence was a uniquely human problem, one he neither envied nor wished for. Elves had enough problems, gods not one.

"I was just saying."

Xander sighed. "What do you know, if anything, about my kind?"

"Hey man, I try to stay out of all that. Mind your business. That's what my dad always said. Nothing good comes from getting involved," Dale said almost too fast to distinguish individual words.

"Relax, Dale. I'm not going to kill you for learning any of our secrets," Xander joked. Though he had thought about it a time or two. "It will help me understand how to explain matters to you."

Dale's shoulders loosened. The tension drained between them as Xander began to speak.

After a few minutes, Dale changed the subject. "What do we do now?"

"How far is it to Elmira?" Xander asked.

"A little over two hours I think."

"Good. Head that way."

"We are," Dale assured. "What are you hoping to get there?"

Xander rubbed a fingertip along his lower jaw. "Something taken from me too long ago. The question you should be asking is can we make it before the others catch up to us before we get there?"

"Others?"

"The same ones trying to kill me since you first picked me up," Xander reminded.

A few miles went by before Dale sorted the comment out. "Xander, I don't want to die tonight."

As much as Xander wanted to tell the man all would be fine, it was a promise he wasn't willing to make. No point in building false expectations after all. He still didn't know if he could trust Dale, for the man belonged to Basil. Nor was he sure if he had enough time to reach Gwen before word of his double cross reached the prime minister. Basil's wrath was legendary. His reach long. Leaving the night to chance, Xander could only stare as the mile markers counted down.

***

Worlds were set to collide. Desperate factions racing through the night on a course that could only lead to heartache and despair.

Far to the west, two women hurried to escape certain doom. They were unaware of the car with two men hoping to find them before external forces converged and shifted the dynamic. An aging man in a helicopter raced west, desperate to prevent a full-blown war. Each vibration in the machine reminded him how he was too old for this sort of work. Far below on a quiet highway leading nowhere a truck full of battered men and one creature pretending to be a young girl, rambled about in the hopes of reaching the prize and putting an end to this whole sad affair.

Tick-tock. The hourglass was running out.

TWENTY-FOUR

Blackmere's helicopter landed behind the chain link fence turning the old prison into a construction zone. Dust and small rocks kicked up as the rotor wash died away: the whines of engines powering down akin to the howl of a lonely wolf deep in the mountains. Soldiers in fatigues rushed out to secure a perimeter, leaving nothing to chance. Too much had already gone wrong.

Agent Blackmere followed, unwilling to sit idle as younger men and women did the dirty work. His time in the Navy might not have been glamorous but it left him with an overdeveloped sense of acting rather than talking. The one difference between the military and civilian worlds he took to heart was how servicemembers were mission oriented and often did not stop until the task was complete. A character trait inspiring many petty arguments between him and his wife.

A cursory glance revealed an empty space. He scanned the ground for signs of remains, but the night and a healthy breeze blowing off the river conspired against him. If any guards had been killed nothing remained. Frustrated and with a growing sense of foreboding building within, he was eager to find answers.

"Sir, the perimeter is secure. Shall we proceed inside?"

He blew out a deep breath and closed his eyes. Blackmere already knew what they would find. The princess was either dead or gone. That seemed to be way it went when dealing with elves. He prayed for the latter. There was no way he could go back to Washington, or the queen, with news of Gwen's demise. Feelings aside, he needed to be sure.

"Proceed with caution and report any findings immediately. Use the analyzer for signs of elf residue. We can't leave anything to chance."

The team deployed, hurrying inside.

Blackmere ran his hand over the ruin of the doors with a frown noticing signs of forced entry. Who did this? Which faction knew of the princess's location and wanted her dead enough to strike on the very night a gathering of senior leaders were meant to be assassinated? He could name a dozen groups interested in shifting the balance of power and rewriting elfkind's future. But who was responsible for this?

The squad returned a short time later with predictable news. The princess was gone. What he didn't expect was word they discovered no trace of remains in the basement cell. Hope flared despite his fervent attempt at keeping it suppressed. Experience being a harsh mistress, Blackmere learned to never trust hope, for it always failed. Still, the absence of remains suggested reason to keep going. With so many wheels in motion, there was every possibility whoever absconded with the princess needed her alive and that gave him an idea.

DESA liked to think they were prepared for any contingency. This being one of them. None but a handful knew Gwen, like so many others incarcerated by the government, had been implanted with a small tracking chip should this sort of event occur. So long as her abductors didn't know of it Blackmere had a shot at finding her.

Just one shot.

His thoughts turned to Daniel Thomas and the team assigned with bringing Xander to heel. Gwen's disappearance changed everything. If they were following protocol, and knowing Daniel like he did they were, they should be hunting Xander down. Blackmere stalked back to the helicopter. He needed to find Daniel's team and fast while there was still time.

His one hope rested in a group of dysfunctional beings who struggled to be in the same room with one another.

Suddenly he chuckled, the noise going unheard. With all this happening simultaneously, how much worse could it possibly get?

***

"Where are you taking me?"

Viviana pursed her lips. The longer she sat with the princess, and it hadn't been long at all, the more she wanted to dump the spoiled brat on the side of the road and wash her hands of the whole mess. *How had I ever been friends with this?* But an assignment was an assignment and the queen had specific instructions. The knowledge, and related implied threat, did little to negate the growing feeling of disgust with the younger woman.

Making matters worse, Viviana had no idea where they were going or how to get where she needed to be. They crossed a curving bridge, walled in by mountains to their left and the promise of freedom escaping from the right. Xander was out there somewhere, but where and how far remained in doubt. *It's not like I can just call him either. This whole affair stinks and I'm stuck in the middle.*

"Princess, when I find out you will too," she said, putting on the pretense of being calm. "This wasn't a well thought out plan."

"Obviously." Gwen snorted. "Why did you feel the need to move me from my cell? Xander would have made his way to me eventually."

That's the problem. He'd stop at nothing to reach you, leaving no one safe, including me. "There are many factions in play. The promise of him surviving long enough to reach you is slim at best. That and you weren't safe at your location. The queen felt it—"

"My mother has many concerns, I have not been one of them for years," Gwen spat. "Don't lecture me on how the mighty queen seeks to redeem old mistakes and past wrongs while becoming the beacon for the clans during these dark times. It is a ruse."

"She is the lone sovereign since …"

"Since I murdered my father? Go on, say it. You think me vile. A stain upon the honor of all elfkind. I can see it in your eyes when you glare at me," Gwen said.

Viviana stiffened under the barrage of implied insults. "Regicide has not been committed for generations. It is not our way."

"Perhaps no longer but dig deep in the histories and you will find a revolving door of kings and queens who met their untimely demise at an assassin's blade. This game we play goes back much farther than either of us."

"How does that change the fact you and Xander all but destroyed the fragile balance between light and dark?" Viviana retorted. "Everything we have worked for crumbles to ruin because of you."

Head cocked, Gwen asked, "Is it? Or is that your perceived reality? What do you suppose would have happened if Xander and I were successful that night? With my mother and father both removed?" Not giving her a chance to respond, Gwen continued. "I'll tell you. We would have discovered peace at last. A reunification of the clans. No more divisions between light and dark. Elfkind would be one again."

"A dream at best. What good would have come from that?"

"The opportunity to regain our proper place in this world," Gwen answered. Her eyes shined with newfound fire. "No longer would we subservient to humans. A whisper from behind. A shadow in the night. We would find strength and remember what we were created for."

As much as she longed for the return to glory, Viviana found no practicality in what the princess offered. Humanity was too developed, too overgrown for the clans to compete with. The time of the elves was ending. They were forced to accept the reality of what was, not what might be. Dreams, she understood, belonged to children.

"Even were you successful you would not find the future as you envision it."

"That is because you lack the vision required for greatness."

"We all have our roles in life, *Princess*. A certain usefulness that often runs dry long before we are willing to accept it," Viviana ground out. "The snake strikes when we least expect. I doubt you and Xander would have found the clans willing participants in your coup."

"Little do you know, then again I expect nothing less from one of my mother's lackeys."

Who has been feeding you poison, I wonder? What grand deceiver filled your head with lies? The longer she thought of it the more Viviana became aware of an intricate web of treachery wove into the fabric of their existence. The list of viable names capable of such mastery was thin, allowing her to narrow down her suspicions.

"Petty insults seem beneath your station," Viviana said, unwilling to disclose her true trail of thoughts.

"You'll forgive me of course. After all, I am a product of my environment," the princess snipped. "We were friends once, weren't we?"

"Such as it was."

Fading memories of better times filled her head. For Viviana, it was a forced relationship insisted upon by the queen: a "Take care of my daughter so I don't have to." How could any friendship born from such disparity last?

Gwen shifted, sliding closer. "Then why can't we be again? It's not too late. Leave my mother, the evil witch trapped in her web, and help us usher forth a new age. We need strong, confident players to forge a new world, Viviana. My mother trusts you. I would like the opportunity to do so as well."

"It is a dream you chase, Gwen. Nothing more. In the end, nothing either of us does will change what is to come. We are trapped in our roles." Viviana's voice carried an edge of sadness.

***

Sergeant Otero stormed to the center of the marshaling area, helmet under one arm and a scowl decorating her face. Those select few who'd accompanied her on the raid to capture the princess were at her back; a silent wall of aggression and weapons. Ahead of them however, stood a mass of the finest marksmen and fanatics elfkind had to offer. Over one hundred of Basil's chosen prepared for war. It was a scene unwitnessed in over seven hundred years. They were the anvil upon which nations broke. And they were all, for the moment, Otero's.

The fire in her soul burned bright with the promise of ending the royal line and removing the Champion of Light. She did not deny her aspirations for the title and the prestige associated with such. The winds of change blew. It was time to escape the restrictions of the past and welcome a new era.

Basil Kadis was the man for the job. Of that she adamantly believed. Great visionaries were rare, but the prime minister shared his truths with those precious few willing to accept his words for truth. Otero was a willing participant in the great revolution.

Halting in the center of the hundred, she recognized many of the faces. Colleagues from the past, comrades through many campaigns. Otero drew a deep breath before beginning.

"Tonight we once again have purpose. Our time in the shadows is ended. Tonight we are charged with the apprehension and removal of two of the most dangerous figures confining our species. Tonight, we hunt and kill Xander and the Princess. Tonight, we win freedom for all. Death to the monarchy!"

"Death!" they shouted as one.

The thunder of their conviction rumbled off into the night.

TWENTY-FIVE

Trapped in the backseat among a host of creatures he did not trust and did not trust him in return, Agent Ralph Murphy couldn't keep his leg from bouncing. The tap-tap-tap of his bootheel on the floorboard beat a nervous report. He caught the gnome glancing his way out of the corner of his eye, Thraken's head bouncing with each leg tap. A curious creature but utterly useless in Murphy's eyes. He hadn't joined DESA to work alongside elves and dwarves. His trust resided in men and men alone. The elves had their chance to rule the world and they blew it. Like so many others found wanting against the tide of machines and progress, they were forced into irrelevance. Yet here he was. Sitting among the worst they had to offer and chartered with preventing a catastrophe.

Worrisome as it that was, Murphy had bigger problems. He needed to find a way to get word back to Morgen's people. To let them know his location and provide an update on the hunt for Xander. Each moment spent confined in the truck reduced his effectiveness and opened the possibility of his removal. Unable to prevent the worry from creasing his face, Murphy lamented ever getting involved with the queen of the dark elves.

But what choice did he have? Bound for prison, or worse, for a botched job that left over a dozen dead, Murphy had been set up to take the fall. It was his first field assignment and he proved himself a miserable failure in every regard. They were supposed to raid a suspected crew of troll bank robbers. A host of complications arose from the onset, including

179

misidentifying the targets. Instead of ending a violent criminal gang they eliminated an innocent family.

DESA, ever quick to punish, were already prepping Murphy to be the scapegoat when the agency of the queen intervened. She offered a one-time chance for redemption. What choice did he have but to accept? Murphy had been in her service ever since. Not the worst scenario, but one chaining him to elfkind and their infernal existence.

His mind raced through how to best approach the coming confrontation, for surely it was all heading for a messy end, when his phone started ringing. Heads turned: Slim's judgmental eyes peering through the rearview mirror. Murphy swallowed and pulled out the phone. His eyes widened upon seeing the caller. Duty conflicted with survival. His fingertip danced over the answer button, suddenly unwilling to commit.

"You going to answer that?" Daniel asked after the second missed call.

Murphy felt his nightmare was never going to end. He clicked the button. "This is Murphy."

From over his shoulder, Jenny clapped and said, "It's Thaddeus. He's a nice man. Hi Thaddeus!"

***

Daniel frowned. Nothing about Jenny made sense. He found her boundless energy in direct conflict with the darkness swirling just under the surface. Everything about her screamed danger. His stomach churned the closer they stood. Nerves jittered when she spoke. The word "unnatural" kept coming to mind. Daniel's imagination was well established, but nothing in his vast research came close to comprehending whatever nightmare Jenny concealed behind a child's guise.

"What does he want?" Daniel asked, forcing those negative thoughts away. Mission first.

Having missed the conversation, as brief as it was, he heard Murphy's response of, "Yes, sir. I understand."

Murphy ended the call and slipped the phone back into his pocket. "He's giving us new coordinates to meet him. The princess has been abducted but she is still alive. We're to link up at a horse track about one hundred miles west of our current location."

Suspicious, Daniel asked, "What is so important he can't just tell us?"

"He wouldn't say, only that it was of the highest importance."

He didn't trust Blackmere any more than Murphy, but Daniel needed this ordeal finished. He turned to Nevada Slim, "Punch it. Let's get this over with."

"For my father," he thought he heard the elf whisper.

The clock inched closer to midnight.

***

Klaus studied his companions, considering the merits and drawbacks of each. Naturally taciturn, he longed to return to his people. Elves were ridiculously aloof, and gnomes represented the worst of the clans. Thieves, pickpockets, and general shysters, they were a constant nuisance he'd rather not deal with. Still, the one snoring softly beside him proved his worth several times during their ill-fated hunt for Xander. Klaus chuckled at the false moniker Thraken introduced himself as: Hugh Jasol. The best part came from seeing so many failing to get the joke or the shock in those who did.

Despite past grievances and personal prejudices, Klaus found it was the two humans who gave him the most problems. Begrudgingly he accepted Daniel's lead. The man was a former soldier and seemed capable enough as a small unit leader, despite their continued lack of success. His exploits during the Long Night, as the clans took to calling the night the high king was assassinated, were well documented and Klaus managed to speak with the Schneider brothers to verify the truth. Solid and personable, the dwarf might warm to the human eventually.

No. It was Murphy who rubbed him raw.

Klaus never liked the thought of having a minder. He was proud to the point of arrogant, and a former soldier in the king's army. Those glory days were far in the past. A bitter memory of better times when the axe was the power of the day. Now he stood, bended and bowed in the service of humans for what they considered crimes. The travesty rubbed him raw. When did it become illegal to collect a blood debt? Reduced to indentured mercenary status, Klaus now found himself working for fools like Murphy.

His gaze bore into the back of the agent's head. Nothing about the man felt right. Lies and subterfuge danced beneath the surface, presenting unnecessary layers of duplicity choking the man's effectiveness. That and he knew Murphy's secret. That one detail transforming the man from an asset to a liability with the snap of a finger. Informing the others might have been the best option but Klaus was nothing if not calculating. There might come a moment when he needed to play that card.

Games within games. Klaus decided to watch Murphy closely as the mission drew toward an inevitable confrontation with elfkind's most vaunted fallen hero.

Which was fine with him. Dwarves loved playing games.

***

Nevada Slim stared at the empty road with dull eyes. The emotion and power of seeing his father die in his hands left him numb, despite countless years of being estranged and ostracized by his family. Ever the black sheep, the dark elf knew his value to society, and it did not lie with stuffy titles and boardroom meetings. He needed the freedom of the road. The opportunity to prove himself to those who thought themselves his betters.

Retreating into himself, Nevada Slim, the ridiculousness of the name inspired by a fatal love of old westerns, tried to imagine a world where he could be himself without repercussions or limited expectations he might never ascend to. Ultimately, he was forced to accept he would never be the man he was born to be. Trapped by birth, Slim rebelled against the notion of becoming a titular figurehead in an oligarchy of limited proportions.

The mission to hunt Xander took his mind off his troubled past. He spent years experimenting with sexuality and drugs, often going beyond the moral constraints approved of by his father. Anything to push the limits and see what happened next. He joined a commune in the 60s. A cult in the 70s. Slim converted priests to unholy causes and unbelievers to the most pious of men. In the 1980s he took up the art of explosives and did some work for the Irish Republican Army north of Belfast. It was all a game, for no matter how heinous his actions, he would always be forced to return to the family and, one day, accept the mantle of leadership. His father's passing hurried the inevitable and that bothered him more than he understood.

Nevada Slim, outside son of the dark elves, turned his focus back to his team and their quest. Xander became his white whale. The impossible target worthy of his ire. They'd crossed paths on rare occasions, though never long enough to gauge the other. Slim came to despise the champion of the light simply because they were on opposing sides of a pointless conflict. He missed the opportunity to eliminate the elf back at the hotel, even if his heart hadn't been in it to begin with. Instead he dropped a bomb on a squad of his own kind. They meant nothing to him, despite their affiliations.

What mattered most was Xander killing his father. Neutrality ended an hour ago in the ruins of a building that should have been demolished long ago. The darkness contained within tore through the veil of life and death. They'd come close to tearing that veil open, before Jenny intervened. Slim was thankful for her, for it allowed him to formulate his revenge on the elf champion.

***

Thraken snored on without a care in the world. He felt comfortable among the others, even if they were a far cry from the familiarity of his people. Gnomes were known for their deep roots and longstanding traditions. Thraken accepted the job with DESA after he got pinched for heisting an ATM machine. Thankless in many ways, he found a new life among the misfits and ne'er-do-wells. Though he might never say it, the men and women he surrounded himself with now were as close to family as he had.

Lost in his dreamscape, the gnome imagined a world where he became the premier bounty hunter, television show and all. Travelling around the world apprehending the worst of the worst. It was a dream he longed to realize.

A smile crept across his face as he nestled into the leather seats, the print of the cushion burrowing into his flesh.

***

Jenny watched her peers with disguised amusement. She was a creature of the old world. A terror born before humanity crawled from the seas and evolved from their primate kin. None living knew what she was, and it had been so long since another of her kind walked the earth she no longer remembered. All she knew was a great and terrible power rested within her childish frame. Not that she needed to appear so. Jenny could be anything she wanted. It was the allure of being a child again, carefree and innocent that kept her from devouring all she came in contact with. The world might be a dark place, but she tried to find a positive side to it. Otherwise …

Humming an old tune she recalled from the late 1600s when she pretended to be the daughter of royalty in France, Jenny reflected on the trapped energies of Craig-E-Claire. So many souls trapped in the darkness, hungry and eager to be free so they may reap a toll upon those perceived to imprison them. She snorted at the absurdity of it. How could the dead know they were gone and forgotten decades after their bones turned to dust? It was a silly game for silly people.

The truth was no one remembered you once you were planted in the earth. Oh a teary eyed relative might visit your grave for a few years but those trips grew distant until naught, but the caretaker ensured the grass was cut and the tombstone free of debris or rubbish. Time was ever a wicked creature none knew how to best.

Her gaze drifted to Daniel. He proved an enigma. A kind soul forced to do vile things for his country. Here was a man she could trust, for he did not willingly commit violence. Perhaps there was a lesson for all in the human.

Content to remain with them a while longer, Jenny began twiddling her thumbs.

TWENTY-SIX

They passed through the quiet city of Binghamton a short while later. Old memories flooded Daniel. He'd grown up not far from there on a mountain in the middle of nowhere. Not cut out for farm life, he enlisted in the Army as soon as he could and a week after graduating high school shipped out. He never looked back. Adventure awaited.

The military sent him around the world, which as an eighteen year old was amazing. He saw and did things too few got to experience. He climbed the tallest mountain in South Korea, stood in an old Buddhist monastery, drank beer at Oktoberfest tents in Munich, walked between the Tigris and Euphrates Rivers, and marveled at the wonder that was the ziggurat of Ur. Not bad for a kid from the country in small town America.

Yet for all his accomplishments and travels, he now found himself right back where it all began. He envisioned those long trucks rides into the city so he could visit his favorite, and only one he knew of, comic book shop. Taking long rides with the girl he once imagined spending the rest of his life. Funny how that never worked out. They'd run out of gas on a long stretch of country road one night then got locked out of their truck on another trip. It was an innocent time. One the nostalgic part of him longed to return to. But life was hard by necessity, and he had done too much to ever return to that youthful innocence.

War changed him. He appeared the same on the outside, but his mind was a conflict of emotions. Sentimentality and sadness welled in him, and Daniel did his best to prevent it from escaping. No one needed to feel sorry for him. Not for him. There were others who needed the support, perhaps even a little sympathy. His wife used to bug him about increasing his disability rating and he considered it, until he ran into an old soldier of his missing both of his arms from the elbows down and was covered with the scars from a vehicle fire. After that it became a moot point.

Daniel caught the reflection of moonlight on the flowing waters of the Susquehanna River on the left. The hum of tires rolling over endless miles of well used concrete droned in his ears, producing a lullaby he almost didn't resist. There was tranquility with the river. He enjoyed spending time floating down in an old john boat or standing on the shores trying to reel in one of the great muskies. Perhaps he'd take the family fishing once all this was over. They could do with a vacation, him most of all.

"Another twenty minutes," he commented as they based a sign for Johnson City.

It struck him again that he was almost home. The irony of it not lost to him. If only Xander knew just how close he was to Daniel's family, the urgent drive to collect the princess might last a while longer. After all, how could the elf resist the urge to eliminate Daniel's bloodline? The chances of being so close at random were miniscule, practically nonexistent. He began wondering who was pulling the strings.

"How do you know?" Nevada Slim asked.

"I grew up near here," he said.

"Sounds fun."

"You have no idea."

They crossed the river and kept moving east, passing beyond the orange glow of the big city, such as it was, and were slowly inching back into the eternal darkness of the country night. Daniel started feeling trepidatious, just as he had during that odd period of time waiting to go on a combat mission. Knowing you were going into a fight and being forced to endure hours of waiting produced heightened nerves, overstimulation and often left the soldiers lagging when the first round when down range. Was the same happening now?

He glanced in the rearview mirror, ensuring Murphy had drifted to sleep before asking, "Do you think Blackmere is on the level?"

"Thaddeus Blackmere is transparent, for a human. He does what he says," Nevada Slim replied. "Good man. It is this one I don't trust."

"Me either, though I can't put my finger on why not."

Slim's voice lowered. "He carries secrets. All is not as he wishes to appear."

Daniel turned, giving the sleeping agent a second look. Nothing special about the man stuck out. Still young and impetuous, the man had a lot to learn and much to prove. Daniel knew none of the team trusted Murphy and that might prove problematic if his life was ever on the line. Still, he didn't feel any duplicity from the man. *Shit. There's one in every squad isn't there?*

He turned back to Slim. "You think he's a spy?"

A shrug. "I don't know, but he is dangerous. Best to keep an eye on him lest he lead us to ruin."

Daniel blinked twice. "What happened to your accent?"

Nevada Slim stiffened, transferring the piece of straw artfully to the other side of his mouth. "What accent, pardner?"

"Uh huh," Daniel replied. "What do you suggest we do with Mister Murphy? Dump on the side of the road and keep moving? Maybe pick him up after the dust settles."

"He would only call whoever else he works for. He is too much of liability to go free."

The Baltic accent, how terribly forced, slipped back into place like a well-worn mask. People like Slim seldom showed their hands, not until the pot was high enough. Daniel wanted to like the dark elf but there remained a lingering prejudice from his first experiences.

"I could put bomb in his pocket. One wrong move and boom." Slim chuckled.

As amusing as the image became, Daniel would never be able to justify why a federal agent turned to body parts and pink spray in western New York. "We keep watching him. See how he handles what comes next. I can't imagine Xander has too much left in him at this point. If that's right, Murphy should be getting a call from his handler soon enough."

"Boom works fine."

Daniel waggled a finger at the elf. "No bombs." A glance at the clock on the dash had him sighing. "Pick it up some. Blackmere should be waiting for us."

"If you insist."

***

The car pulled off the side of the road at a rest stop. Viviana threw it into park and yawned. They had gone far enough from the prison in Elmira to warrant a stop, even if just to stretch. She despised travelling by car. Once, she'd crossed entire continents on horseback or as part of a caravan. She longed for the feel of the wind in her hair and the spring chill across the open steppe. Her bloodline came down from the Norwegian mountains. They proved the inspiration behind many Viking myths and legends, an amusing premise she helped play up at the time.

Now she was reduced to being a babysitter. Viviana regarded her charge with unusual familiarity.

Their previous conversation chilled the atmosphere and neither had spoken since. She resisted the urge to confine Gwen to the vehicle, knowing the beckon of freedom was but a stride away. Enough damage had been done this night, if what the queen told her was true. Losing the princess might prove the final nail in the coffin.

Ignoring the warning in her mind, Viviana allowed Gwen to get out and stretch. It was a mistake. Separated by the width of the car, the elf princess raised her arms above her head, interlaced her fingers and pulled up. Viviana relaxed just enough to blink. By the time she opened her eyes Gwen was sprinting away.

"Fuck!" she shouted and took off after her.

They wove through the mostly empty parking lot before slipping into the row of shrubs and down the long slope of the ditch leading toward the highway. Viviana, always the more agile of the pair, ran her counterpart down with the skill of a lioness. They collided halfway down the slope, the impact knocking both off their feet. Bodies intertwined, they tumbled to the bottom. Sticks, grass, and leaves clung to them; clothing was torn. Out of breath and angry, Viviana wrestled the princess to her back, taking a knee in the lower ribs.

Pain lanced through her side, up into her stomach in the instant Gwen flipped her off. Blood smearing her teeth, the princess gave a feral grin and crawled back to her feet. She made it to her knees before Viviana tackled her from behind. This time she pinned Gwen facedown, forcing an arm behind and jerking it up to the point of dislocating.

Gwen kicked back, striking Viviana in the lower back with little effect. The elf pulled harder and was rewarded with a slight pop—Gwen screamed. She took a blow to the side of the head, knocking her unconscious. Viviana waited until the princess's head dove into the dirt before she released the pressure on her arm. Clutching her side, Viviana struggled to her feet. The temptation to kick Gwen whispered to her, but the elf ignored it.

"What was I thinking?" Viviana began pulling dead leaves and twigs from her hair. This was not how it was supposed to go. Whatever happened to honor?

The princess, softened by her time in a DESA cell, remained a threat. One Viviana sorely underestimated. It was a rare moment of weakness. One she vowed not to allow a second time. She slumped down beside the unconscious woman and laid her forearms over her knees. Crisis averted, for the moment, she was left with a greater problem.

"How in the world am I going to get Gwen back to the car?"

The thought of dragging royalty through the dirt and mud proved amusing. Nothing satisfied the masses more than seeing royals suffer indignity. But if she did there'd be no end to Gwen's complaining and baseless threats. Viviana glanced at her watch. She still had time. Then again, every action was induced through the fervent need to transfer the princess out of her control, and into the arms of the one person who could control her.

The risk was high, for reuniting Gwen with Xander might prove the catalyst capable of bringing down the entire elf hierarchy. As dedicated as she was to the queen, Viviana often wondered if that would be such a bad thing. The current family had done nothing but march elfkind toward the cliff at a slow but steady decline. Perhaps Xander was the storm they needed to reignite the passion with which they had once strode across the world.

Orders were orders, however. Morgen didn't want her daughter anywhere near the disgraced champion. Any deviation now might result in Viviana losing her head.

The queen's wrath was well documented and, no one would ever admit aloud, she had grown increasingly unstable after the death of her husband and foe.

Gwen groaned, fingers twitching.

Disturbed, Viviana grabbed the woman by the hair. "Get up, little bitch. Time to see you get your due."

Gwen cried out as she was dragged to her feet. "My arm!"

"You're lucky I didn't stick a knife in your heart for that stunt," Viviana growled.

Any pretense of friendliness was gone.

TWENTY-SEVEN

They crawled past the open gate and into the vacant parking lot. Daniel ordered the headlights cut to reduce their silhouette. Windows lowered enough for rifle barrels to poke out. They'd been told the SUV was bulletproof, but it was a risk no one wanted to take. Losing one of their group early, Daniel needed the rest of them alive if he was finally going to be free from the threat Xander represented. Better to be ready for war than caught unprepared.

A short drive down the service road to the horse barns and they found Blackmere's helicopter. Red lights bathed the interior. Heads bobbed and a door opened. Daniel, ever suspicious, had Slim stop the truck at a distance. He ran a finger over his chin, mind swirling. Too much remained at stake. Grunting in frustration, Daniel double checked his magazine.

"Everyone wait here. This shouldn't take long. Murphy, you're with me," he said and hopped out the car. A split second later a second door opened then slammed shut. *Good. That's one less problem I need to worry about.*

Murphy came beside him, and the pair headed for the helicopter, where Blackmere had already exited. The glow from the half-moon bathed the surrounding area, from the grandstands to the small casino attached in a haunting blue light. Leaves swept across the horse track. A chill pulsed off the nearby river, enough to send shivers down his spine. Daniel adjusted the grip on his rifle, careful to present himself as a non-threat while remaining capable of engaging any hostiles should the need present itself.

"What do you suppose he has to say?" Daniel probed.

Murphy shrugged. "He's already told us the mission has changed. Hopefully Agent Blackmere has discovered new intelligence that will help us run Xander down."

"Pretty vague answer, Murphy. What do you know you're not telling me?"

The crunch of their boots on cold hardened dirt sounded like glass breaking. Each step heightened Daniel's nerves.

"There's not much I can say, is there? I've been in the truck with you this whole time."

"Have you come looking for a fight, Daniel?" Blackmere asked once they halted. His eyes drifted to Daniel's trigger finger lightly tapping the magazine well.

A plume of breath escaped as he huffed. "That all depends on you, Blackmere. I've taken enough thumps this night to be wary."

"Understood, and I'm sorry this hasn't gone the way you or I imagined, but I have news you need to know."

"Let me guess. You miraculously tracked Xander down and know his present location?" Daniel asked, tone dry.

"We—"

"Save it. We've been a step behind him since you brought me aboard. I'm starting to think you want him to get away."

Blackmere stiffened. "Why would I have come to you if that were true? Think, Daniel. Xander is a proven threat to us all. He's already killed. Who's to say he won't try again? Only one name on that list died."

"The others fled once the building collapsed. Shouldn't you be worried about them?"

"We have teams in contact with both light and dark elf leadership. They will be protected should Xander, or his employer, decide to strike again." Blackmere caught Murphy's nervous expression and asked, "Something bothering you, agent?"

"No, sir." Murphy jerked back; eyes averted.

Daniel spat. "He's lying. This bastard is hiding something and, until I know what it is, I don't want him back on the team."

"He's your liaison with me," Blackmere replied. His brow furrowed.

"Wait a minute!" Murphy cried out. "I've done nothing wrong. Everything I've done has been for the good of this team! It's not my fault none of them accept that. They've turned him against me."

Daniel sidestepped, slipping his finger into the trigger guard of his gun. "Doesn't sound like any defense an innocent man would use."

Blackmere's frown deepened. "Agent Murphy, would you care to explain? Daniel doesn't seem to believe you and I need to know everything so we can put this to rest and move forward. Are you hiding something from the team?"

Trapped in an impossible scenario, Murphy's shoulders sagged as he began to speak.

"And so I now—"

Daniel acted faster than either of them anticipated. In one motion he let his rifle go and landed a blow to the side of Murphy's head. The younger agent crumbled, unconscious.

"Daniel, I believe that is enough. It wouldn't do to have you kill one of my people," Blackmere cautioned as Daniel drew his leg back to deliver a kick.

"This son of a bitch has been playing both sides from the start. He's lucky I don't put a round in his head,"

Daniel vented, reaching for his weapon. The last time he'd pointed a weapon at one of his own was back in Iraq when a particularly ignorant young sergeant forgot his assignment and nearly got them all killed. When it came to personal security and the lives of his people, Daniel was unforgiving.

"That's my problem to deal with. Agent Murphy will be handled accordingly, though I suspect he has not committed any treason or crime worth punishing."

Confused, Daniel asked. "How do you figure? He's been funneling information back to Morgen. Remember her? The woman who wanted me dead not so long ago."

"Morgen is not the issue. The queen has been quiet lately. There are greater players in the game we need to worry about," Blackmere countered. "We believe it is the prime minister who is responsible for this debacle."

Daniel grunted. "I don't know him."

"Basil Kadis is a vain man often accused of being jealous of the crown. His desire for power is well documented. I have it on good authority he all but threatened to overthrow Morgen."

Disgusted, Daniel moved away and started pacing. Prime Minister? Where did this clown come from and why was he just now being made aware of the situation? His sole focus had been on Xander since leaving his house two days ago. Now he had to contend with one of the most powerful men in elfkind? Life continued dumping on him without mercy.

"You're telling me we have a greater threat? One running his own con?" Daniel asked. "Blackmere, this is pushing it. My people have already been tested enough. They don't have much left in the tank."

"I understand Slim's father was the lone victim at the castle. He has my condolences."

"Yeah, you go tell him that," Daniel snapped. "Look, how can I fight what I don't know?"

"That is the age old question, isn't it? The elf clans are as enigmatic to me today as they were the first time I discovered their existence. None of it makes sense, Daniel. DESA is all that keeps them in line and even that is done poorly." He paused, uncertainty awakening in the darks of his eyes. "Your mission parameters haven't changed. Find and stop Xander at all costs and I might have the tool to make that happen."

Still dubious, Daniel stopped pacing long enough to listen.

"When she was first imprisoned, the princess was fit with a tracking beacon. Nothing invasive nor out of the ordinary. Every prisoner in our facilities has one for just such an event. Gwen was moved earlier tonight. Unauthorized, I might add. Whoever raided her compound knew what they were doing. As best we can tell the guards are dead."

"I feel myself getting older, Blackmere. Get to the point."

"We can follow Gwen and set the trap for Xander," Blackmere finished, his voice growing heavier as his own patience wore thin.

"Presuming Xander has slipped his leash from this Basil Hayden guy," Daniel countered.

"Kadis."

"Same thing."

Daniel admitted the plan had merit. Getting the princess back in custody certainly allowed more flexibility for his team. A way to cut the head from both snakes, freeing them in the event the prime minister decided to take a more active role. It was a risk needed to be taken. There was only one problem.

"What do we do with him?" he gestured to the fallen Murphy. "If I take him back to the truck the others will tear him apart, especially the dwarf."

"I think Mr. Murphy will be of some use to us yet. Help me get him up. We have much to discuss," Blackmere said.

***

"So, there's that," Slim said after Daniel knocked Murphy out.

Klaus grunted. "Hmm, never liked that little prick. Think we should go out there?"

"Daniel said we wait here," Jenny added.

The strain in her voice put Klaus on edge. He half turned to face her. "When are you going to tell us what you are?"

Smiling sweetly, Jenny said, "A girl has to keep her secrets, silly."

"She's got a point," Thraken chimed in.

"About secrets?" Klaus demanded.

Thraken shook his head. "No. Daniel said to wait here. We'll know if he needs our help."

"Doesn't seem like it right now," Nevada Slim added. "We wait."

Grumbling, Klaus slumped in his seat.

***

"Your majesty, an urgent call just came in."

Morgen set the nearly empty glass of red wine down and pursed her lips. The fragrance danced upon her flesh, prompting her to admit humans came up with a good idea every once in a while, though not with white wine. That she never figured out.

She glided to her desk and answered the phone in the center of the table. "This is Morgen."

Silence, whether from nerves or delay in transmission left her guessing until a voice spoke, "Morgen, we have a problem and only you can solve it."

She failed to recognize the voice. "Who am I speaking with?"

"Agent Thaddeus Blackmere. We've met before."

Morgen searched her memories, vaguely recalling the aging man in a sharply tailored black suit and a no-nonsense demeanor. She appreciated such men for they were a dying breed. "Agent Blackmere, how pleasant it is to make your acquaintance again, though I do question what could possibly be so important as to disrupt my night."

"M-my apologies, your highness but there is a situation you need to be aware of." He went on to explain the events of the last two days.

Morgen already knew most of it, especially the events concerning her daughter. The rest served as confirmation for her suspicions. Allowing him to finish, her thoughts twisted to diabolical revenge and endless stream of torments the likes of which hadn't been seen in centuries. Basil Kadis was going to pay for his meddling. This she vowed.

"I have been in contact with my daughter since she was removed from your prison but have not been made privileged to Xander's whereabouts. Tell me, Agent, where are you located now?"

"Where are we?" he said to someone else, Murphy no doubt. "Tioga Downs Raceway just off the interstate."

So close. Morgen smiled as a nearly forgotten memory crept into her mind. "There is a place not far from you, or my daughter. Go there. I will send Xander to you, but it may come at a cost."

"How are you going to manage that? And go where?" Blackmere demanded. Suspicions aroused, he knew nothing came without an associated cost.

"Why, I'm going to make a call," she teased, almost laughing. "You need to head to the Fainting Goat Island Inn. It is a most cozy place I'm told. Leave the rest to me." Morgan reached for her glass of wine. The dark red tinge swirling in the crystal grooves. "Goodnight, Agent Blackmere."

TWENTY-EIGHT

Originally intended as a hotel when the steel giants snaked westward, the Fainting Goat Island Inn was the kind of house you drove by without looking twice. Nothing distinctive set it apart from the others running along the river road between Waverly and Nichols, New York. Blink and you would miss it. Yet for all of the quaint coziness of home, there remained an air of mystery surrounding the Inn. A whispered darkness settled in the old bones, reminding guests and visitors they were not alone in this world.

Viviana knew nothing of the Inn's history, nor did she care. Her sole focus remained of what lay just ahead. An end to the foolishness of this night and, she hoped, a shower and change of clothes. Stains covered her jacket and pants; the byproduct of her altercation with Gwen. The foolishness of her deeds, while necessary, further reminded Viviana how times had changed. Once, so long ago the names and locations were little more than hazy blurs, she had but to snap her fingers and whatever problem she experienced was handled.

Now she was reduced to little more than a chauffeur. A shell of her former authority. She wasn't alone. All of elfkind languished under their inability to adapt to the new, changing world. They were, she realized, obsolete.

Viviana pulled the car into the driveway and made a quick survey of the landscape. The Inn was two stories and backed up against a wide river. Shadows of an island behind suggested there was no easy way to infiltrate from any angle but the front—she nodded. At least something had gone right for her tonight.

201

A lone light shined like a beacon from the front window. Taking that as a good sign, she turned to the princess. "Stay here and don't try anything stupid. Next time I won't be so kind."

Hatred spilled from Gwen's eyes, but the princess stayed silent. Some threats didn't need saying and the fact that she'd been tied up and secured to the vehicle made Viviana's speech moot.

Satisfied, Viviana slammed the door shut behind her and cursed herself for the momentary weakness. For a split second, so brief she almost missed it, Viviana considered untying the princess so they might work together. Foolish. She clenched her fists and stomped to the front porch. It took great effort for her to calm enough to knock on the front door. The hour was late. If anyone did open the door she would be met with suspicion, or worse.

She blew out a steadying breath as the sound of footsteps accompanied the shadow she noticed approaching. Rich, orange light spread through the crack as the door opened.

"Can I help you, miss?"

She found the man opening the door mildly attractive, for a human. His scruff of beard and moustache complimented the lines on his face and the gentle pulldown of flesh around the corners of his eyes. Middle aged, he wore a long flannel housecoat and, much to her amusement, an old pair of combat boots, unlaced. It was the eyes she studied most. This man, whoever he was, had not lived an easy life. One of quality perhaps but lacking the ease with which she'd grown up.

Viviana put on her sweetest smile, which she reckoned must look terrible given her inability to clean up after the fight, and said, "My apologies for disturbing you this late at night."

He glanced at his watch. The indifference of his expression unsettling.

"My friend and I have been traveling all night and, well, we just happened to be heading down this road and you just happened to have a light on ..."

Not lies, exactly, but neither was it the full truth. By accepting them into his home, this poor man invited the host of trouble coming with it. As much as she wanted to give warning, doing so put a target on her back and, being far from home, Viviana wasn't in the position to trust anyone. Especially in the middle of the night. Part of her wanted to leave, to spare this man the injustices racing toward him, but the queen had been adamant about where she wanted her daughter taken.

"We don't usually take many guests this late."

"Nor do I blame you. The world has become a crazy place and you never know who you can trust. I'm Viviana, by the way." She smiled and extended her hand.

He glanced at the hand, then the leaf that fell from her hair as she shifted forward, before accepting it. "Willard. Who's the lady in the car?"

Viviana looked back, watching the exhaust plume trail away under the red glow of taillights. "It's best if you don't know."

"Uh huh." Willard frowned. "You a cop?"

"You might say that," she replied. "I promise we won't be much trouble and out of your hair come the dawn." *One way or another*.

Willard stared at her until Viviana grew unsettled. There was something in that gaze she couldn't identify. And that bothered her.

"Fine. Grab your friend and come inside. I'll wake Moose and get you checked in," he said. "I hope you know what you're getting into."

He left Viviana staring at his back. Suspicion and confusion mixing in her gaze.

***

Daniel watched as the marker halted then asked, "Do we go now?"

Blackmere shook his head. "The princess isn't the target. She's just the bait."

"It could be a while before Xander makes his way here. Hell, are we even sure he's been given her location?"

The DESA agent felt his age. Endless questions, wargaming what might happen, and the eternal prospect of total mission failure hounded his thoughts and footsteps. Just like old times. Daniel, and by extension his team, were invaluable assets, but their lack of discipline made them unstable and slightly unreliable when it came to following orders. It also showed him another side of what the strike force could be once freed from the restraints of a proper chain of command.

Right now, Daniel provided a running line of questioning Blackmere didn't want to answer. Though, he didn't question the man's eagerness to complete the task. For many soldiers the need to act remained throughout their lives, often to the irritation of those around them. Task oriented people usually rubbed others the wrong way and Daniel certainly fit the mold. Normally he found the trait attractive. Tonight was not one of those times.

"They have loved each other for almost five hundred years," Blackmere explained. "The one motivation Xander has is Gwen. He'll show. We just need to give it a little time."

"You seem pretty sure about that," Daniel replied.

Blackmere said nothing.

Frustration producing tight lines from the corners of his eyes, Daniel rubbed his chin. "At least let my team move into a better overwatch position. We're too far away here."

"It's less than a mile away," Blackmere exclaimed.

"Precisely. By the time we move our targets could be gone," Daniel pressed. "Unless you have aerial surveillance on the area?"

Smug bastard. You're guessing too close to the mark for my liking, but I'll be damned if I ever admit it to you. "We have adequate support to complete the assignment. That's all you need to know. Unless you wish to become part of the team?"

Daniel's eyes widened. "Wait, you're serious?"

"Why not? You have an intimate knowledge of the elf clans, more than most of our field agents. You've been involved directly with the upper tier of their leadership. Those you don't know sure know you. It's the perfect match."

"Tinkering around with elves for the rest of my days doesn't appeal to me much after Raleigh."

"I understand that, but you are the perfect candidate," Blackmere said. "I don't expect a decision tonight, but at least think about it. Talk it over with your wife. This is too big a decision for one person to make. Besides, look at what else I have to work with."

***

Daniel followed Blackmere's gaze across the parking lot to Murphy. The younger agent lamented his redefined role. Sorrow twisted his features, even in the quasi-darkness. Sitting on an overturned barrel, Murphy's head hung low, defeated.

Despite the man's betrayal— Daniel didn't feel any malicious intent coming from Murphy. Youth propelled rash decisions. Guilty of his own past discretions, Daniel knew pushing too hard would break the man. He'd already been torn down. Now it was time to start building back up and see what was left. Did he want the job? Did it matter? With Xander still on the loose, Daniel needed all the assets possible.

"He's not so bad. Sure looks up to you," Daniel said.

Blackmere stiffened. "Does he? That's interesting. Do you think you can fix him? Get him back in the game?"

Understanding few men were truly useless, Daniel shrugged. "I can try. He's not the first man I've had like that. Might not be enough time though."

"Do what you can."

Daniel nodded.

"Move your team into overwatch of the target location. There should be a cemetery across the street giving you a good vantage point. You'll be able to react swift and sure once Xander is confirmed on target," Blackmere relented.

Daniel grinned. He slapped Blackmere on the shoulder and headed toward the truck. "Murphy! Get up off your ass and get in the truck. We've got a fight to finish."

"Don't forget my offer, Daniel," Blackmere called.

***

Tired, Dale's eyes burned. Cramps in his left hand made driving almost impossible. Endless miles without a break in scenery dulled his senses. They'd been on the move for almost two full days. He didn't know how much more he could take before his body collapsed from sheer exhaustion. That Xander didn't suffer from the same amplified his irritation.

"You are certain of this?" Xander repeated for the third time.

Dale rolled his eyes. Whoever he was speaking with, Dale assumed it was Basil, was either irate or redundant. Neither appealed much to him. His sole focus was on finding a nice soft bed and a bottle of bourbon.

"I'll punch it into the navigation now." Xander plugged in the address Basil provided and lit up upon seeing they were but ten miles away. "We will be there momentarily. Thank you."

"What did Basil have to say?" Dale asked between yawns once the call ended.

Xander's eyes narrowed. "That wasn't Basil. It was the queen."

"The queen!" Dale exclaimed. "Wait, how did she get your number?"

"I don't know," his said, voice lowering. "Making this suspicious at best. Slow down."

There was no love lost between Xander his potential mother in law as much as Dale could tell.

"Pull over at the next place you can," the elf ordered.

"We're not going to get the princess?" Dale asked.

"We are, just not the way the queen expects. Pull over. We have work to do, Dale."

Unhappy at the prospect of continuing their epic crusade across upstate New York, he never understood why people called it that, the Pennsylvania border sat just a few miles away, Dale looked for a place to park.

The car rolled to a stop under the scrutinizing glare of a small herd of deer.

TWENTY-NINE

Gwen glowered at her captor from the corner of the room. This new hate burrowing deeper within as the minutes passed. Any semblance of friendship they might have once enjoyed crumbled away under the mounting pressure of conflicting desires. She'd shown no qualms with killing her own kind, ask her father, but this went further. The princess hadn't spoken since Viviana knocked her out and dragged her back to the car. She chose to lick her wounds instead, biding her time until Xander arrived.

Viviana would not live to see the dawn; Gwen vowed it. Hurt demanded repayment with hurt.

Aches spread throughout her body, she wanted nothing more than the opportunity to crawl away and recover before unleashing vengeance. She should have known better than to trust her mother's henchwoman. Viviana had ever displayed signs of a cruel heart and, in a moment of weakness, Gwen allowed herself to believe things might have changed between them. That she was being rescued out of a sense of obligation. How wrong she had been.

The part making no sense to her was why. Why had Viviana absconded with the princess now? Her jaw throbbed, bruised where knuckles struck her. Gwen worked her mouth to numb at least some of the pain.

"What is this all about, Viviana?" she asked, breaking the silence. "Has my mother had a change of heart?"

Without turning from the window, Viviana replied, "The queen's desires are none of my business. Whether she wishes you by her side once more or has chosen to take care of you herself, I don't care. I was sent to do a job."

"That's all I've become to you, eh? A job? A thankless task best completed and forgotten before the dawn," Gwen spat. "Kill me now and be done with it."

"That's not going to happen. The queen will decide your fate."

The finality in her voice shut down the conversation, infuriating Gwen that much more. She decided to shift tactics. Anything to keep Viviana talking lest the silence become maddening. "You could let me go. No one needs to be the wiser."

"Let you go? I've risked my life getting you." Viviana's laugh bit deep. "No, Gwen. There is no freedom for you. Too much has happened to let you slip away."

"Not enough has happened for my liking. I was fine in my cell."

"But you weren't. You still don't get it." Viviana shook her head. "None of us are safe tonight. You most of all. The Prime Minister has begun his coup. It started when Xander was freed from the Grinder."

"You're certain of this?" Gwen asked, perking up at the mention of her lover.

She longed to be back in his embrace, forgetting their cares as the world forgot them. Whatever dreams they'd once shared for ruling the clans dissolved that fateful night but she never stopped yearning for Xander. He was her rock. The one constant she never found from either parent. Separated for so long, she wondered if he thought of her the way she did him.

"Reasonably. If this is accurate you can bet he will not stop until the royal bloodline has been wiped out, along with the major clan leaders and influential members of our society."

"And why—"

"Ssh." Viviana cocked her head and scanned the room. "Do you feel that?"

"Feel what?"

"We are being watched. There is another being in this room."

Frowning, Gwen looked about. She detected nothing. *Are you losing your grip on sanity, Viviana? Has the pressure of serving my mother for so long at last taken its toll?* "You need sleep. There's nothing here."

Viviana's hand dropped to the weapon concealed at her hip.

Gwen, enjoying her obvious discomfort, suggested, "Perhaps this inn is haunted."

Viviana's head snapped to her, recognition flaring wild in her eyes. "What did that man say the name of this place was?"

"Something about goats." Gwen shrugged. "I don't remember, why?"

"You might be closer to the truth than you imagine."

Wind rustled, jarring the old wooden shutters. They both stared, jerking at the sound.

***

"Here, pull in here and cut the lights."

Nevada Slim followed Daniel's finger and parked behind a small stand of pines. Just far enough to be out of sight, but too far to conduct full surveillance, forcing Daniel to make a decision.

"We take turns watching the building. Two at a time. I'll go first, who's coming with?"

Groans, and one odd snore, followed. Not reassuring. Daniel couldn't blame them. No sane person volunteered for guard duty in the middle of the night.

He decided choosing the team's sniper most prudent, and coerced Klaus to join him, much to the relief of the rest—except Jenny who all but begged to go. He felt them all staring at him as he and the dwarf headed to a good vantage point.

They settled in among a small corpse of pines with drooping lower boughs. Daniel had done a little time as a spotter for the company sniper during one of his deployments and fell into the role as Klaus set up his rifle. That the dwarf left his light machinegun behind was a minor miracle.

"That's the place? Doesn't look like much." Klaus grunted and swept his scope over the grounds. "Looks like the princess is the only one here."

Using a small pair of field glasses, Daniel focused on the windows with lights on. "I'm not seeing any movement. Make sure you have the front door covered."

"Got it. I can sweep across the property if anyone squirts out the back."

"Unless they have a boat waiting," Daniel speculated. The prospect of their targets escaping by river hadn't occurred to him until now. Lacking contingencies, the DESA team might be in trouble.

He pulled his jacket collar up to keep the wind from sneaking down his shirt but the chill coming off the ground was unstoppable. He fought back a yawn and set the glasses down.

"It was my favorite time," Klaus revealed after noting Daniel's lack of interest in their assignment. "Alone in the night. No pointless conversation to distract me. It was just me and a potential target. There's something pure about that."

"When were you in?"

"Europe, 1944," the dwarf replied, grinning. "Those were different times."

He shouldn't have been surprised given the longevity of the race, but to sit beside a World War II veteran who didn't look a day over thirty left Daniel awed.

"Makes your war look like recess," Klaus added.

Daniel couldn't argue. He remembered flying into Bangor, Maine after his second deployment. The hall was filled with Korea and Vietnam era veterans all thanking them for what they had done. He felt wrong, as if he wasn't worthy of their praise. After all, what those men went through in their respective wars overshadowed anything those who spent time in desert did. It took many years before Daniel finally understood those old timers weren't doing it out of a sense of duty. Perhaps they decided to right old wrongs and give this new generation of soldiers the welcome home they never received. That thought still humbled him to this day.

"What was it like seeing the Allies invade?"

"Funny guy," Klaus retorted. "Do I look German?"

To be fair, most of the dwarves he'd met did, but Daniel kept that to himself. "At least you won your war."

"Like I said, different times. Men were men. None of this no sock wearing, man-bun nonsense." He paused. "I'm sure you have good stories from your war."

"Wars," Daniel corrected. "I fought in both. I do, but they aren't as intense as what you went through against the Nazis."

"I don't think I ever saw a real Nazi. Them German farm boys gave us enough grief, though I wouldn't have minded putting a few holes in some of the SS asshats." The dwarf shifted his weight to the opposite elbow, a pensive look consuming him. "Ah well, it's all in the past, ain't it?"

Daniel reflected on his first deployment. Over twenty-five nations sent soldiers to Afghanistan: Germany, Italy, and Japan among them. He imagined his grandfather turning in his grave to see how enemies became allies in the span of decades.

"How did you get roped into this gig?" Daniel asked.

"I missed the fight, and this sounded like a good idea. Blackmere approached me and I said yes."

"Does it bother you, hunting your own kind?"

Klaus bit back a laugh. "Not sure if you noticed but most of my kind are assholes. I look at it as doing the world a favor."

That was one way to put it. His one interaction had been with the notorious Schneider brothers. They were the most difficult people he'd ever worked with and, by the time it was over, Daniel never wanted to see another dwarf. He wondered if Klaus knew how close he was to fitting that bill.

He decided to shift the conversation, knowing that while there might be judgment from the team, chances of running into any of them after this were slim. "Blackmere offered me a job."

"On the teams?"

"I'm not sure. He said I'd make a great field agent since I've already dealt with the clans."

"I suppose it helps most of us know who you are," the dwarf said.

Daniel groaned. "I need to pick another genre to write in."

Klaus laughed. "Like that matters. You're famous and hated. Hell of a combination."

"I'm never going to live it down so I might as well embrace it."

"Yeah. The only way to handle situations is by tackling them head-on. You should know that, soldier. Can't hide behind the curtain and expect it to go away." Klaus scanned the perimeter again before asking, "What did you tell him?"

"I didn't."

Klaus fell silent and Daniel went back to his thoughts. Sometimes all one needed was a sounding board to figure things out. Joining DESA was sure to keep him busy, though it might tear a hole in the fabric of his marriage. Daniel admitted to not being the best husband, despite the mug in the cupboard stating otherwise, and the last thing he needed was to add unnecessary strain to their relationship.

Still, the idea of becoming part of a clandestine organization falling outside of the normal government parameters intrigued him. How could it not? He'd grown up on ridiculous spy movies and fantasy novels. Daniel missed his time in uniform. Missed being part of something bigger than himself. There was no comparison between the camaraderie among soldiers and the callous distance civilians treated each other with. That alienation, perhaps some of it self-imposed, left him feeling ostracized for many years before he realized he was the one who didn't quite fit in with the rest of the world.

Veterans were an interesting breed. He'd lost count of how many people gave him the 'I thought about joining the army' talk when he introduced himself. Daniel took it personal, as if being pandered to when in truth it was the feeling of being unable to relate being expressed. Truth be told, he didn't care if anyone served or not. It wasn't for everyone and, given roughly two percent of the population donned a military uniform, he was most likely the one who didn't fit in—that cross he bore with pride.

Joining DESA offered the opportunity to be part of something again. Give him a reason to leave the house and, he admitted, find new material for future books. He couldn't deny the desire to crank out a hard hitting expose on the clans to throw in their faces grew stronger the more he interacted with them. Just for a moment, Daniel allowed himself to dream of a day where he controlled his fate. Was he really willing to cast his fate with this crowd, after promising Sara a long life in peace?

Head lights cutting off as they crept up the road disrupted his train of thought and he shifted right to see who the intrude was. The audible click of Klaus taking the safety off was like music to his ears.

THIRTY

They sat in their room. Neither spoke. They didn't need to. Moose and Willard had been together long enough to pick up on each other's moods and know what the other thought. That unspoken understanding proved the envy of many of their friends. It became a tribute to their love and a source of unshakeable strength.

Golden hair cascading over her shoulders, Moose resisted the urge to close her eyes. She anticipated Willard speaking his mind in the hopes of learning more about their unexpected guests. He'd already opened and closed his mouth several times, heightening her nerves with each false promise.

"Oh, will you just get to it," she said, unable to take it any longer.

The hint of a smile haunted his face. "I don't know what to say. The lady who came to the door didn't say she was law, but who else would have another person handcuffed in the car like that?"

"She might be a kidnapper. Or a bounty hunter."

That had crossed his mind, though the likelihood of it seemed small. Their quiet part of the world seldom sparked intrigue or controversy. The last time anything of great import occurred had been a few miles down the road when the Feds raided what became known as the Apalachin Meeting back in the 1950s. Folks in these parts enjoyed a quiet life away from the spotlight. They were hard working famers for the most part. Up before dawn and crawling into bed long after the sun went down. It took little imagination for either Moose or Willard to see the town abuzz when word got out of these late-night visitors.

And word always got out.

"Oh come on now, Moose. A kidnapper? Can you imagine? The police wouldn't know what to do," Willard chided.

She shrugged. "It's not the craziest thing we've seen. Remember when they found those bodies stuffed in the storm drain at the bottom of Peck Hill?"

"What has that got to do with this? It was what, two decades ago?" he asked.

"Doesn't have to have anything to do with it. I'm just pointing out how we never know what might happen or when."

Moose had a point. The unknown had become a major part of their lives since buying the inn. Whispers and rumors circulated the local communities and neither did much to stop it. After all, who didn't enjoy a bit of intrigue to take the chill off the cold winter nights?

"Still, I don't think she's kidnapping anyone. I will say this, there is no love lost between those two," Willard said. "Did you catch the look of hatred in the other one's eyes? There's a lady who could kill."

Moose grunted. "There're too many unknowns with this, Willard. I'll sleep better when they are gone. We don't need trouble, not after all that has happened lately."

He laid a reassuring hand on her shoulder and squeezed. "I know, Moose. I know. We'll see what happens."

***

Unable to sleep, Viviana took a quick shower. The hot water stole her chill and infused a rush of much needed energy. She placed her hands on the tile and let the water strike the back of her head with unabated enthusiasm. Ever thankful for the little things in life, she tried forgetting about the nightmare situation with Gwen.

She'd just turned the water off when that familiar sensation of being watched returned. A haunting feeling of eyes boring into her from behind. Ever hidden. Ever gazing. Her stomach fluttered. Viviana reached for the towel and wiped off her face. Steam clouding the mirror, she cast sidelong glances through the small bathroom.

Nothing. She saw nothing.

Frowning, she dried off and slid back into her dirty clothes. The idea disgusted her, but she'd never planned on getting dirty. Indeed, she hadn't planned on any of this night's events. That inadequacy alone proved disturbing to a degree. She was better than that. The queen expected her to be better.

A slight breeze slipped under the door causing her to whip her ahead around. "I know you're here. Who are you?" she seethed between clenched teeth.

Viviana thought she heard the faintest whisper of laughter mocking her. She wiped a hand over the mirror and saw a flicker of movement.

Spinning, the elf found no one. "I'm losing my mind."

Viviana wrapped a fresh towel around her hair and returned to the bedroom. She contemplated telling Gwen her experiences but thought better of it. The less they spoke the better, for both of their sakes. To her surprise, Gwen sat upright, eyes wide. She searched about the room, seeking the cause of the tremble in her flesh.

"You saw it as well," she surmised.

"I don't know what I saw, but we are not alone in here," the princess admitted.

Not good. We don't have time for this. Where is that blasted Xander? The one time I need him and he's nowhere to be found. "What did you see?"

Gwen frowned, trying to put into words what her mind refused to reconcile. Worry creased her face. "I ...

I'm not sure. It might have been a person. Just the hint of a child perhaps. It felt …"

"Unnatural," Viviana finished. "I felt the same just now in the shower."

Gwen nodded. "Like you're being watched."

"Do you suppose this place is haunted?" Viviana asked. The word sounded foolish as it slipped off her tongue. She never believed in ghosts or specters. Those reported incidents were almost always dispelled with common sense or modest investigation. Reasonable explanations solved many mysteries.

"We aren't the only mysteries in this world, Viviana. Remember the fae?"

The word produced ill feelings. Reviled and feared, the fae stood for everything elfkind did not. They were violent, often ruling through fear. Predecessors to the elves, the fae were brutal tyrants who became obsessed with eternity. They never imagined the downtrodden elves and dwarves might one day seek to cast off their shackles and demand freedom.

The war was swift and brutal. Thousands died on both sides, but the elves outlasted their oppressors. What few fae remained fled to the dark corners of the world and hid lest they too became targets of vengeful persecution. Viviana recalled the last few days with trepidation, for though her kind won, victory remained elusive. The threat of the fae returning remained all these thousands of years later.

"I doubt they have come from hiding after all these years to haunt us, Viviana," Gwen replied without conviction. Her eyes retained their wild look.

"We have no weapons to fight them. I don't like this."

What game did the queen play to send her and the princess here? Viviana wondered if she'd been betrayed.

Deceptions ran rampant among the upper tiers, making the doubt legitimate. Whether the queen orchestrated this night, or it fell to mere chance, the elf needed to focus on the matters at hand. Clear the building and then worry about her future.

Gwen made a show of pulling against her restraints. "I can't fight much of anything so long as I'm tied up like this."

Torn between the anticipation of Gwen's escape and the need for an ally, Viviana raced through possible scenarios. Depending on what haunted the inn she stood a chance at being defeated, or the slightest margin of victory might sway in her favor. The chance for failure remained far too elevated for her liking, yet Gwen would not sit still for long.

"If I cut your bonds will you remain here?" she asked.

"Xander is coming. Where else would I go?"

Fair enough. Viviana drew the slender blade from her boot and set it to the plastic zip tie. "Don't make me regret this."

***

The john boat drifted down the river unseen by all but the owls. The pale glow of the moon turned the serenity of the cold water to a sheen of wavering glass. Two men dressed in black crewed the ends. In the center sat bags of weapons and ammunition, first aid kits and random supplies. Neither man seemed concerned with that just now. Chills permeated their clothes, stretching deep into their bones. The one astern shivered, unable to keep the cold out. The man in the bow did not move. His eyes were focused down river and on the prize awaiting. Just a short distance to go and would at last find closure to an ordeal that had gone on far too long.

***

The thunder of engines droned in her head. Otero watched the mile markers flash past with limited interest. Lasting frustrations from earlier made her ground her teeth, the sound producing a quality headache. They'd received word from the prime minister an hour ago with new target parameters and an accurate destination. The enemy, for she could view the princess as nothing less, was close by. No doubt with the intent of slipping away and disappearing before justice could be brought upon her. Otero's force was to intercept and eliminate all obstacles with extreme prejudice. If the princess died in the process so be it.

"Do we have their location yet?" she growled through the headset.

Static flooded the open channel. "Downloading now, Sergeant. Anticipate contact within the hour."

Frustrated, Otero said, "All elements, this is task force leader. Prepare to engage. You have been briefed on your deployment orders. Strike teams will assemble and assault within five minutes of infil. I want a clean insertion. No mistakes. The princess must not get away. Copy?"

One by one the squad leaders responded until Otero was left with nothing but the night and the limited drone of headlights struggling to push the darkness back. A futile effort she hoped was not replicated when they arrived on scene.

"I'm coming for you princess. There's no escape this time. Not tonight," Otero whispered. "Tonight, you're mine."

***

Blackmere yawned, fighting off the urge to sleep. His eyes were burning now. An unfortunate byproduct of too many hours on the screen. His mind swirled around the series of events playing out just a mile down the road.

His team, shorthanded and riddled with mistrust, were heading into a potential buzzsaw and there was nothing he could do about. A convergence of forces, all determined to be the victor in a hopeless situation, promised to swallow them whole and it was his call to send them in.

Far from the first time he'd directed troops into combat, Blackmere felt an unusual wariness. So much was at stake, much more than he dared explain to Daniel, lest the man change his mind and go home. Blackmere needed his reluctant recruit.

The queen. Prime minister. Xander. DESA. All factions were playing their separate angles with the potential of bringing the fragile balance between elf and man crashing down.

His thoughts were disturbed by the heavy thump of helicopter blades echoing through the mountains. Experience told him it was military: every helicopter had a distinct sound. Blackmere frowned. There shouldn't be anyone else in the area and, with no military bases nearby, that spoke of ill portents. Another faction he hadn't accounted for must be involved.

He looked at the scattering of DESA agents and security personal on his team. A paltry amount, but they were all he had. "Saddle up! We're not going to sit here all night."

Blackmere reached for a rifle.

THIRTY-ONE

They slipped into the hallway without a sound. No creaking boards or heavy footsteps. Yet they staggered under the unseen presence surrounding them. Viviana expected to find cobwebs drooping from the corners, dust on the faded wooden floors, not the immaculate bed and breakfast they were in. Had circumstances been different she might have taken a moment to appreciate the cleanliness.

"What are we looking for?" Gwen winced at her glare. The sound of the princess's voice carried down the corridor. "Sorry."

Viviana didn't bother replying. It was her experience that the owners of old buildings became versed in the nuances of their property. No doubt the couple downstairs were the same. She'd been adamant about getting a room on the ground floor, but Willard had insisted, without offering reasoning, otherwise. To compensate the lack of exit points, she took first room overlooking the main entrance.

"If I knew I might not be so nervous," she whispered eventually.

Nonplussed, the princess added, "I'd feel better if I had a weapon."

"Not happening."

"I gave you my word, Viviana."

The heavy click of a door opening froze them both midstride. Viviana clutched her knife tighter, slipping into a fighting stance. A soft yawn followed by six footsteps before another door opened and closed told her one of the owners was heading to the bathroom. No ghosts there.

"Seems like we solved the spooky mystery of the midnight bathroom goer," Gwen chided. "I wonder if they have hidden passages in the walls so they can spy on us through the false eyes of different paintings while we sleep."

Rolling her eyes, Viviana bit her tongue. There wasn't time for foolery. The only way to clear her conscience and focus on the impending reunion was by securing the inn and ensuring there was no supernatural threat.

Viviana got moving. She reached the end of the hallway, pausing at the top of the stairwell. Most of the inn was pitch black, save for a few small lights with dim, flickering bulbs. She glanced down and froze. There, at the bottom of the stairs, was a young boy smiling up at her. He waved then melted into the darkness.

"What the fu—"

Gwen crowded her from behind. "What did you see?"

She pointed with the blade. "A small boy. He waved and … and disappeared."

"A ghost? I thought you didn't believe."

"What other explanation is there? Come on."

Gwen drew back. "I'm not going down there. This is your crusade, not mine. You want to spend the night chasing ghosts and demons, fine by me. Don't expect me to play along. I'll head back to the room."

Coward. You never had the fire to march into battle, did you? "Fine. Go back and stay there. Xander should be here soon and our association ends."

"I can't wait," the princess said, smiling. "Now go find your ghost so I can get some sleep."

***

Gwen slipped back down the hallway. Her hand curled around the handle of their room's door when she felt a strong grip on her shoulder jerk her back. Grunting, she spun and swung. Her fist slashed through empty space. Fueled by rage and indignity, the princess caught the top of Viviana's head going downstairs. The elf was too far away to have grabbed her. So who did?

"Princess."

The voice dug into her flesh. She curled her fists, tracing the lingering sound to the far corner swathed in total darkness. There, buried in the shadows, stood an immobile figure. Waist high and vaguely humanoid, she found herself staring back into ice-colored eyes.

"Princess. Come with us."

Dropping her right leg back, Gwen rocked her weight as she contemplated attacking. The figure robbed her of the decision and charged. Shadows swirled. The cackle of static energies electrified the area. Knowing she was outmatched, she reached again for the door and plunged inside. She slammed it shut and locked it in the same move before pressing her back against it.

Heavy pounding jarred her. Dust drifted down from the ceiling as the intensity picked up. She screwed her eyes shut. A crack in the wood. Heavy pounding. The door started bucking against the deadbolt. Gwen pressed back with all her weight.

"Princess! Open the door! You belong with us!"

"Go away," she whispered. A sliver of a tear crept through her pressed eyelids.

The pounding stopped.

"Tonight, Princess. Tonight we shall feast upon the agony of your soul. We come for you, Princess. An eternity of torment awaits."

It was then she picked up the rotor thump of an approaching helicopter.

***

Frustrated, Viviana began the slow climb down. Whatever the creature, she was certain it wasn't human, or alive, was demanded attention. Why else take the risk of showing itself to one of elfkind? Magic no longer graced the elves, its influences bled dry through a thousand generations. Once, she would have enlisted a witch to assist her hunt. Time and lack of resources reduced her options to the blade in her hand: A small thing incapable of severing the lone strand of energy connecting the dead to the world of the living. It was all she had.

A toilet flushing followed by the sink running gave her pause. She had no explanation for being in the middle of the staircase with an open blade should one of the owners confront her. Viviana pressed against the wall and blended with the shadows.

Willard stomped by, scratching the scruff of his beard mid-yawn, and returned to his room. In his wake stood the boy. Steeling herself to the improbable, she descended the final few steps only to watch the boy melt away a second time.

"I'm being lured," she muttered. "What secrets do you wish me to find?"

A draft in the house tickled the back of her neck as she stalked deeper down the hall. She caught flickering images of the boy, each time several paces back from where he'd been. The game stretched her patience but dealing with the fae ever proved problematic. Though Viviana convinced herself this was more supernatural than the elder race.

The boy stood in front of a door on the far side of what had likely been the living room. His smile remained fervent, a silent beckoning.

Viviana peered closer and was rewarded with a glimpse of dirt-streaked flesh, torn clothes, and threadbare shoes not worn in the past hundred years. What strange fate befell this child now threatened her. He waved a final time before dissolving into the door.

"Fine, kid. Let's see what you have to show me," she muttered.

Her strides gained strength as the fear bled dry. Viviana felt at peace now, alone in the cold darkness. Laying a hand on the knob, she opened the door and wasn't surprised to find a stairwell leading down.

"Of course it's the basement. Where else would the body be?"

She'd seen enough paranormal shows through the years to expect the impossible. Humans were mundane and terribly unimaginative with their demise stories. No one ever died in the kitchen. No bodies left to rot in the parlor. No. They preferred dank places investigators were sure to check first once warrants were issued. No matter how clean the perpetrator thought they cleaned the crime scene, they always left behind clues, followed similar patterns.

She expected to find a furnace below, filled with forgotten ashes and children's bones. Perhaps a hole in the wall revealing the desiccated remains of a human face. The truth of the matter often proved fragile and far from wild expectations.

Viviana skipped down into the dwelling darkness, her mind racing through limited possibilities of what she might find. The air turned humid, almost rank. A musky odor clung to the walls. At last came the cobwebs, friendly reminders that not all was wrong with the world. The dirt floor had undeniable moisture. Her boots left prints. Perhaps the final tribute to an inglorious demise. Moss-stained rock walls completed the small room.

Nothing surprised her. She'd been in far worse.

227

And yet the dozens of ghosts lining the far wall, the child in the center, stole her breath, leaving her stunned. Hands trembling, she almost dropped the knife.

"Welcome, elf maiden. We have been expecting you."

A slender man stepped forward; his face concealed beneath the wide brim of a black hat. His clothes suggested he had once been a man of God. The remains of a Bible in his right hand confirmed it. Wisps of stark white hair draped his shoulders.

Viviana focused on the worm crawling from a hole in his cheek. "Me? Impossible."

Holding out his hands, he said, "It was foretold. You would come to save us. To set us free from this eternal torment."

She reeled back, at a loss for words. Many things through the years, she had never been a savior. The ghosts crowded closer, leaving her claustrophobic. Instincts screamed to flee. Run back upstairs and hit the road. Yet even as these thoughts warred within her head, Viviana understood a deeper truth. One she had always been loath to admit. She knew, though could not bring herself to admit, she had always been a coward at heart.

The boy she'd first glimpsed upstairs stepped through the crowd, slipping between legs until he stood before her. The smile was gone, faded like the detritus of abandoned dreams only the dead understood. Tears streaked his soot covered face. He reached a hand toward her, and Viviana's stomach clutched.

"Please," he begged. "I don't want to be here."

Her heart nearly broke, so powerful the desire. The temptation to reach back arose. Few creatures deserved their fates. Whatever transgressions these humans once committed happened long ago. It was her experience judgment often outweighed the crime. None of that changed the horrors of the past, or the sense of dread clinging to her. The situation felt wrong. She forced her hands to her sides.

"You have the wrong person. I'm sorry," she whispered.

The preacher clutched his weatherworn bible with both hands, raising it high above his head for all to witness. "It has been foretold! You shall deliver our salvation, or you shall join us! Choose your destiny, elf."

Hands stretched forth, arms elongating to clutch at her. Warrior instincts settled and Viviana fought for her life. She swatted and pushed the dead away, their incorporeal forms dissipating under her ruthless assault only to form again further away from her.

Elf and ghost.

Power and desire.

The clash between reality and fiction raged throughout the basement.

Each victory proved fleeting but allowed Viviana the opportunity to collapse back on the staircase and her only shot at freedom.

A misplaced step on a loose rock tripped her. She fell backward, striking the dank ground. Her knife skittered away, leaving her unarmed. Not that it mattered. The dead could not be banished with mortal steel.

She braced for the end.

The ghosts halted in a half-circle several paces away. The child and the preacher stepped closer. One bore the look of helpless resignation. The other one of the false promise of hope.

"I offer a final time," the preacher said. "Lead us to salvation. We are the damned and cannot escape this mortal realm alone. Fulfill your destiny and save us."

Viviana squeezed her eyes shut and shook her head. Locks of dirty hair swayed across her cheeks. "No.

You have the wrong woman. I … I don't have the power you need."

Kneeling before her, the preacher chuckled. "That is where you are wrong, elf. You are the only one who does."

THIRTY-TWO

The convoy roared past the racetrack and casino and into the front yard of the Fainting Goat Island Inn. Dust kicked up in great clouds, deepening as a hundred sets of combat boots stomped about. The jingle of weapons and gear clashing sang a proud song replicated through the ages. Elves set about establishing fighting positions across the frontline of the property. Heavy weapons placed on the vehicle rooftops through oversized sunroofs swept along both avenues of approach.

Sergeant Otero set foot on the property and felt a tremor rise from the earth to nestle deep within her marrow. What strange power lurked beyond sight quested for her blood. Unsure if the others felt similar, the elf warrior adjusted her rifle sling and swept her gaze over her deploying task force. They were in the correct position, though she had yet to establish if the princess was indeed within. Her gaze was drawn to the aged building. There was a haunting quality to the structure, one transcending space and time.

Shadows moved in some of the building's windows. Otero shivered. Such locations were spread across the globe, interconnected through invisible powerlines demarcating realms of impossibility. Never one for believing the old stories of ghosts and demons, Otero chose to place her faith in a live weapon and proven targets. Yet she could not deny the raw energy pulsing through the building. Beckoning.

Growling, she keyed the intercom. "All squads establish an outer perimeter cordon. I want heavy weapon emplacements with clear lines of fire up and down this road. No one gets in or out. Assume any approaching vehicle is hostile. Breaching teams assemble on me. I want this building cleared and targets secured in ten."

Muted and clipped acknowledgments came in from the various squads. This was the largest force she'd commanded in the field in over a hundred years. The risk of failure rose the longer the mission went. Her nerves already on edge from mounting pressure and the unexpected energy of this place, Otero expected nothing to go right.

The drone of muted rotor wash forcing cool air down the back of her uniform refocused her attention on the mission. Pushing thoughts of the paranormal aside, she readied for the most important task of her life. Once the dust settled, she would become one of the most lauded heroes of elfkind. In a revisionist sort of history of course.

Otero gave the aged building a daring glare and spat. Tonight belonged to her.

"Team one move into position. Everyone else stack on me," she ordered. "The princess lives. Kill all others if they put up a fight. Let's get this over with."

Commandos raced through the lawn and up the short flight of stairs leading to the front door. The lead elf looked for her signal before drawing the handheld ram back. Light bathed the front porch and the door opened revealing a bewildered husband and wife.

***

"Shit. I think we're compromised," Daniel muttered.

Klaus ground his teeth. A disturbing habit developed during downtime in the war and on he hadn't been able to shake in the years since. One eye closed, he scanned the scene through his rifle scope. They'd only been in position for a few minutes before the vehicle convoy rolled in. He recognized the commandos and felt his nerves rise. There could be but one reason for the prime minister to deploy his personal forces. "We're not walking away from this one."

Daniel watched as a handful of elves hurried to the porch then glanced at him. "What makes you say that? Who are these guys?"

"Prime minister's death troop. They don't leave witnesses and do the dirty work that needs doing," the dwarf replied. "Nasty bastards all around."

An eyebrow arched. "Nastier that you?"

"You have no idea."

***

Fighting the urge to scream obscenities to the skies, Daniel punched the ground. The unexpected arrival of at least a company of commandos changed the mission dynamic. There was no plausible way for his handful to sneak in, grab Xander, and end the threat tonight. He considered radioing Blackmere, but the circling helicopter stole his attention.

"I'm at a loss, Klaus. What do you think we should do?" he asked. With no answer presenting itself, he felt indecisive and frustrated.

"Cut and run is the prudent option."

Daniel shook his head. "I've never known a dwarf to suggest retreat."

"You've never met one who knew what's good I guess. And don't say those damned Schneider brothers. Backyard bullies, that's what they are. Neither one had any sense beaten into them by their mother."

"We can't move, not like this. A few more minutes and they'll have this entire road locked down. Unless we crawl back, using the ditch for cover."

"It's a fair bet they have thermal tech," Klaus said. "Probably monitoring radio traffic too. We're screwed, Daniel."

Unable to move forward, unable to move back, the unlikely duo pressed deeper into the cold earth and struggled to come up with a viable solution.

"At least one thing feels right," Daniel said.

"What's that?"

He flashed a quick smile. "Nothing has gone right from the beginning. Why would this be any different?"

"Shit."

***

"What's the meaning of this? Who are you people?" Willard demanded.

Crowding over his shoulder, Moose attempted to get a better look.

"Apprehend them but do not kill," a woman ordered before turning and addressing them. "Do as we say, and no harm will come to you. We will be gone before the dawn, and you can forget all about this night."

Assault rifles were pointed at his face and chest, Willard swallowed. "Fine by me."

"Good man. Now, we have reason to believe there is a fugitive in your establishment. My teams are going to search your inn."

"What is she saying, Willard?" Moose hissed in his ear.

"Quiet, woman or you'll get us both killed," he whispered back and stepped aside.

Standing in front of his wife to protect her, Willard watched helpless as a squad stormed into his inn. The green glare from their laser targeting scopes pinpricked the walls. His heart raced as it remembered days long past when he wore a uniform. In another time and place he might have acted, but age and common sense conspired against him. Past his prime, Willard figured he had one good run left in him. This wasn't it.

The angry woman standing before him confirmed it. When the last commando entered she faced the innkeepers. "You will be escorted back to your quarters and held under guard until we leave. For your sakes, do not make this more difficult than it needs to be. I am under strict orders but have no qualms about killing humans." She gestured to the trio of guards. "Take them away."

Once they were safely secured in their room, Moose leaned her head on Willard's shoulder. "Willard?"

He hummed. "What do you suppose she meant by humans?" he asked hearing the door's lock click into place from the outside.

She pressed tighter against him. "I don't care. You never should have let those two women in here. We'll be lucky if we live."

Willard patted the back of her hand. "It'll be all right. You just wait and see. We'll be fine."

He could tell she didn't believe him but knew better than to bring it up. Right now they needed each other more than ever before. She started to relax against him an instant before gunshots rang out from the second floor.

***

"Move!"

The command echoed up the stairs. Otero pushed aside the man in front of her and charged ahead. Adrenalin surging, she clicked her rifle off safe and took a kneeling position beside the lead commando. Smoke issued from a pair of rifles. Splinters and fragments of wall decorated the floor.

"What did you see? Is it her?" she demanded.

The lead elf shook her head. "I don't know, Sergeant. There was movement at the end of the hall. It appeared to charge but disappeared when we fired."

Otero squinted, desperate to find any trace of a dead elf. She found nothing. There should have been residue. There was always residue before the winds conspired to erase the fallen from all but memory. A thrum of invisible energy pulsed up from the ground. Her teeth chattered; every muscle electrified as dust knocked from the ceiling.

An elf to her right suddenly pitched sideways and lay racked in convulsions. She smelled singed hair. The faintest hint of a bowel movement. Urgency filling her, Otero steadied herself and hurried ahead lest the house destroy them all.

"Which door did it enter?" she asked.

Her breath was fervent, pitched.

An elf gestured but drew back.

Drawing upon her courage, Otero sped across the hall and smashed into the aged wooden door. Shattering upon impact, the door swung open, and Otero ducked into a combat roll before coming up on one knee. She heard the scream before it registered. A figure darted from the side and crashed into her. They went down in a heap of flailing limbs, though her attacker got the better of her with repeated body blows that might have incapacitated her had she not been wearing armor.

An elbow smashed into the side of her head, driving the helmet into the floorboards and cracking her visor. Otero threw a blocking arm up to halt the next attack and spun right, away from her attacker. Using the assailants force against them, Otero slammed them against the nearest wall and crawled to her feet. She ripped her helmet off and got a good glimpse of her target for the first time.

Princess Gwen.

"I'm supposed to take you alive," she threatened. "I don't mind if it goes the other way."

Fists clenched; the princess appeared much smaller than she was. Otero took in the bruises she had along with the clear weight of fatigue. The princess looked worse for the wear, marking her an easy target.

"Basil sent his attack dog, I see. Did the worm not come himself?" she asked.

Otero shrugged. "Come now. You are better than petty taunts. Surrender and let me do my job. No one needs to get hurt. Especially that lovely couple who run this dump."

Gwen scoffed.

Otero moved closer. "Where's Xander? He's the real prize, not some washed up remnant of a fading royal lineage. Your family's time running the clans to the ground is at an end, Gwen. A new age is dawning. One that has no need for the likes of you, or your lover boy. Tell me where he is."

"Not if you had a gun to my head." Gwen's defiance asserted itself in her stance. No longer meek and weary, she stood tall, proud. "Do you worst. My mother will erase your name from history."

Now Otero scoffed, brushing off the threat she'd lived with since signing on with the prime minister. "Is that the price for victory? My demise? That is a price I am willing to pay. Are you?"

"Try me and find out," Gwen retaliated.

Otero straightened and began removing her armor. She clicked the safety on her rifle and set it down under Gwen's watchful gaze. Making a show of rolling her neck and shoulders, Otero cracked her knuckles before settling into a fighting stance; Gwen imitated her.

"I am going to enjoy this more than you know."

The princess blew out a deep breath. "So you think."

They charged each other; fists raised high.

THIRTY-THREE

The pair of roving guards finished their turn and headed back toward the front of the house. Enough moonlight bathed the ground night vision was unneeded. Like most deployed in similar situations, the guards were complacent with supposed superiority. Weapons lowered, they moved without worry, believing in their overwhelming firepower and tactical advantages. After all, what fool dared risk crossing a river in direct light?

Waves sloshed against the bow as the john boat pulled to shore. Without waiting, Xander leapt out. His shoes crunched on the combination of gravel and freshwater muscle shells. Crouching, he drew one of the three pistols strapped to him, ensured the magazine was full, and clicked the safety off. There would only be one chance at this.

He took in Dale's paling color and wide eyes. The logical thought process suggested he needed the human's help. One additional gun provided firepower and distraction. Xander briefly considered dragging him along, if for no other reason than to draw fire away from him while searching for Gwen. Little more than a necessary inconvenience, Dale proved his worth in navigating them into the correct position. Leaving the man behind might just save his life tonight.

Xander fixed Dale with a menacing glare. "Stay here until I call."

Leaving Dale to his stuttering, he bolted up the slow bank and took cover behind a stand of wilted brush. His senses were heightened. Awakened during the botched raid earlier in the night, he used what adrenalin remained to fuel his rage, knowing he would need all of it to survive what he assumed was a full company of Basil's elite private army. Their uniforms stood out in their anonymity, marking them as the most dangerous among elfkind. Fortunately for Xander, they were untested in battle.

A loud snap twisted him around, pistol level. Xander and the elf soldier were meters apart, both caught unaware. Shock registering in his eyes, the guard raised his rifle. Xander was faster. He fired twice, aiming for the joint between armor and flesh. Both rounds struck true. The soldier pitched back and burst into ash before hitting the ground.

With no other targets in sight, Xander sprinted to the fallen gear and secured the assault rifle.

Running footsteps announced approaching soldiers, perhaps a squad. Xander retreated to the shadows of a stand of trees and huddled down to reduce his profile. Double checking the rifle, he sighted in on the gear and waited. Moments later a half dozen soldiers swept into his line of fire—Xander opened fire. Two dissolved and a third dropped before the others regained their composure and returned fire. Branches and bark rained down on him, forcing him to duck lower. A ricochet from a rock slashed his upper arm. Blood welled. Gritting his teeth, Xander resumed firing.

Another two soldiers died before those remaining retreated to cover. The whump of the helicopter neared. Fearing the potential of an aerial assault, Xander crawled back and rolled to his right. The house loomed ahead and within waited his love. All he had to do was make it there alive. No easy task.

***

Dale stared at Xander's back as the elf hurried away, leaving him alone, again. Already plagued with longstanding abandonment issues, Dale hated being relegated to the sideline, even in a hostile situation like this promised to be. He'd spent his life being underestimated and underutilized. Not that he had much to offer. Dale was no genius, nor was he a hero. A simple man trying to make a living, he looked out for the one person with his best interests in mind: himself. No one and nothing else mattered.

Dale pulled the phone from his jacket and made the call.

***

Viviana ducked from the preacher's grasp but not before the cold penetrated her flesh, questing deep for the core of her soul. The elf shuddered, eyes rolling back in her head.

Power. The dead held so much power!

She felt him attempting to gain control. To show her the extent of their nightmares. Mind numbing, Viviana fell to her knees and lowered her head. Visions flashed, far too fast to comprehend. She felt pain, misery. Each time she gasped produced an echo of the suffering one of them felt, yet there was something more. An entity ever out of reach. There, but ill defined.

Mouth agape and drool running down her chin, she convulsed as divergent powers collided. The aggression played out within her, threatening to subsume all she was and reduce her to little more than a hollow shell.

Elves were far from defenseless, however.

Viviana fought.

Her inner fire awakened, forcing back those in contempt. The war abated, but not before a final lance of pain ran down her spine.

Collapsing in a heap of ragged flesh, steam pulsed off her. Through narrowed eyes, she watched the ghosts drawing back, all in mute shock. The preacher flickered, his pale green glow dimming.

"Wha—" She vomited, expelling the darkness from her soul in a cleansing manner. Wiping her mouth with the back of her sleeve, Viviana pushed herself up to her feet. Muscles betrayed her, threatening to send her back to the ground. Sheer determination kept her afoot.

"What was that?" At the lack of response, her anger grew. Fixing her gaze on the preacher, she snapped, "Damn it, answer me. What did you do to me? What is this? What was that figure you battled?"

"Its name must not be spoken," the preacher bemoaned. "Ever have we been captive to the darkness, kept here instead of going to join our families. There is no rest. We are trapped. Victims of an eternal hunger for punishment. You must save us, for we have not the strength."

Stomach still rebelling, Viviana asked, "Is it a demon?"

"Such as you name it."

The confirmation chilled her. Possessions occurred throughout history, though she had never been a true believer. The supernatural aspect of it all felt childish. A fairy tale meant to keep ill-behaved children in line when naught else worked. Viviana couldn't deny the raw power occupying parts of her soul. Why did the dead think she held the power to destroy a demon? Her conflict of faith alone should have eliminated that possibility.

The boy stepped forward again, the same desperate look intense in his eyes. She wondered who he was, why any creature would strive to keep him in endless torment. The sternness of her heart softened, and she struggled to keep from crying. There was inherent sadness flowing from him into the tattered remnants of her soul.

Viviana sank back to her knees, beckoning the boy to stand before her. "I do not know what strength lies within me, but I will attempt to save you," she whispered.

Satisfied, the boy broke into a wide grin and jumped. Viviana's heart warmed, imbued with strength pouring into her from the others as they moved closer.

She rose and faced the preacher. "What must I do?"

He stretched forth his hand for her to take.

***

Pain blossomed up his ribs, but Xander kept fighting. He hammered the butt of his rifle into the downed soldier's face. Each blow resulted in a satisfying crunch bone and tissue. Crimson spattered the plastic stock. Fury filling him with strength, Xander didn't stop until the man gasped a final breath and collapsed in a pile of dust and ash. Unspent energy bulged in his arms as he drew back to strike again. He shouldn't have been caught like that—a rare mistake. Xander had been closing on the house when the soldier tackled him from the blind side. The ambush nearly finished him.

Reaching Gwen felt impossible. There was no way he could breach a cordon of almost a hundred soldiers and stay alive. Each minor engagement threatened to push beyond the edge. His ammunition was running low. He bled from a dozen cuts and scrapes. Bruised and battered, Xander knew if he sat down he might not get up. It was a valiant effort, but one doomed by foolish bravado. Perhaps against a lesser trained force he might have stood a chance, but these were Basil's elite. Surviving already difficult enough, Xander prayed their long years of inactivity worked in his favor. Otherwise…

The helicopter swinging around for another pass got him moving again. He wasn't out of the fight yet, despite the war between his mind and body. Xander snatched a few magazines from the gear at his feet and hobbled closer to the house. The snap-hiss of rounds zipping past his head hurried his step. With no exit to the boat and no entrance to the house, he was trapped. It was but a matter of time before the soldiers surrounded him and pinned him down.

Pressing his back against the far side of an aged pine, Xander gathered his composure and thought. He wondered if the soldiers knew who their target was. If not, there was the sliver of a chance he might escape alive. Not much of one, granted, but he reckoned any chance was better than not.

The helicopter passed on.

Xander surmised he wasn't the target, merely an unfortunate coincidence they hadn't counted on. This alone confirmed Gwen was within and, knowing Basil lacked the strength to execute her on the spot, Xander found his chance. He began stripping away the weapons accrued during the firefight. Once unarmed, the champion raised his hands above his head and stepped into the open.

"I'm unarmed!" he shouted. "I don't wish to fight any longer."

Excited shouts broke out from around the house. Xander's heart sank, for he had just admitted defeat for the first time in recent memory. The desire to fight, to keep going until his last was spent threatened to undo his plan, but he remained strong to his purpose. All that mattered was getting inside and next to Gwen. The rest would figure itself out, or it wouldn't. He'd worry about that when he got there.

Soldiers rushed in from three sides, surrounding him in short order. Xander felt the vitriol pulsing off each one, for all had lost friends and valued comrades. He smirked, as it was the cost of war.

"Show me your hands!"

He complied. The helicopter hovered overhead, bright search light beaming down on him. A pair of elves hurried behind him, kicking away pistols and rifles. Xander turned his head and was rewarded by pain exploding from the back of it as the rifle butt cracked his skull.

***

Shoving the john boat away, Dale started rowing. Fighting the current proved difficult for one man but his heart sang from being released from his duty. Basil was pleased and sent him home. His nightmare ended, Dale rowed as hard as he could to get back upriver and to the waiting car.

He never felt the bullet enter the back of his head.

THIRTY-FOUR

Daniel knew he'd never be able to explain what happened next no matter how long or many times he was given. Trapped in position, he and Klaus waited for the opportunity to break loose. Nothing in their mission parameters detailed tangling with a heavily armed force with tactical superiority. Recognizing a losing proposition, Daniel decided an organized retreat best served their purposes. From there the team could regroup and figure how best to capture Xander.

Like all good plans, his fell apart in the span of mere heartbeats. The helicopter, which had been hovering like a dark menace over the inn, sped off and banked back toward them at sped. All but those assigned to defensive weapon emplacements left their positions and hurried to the rear of the building, leaving the slimmest margins to fall back. Daniel couldn't believe his luck. They'd been given a chance.

"We need to move," he told Klaus.

Gunfire erupted in the night. At first a trickle, then escalating into a full-blown firefight. Muzzle flashes dotted the night, accompanied by screams of pain and the grunts of those dying. Confused, Daniel froze. He watched the helicopter return and blast a spotlight down on an area between the inn and river.

"Looks like Xander's here after all," Klaus said.

"What makes you say that?" Daniel asked.

The dwarf pointed. "Who else is going to spark a gun fight in the middle of the night? Changes things, don't it?"

"Maybe." Daniel tried to think how though. "It makes getting our hands on Xander more difficult."

245

"Let the prime minister's people take him in," Klaus suggested. "It's not like we're getting paid for this."

Daniel paused. He hadn't considered until now the negative financial compensation. In fact, Blackmere never so much as hinted at recompense. Sneaky bastard. Add it to the list of topics he needed to bring up once the dust settled. Knowing the others as he did, Blackmere must hold something over each to get them to cooperate. No one did anything for free.

"We can figure it out once we regroup at the truck," he said.

The radio on his web belt squawked to life.

"Daniel, this is Murphy. You need to look up."

He did … His mouth fell open. Several dark shapes dropped from the sky in a cluster of parachutes. Then he spied the plume of exhaust. Daniel tracked the missile and watched in muted disbelief as the helicopter erupted in a ball of flame and twisted metal. The wreckage plunged into the river beneath a cloud of black smoke.

"Son of a bitch," he muttered. His mind raced back to a similar scene during that fateful night in North Carolina. That time he, and the others, nearly died as a helicopter crashed into the church they were taking cover in. Watching the event proved doubly traumatic, at least until the figures in the sky hit the ground and began their assault.

Still feet off the ground, the airborne attackers released their harnesses and dropped the final few feet. They attacked with unprecedented fury, quickly overwhelming and destroying the heavy weapon emplacements. Puffs of black ash and dust filled the night. Daniel watched three figures strike the side of one of the trucks, throwing their weight into it, and pitching it over. The elf in the sunroof climbed free and was stabbed in the back by a glowing yellow sword.

Ten figures, all dropped from the sky, secured the immediate area. Each held a similar sword, and all were armed to the teeth. Daniel thought the prime minister's soldiers were impressive. This went beyond any unit he ever witnessed in the field. Their professionalism and tenacity showed in each movement. Soon, naught but smoldering remains, and ruined vehicles were left in front of the inn.

Klaus tensed, his index finger tapping incessantly on his rifle. "This ain't good, Daniel. Those are the Old Guard."

"What does that mean? Who are the Old Guard?" he hissed in awe.

"It means we're fucked."

***

Constantin Andros stood in the center of the battlefield surveying the damage. All enemy forces in the vicinity were terminated. The hum of his sword vibrated deep in his bones. A familiar sensation reminding him of his responsibility to the throne. Much more than soldiers, Constantin led the Old Guard with the fervent devotion of a fanatic. They were chosen from the royal families at birth and honed into the ultimate fighting machines. None in the clans withstood their power or denied their authority. They acted in the name of the crown, beholden to two.

Here, let loose from the leash, he rediscovered purpose.

The Old Guard struck with blinding precision, slaughtering all who stood opposed. Their mission was simple; destroy those responsible for the ambush and murders of their brothers and exact retribution. He approached his task with enthusiasm. Constantin struck down the elf scrambling free of the overturned vehicle, grunting as a lucky round struck his shoulder pauldron.

"Report," he snarled into the headset woven into his helmet.

"Commander, all clear. Remaining enemy forces have collapsed on the rear of the building. They appear unwilling to engage."

Face twisted with disappointment, Constantin replied, "Then we take the fight to them. Fall in on me."

They complied, swift and silent as shadows. Much larger than normal elves, the Old Guard were akin to living armored vehicles. They were all but unstoppable once unleashed and his orders this night were specific: kill all but the princess.

Constantin liked simple orders. They made his life easy, and easy was good.

***

Daniel set his rifle on the hood while resisting the urge to punch the cold metal. Tired, exhausted, frustrated from repeated setbacks and failures, and done with elfkind, he struggled with the growing desire to get in the truck and head for the nearest airport. A quick look at the others told him they felt the same.

"I fought in two wars, and I've never seen anything like that," he said after a long drink of water. "They jumped *out* of their parachutes! Who does that?"

"The Old Guard," Thraken replied.

"Ooh, I would like to see that. They'd be fun to be around." Jenny clapped.

They'd been together long enough that she failed to get a rise from any of them this time. Daniel toyed with the idea of sending her to solve their problems. Entertaining as the idea was, he needed a better plan lest they all fall victim to the indiscriminate slaughter begun down the road.

"Any chance we can still grab Xander?" Nevada Slim asked, his accent absent.

Daniel gestured to the gnome. "We can send Hugh to knock on the door and say hi."

"Me?" Thraken gulped.

Daniel held up a hand. "Relax, no one is going in there unless we have to." *Which we might need to do.*

"Xander must die," Slim insisted. "He killed my father."

"You want to head into that nightmare be my guest," Daniel countered. "I don't want to die tonight if I can help it."

The gunfire erupted again, heavier and more intense than before. Daniel caught the whump of several grenades exploding: Flashbacks from Afghanistan sprang to life. He remembered the cries of Specialist Forbes after he got hit by a sniper while clearing a village. Daniel had a moment of hesitation before sprinting across the open area to his fallen soldier. The second round, he was convinced, had been meant for him, but Forbes took it in the throat instead. He died in Daniel's arms.

"We need to get over there," he said, reversing all he'd argued for.

Klaus gave an approving look, having already switched his sniper rifle for his favored light machinegun. "Thought you didn't want to die?"

Daniel shrugged. "I figure it's not up to me. We got a job to do. Let's finish it."

"That's the spirit!" the dwarf roared. "Been too long since I was in a proper fight. You got dibs on the Old Guard."

"Or we just avoid them for as long as possible," Daniel countered. He looked at the others. "Are we ready for this?"

No one answered.

Good enough.

***

Xander awoke on the floor. His hands flex cuffed behind his back and jets of pain pulsing through his skull. A sharp kick to his side brought him out of the fog. Captured, he had been taken inside and presented to the enemy forces commander. It was where he wanted to be, though perhaps under better circumstances. He received a second blow after testing his bonds.

"Leave him alone!"

The voice penetrated his conscious, bringing him back to reality and his reason for being in New York. Such a simple sound inspiring both heart and mind. Xander blinked through the tears.

"He lives only because I haven't decided how best to hurt you yet, Princess."

Xander frowned. He knew that voice too but couldn't put a face to it. One of the drawbacks of living such a long time, he often forgot trivial matters.

"Hurt him one more time."

"And you'll what? Defend your fallen hero?" A snort. "Look at him. Beaten to the point of breaking. His hopes of rescuing you brought to a disappointing demise. Is this the romantic interlude you dreamed of locked away in your cells?"

Boots stopped in front of Xander's face, and his assailant crouched down to grab his chin and tilt his head back.

"You don't remember me, do you, Champion of Light?"

He spat a mouthful of blood and saliva. "Should I?"

Fingernails dug into his cheeks. "We were once contemporaries. I sought to replace you, but you sabotaged my prospects, all but ruining my family in the process. I have awaited this moment for a very long time. This is your final night on earth, Xander. How fitting you die in front of the one you cannot save."

He closed his eyes and a host of memories flooded back. The last time any from the clans challenged his position was almost two hundred years ago. He defeated the young upstart, retaining his title and reinforcing the love shared between himself and the princess. It was that moment the thought of overthrowing the king and queen first arose. All thanks to a rogue woman seeking to make a name for herself.

"Otero," he muttered and opened his eyes.

Her eyes blazed. "You do remember after all. I have been looking forward to this, Xander. You have no idea."

He tried to laugh, stopping when it hurt too much. "There's always someone like you trying to be someone they're not. They always fail, you know. Returning to anonymity with shame and disgrace. I thought you were dead."

Her slap rang through the room.

He felt a tooth wiggle loose.

"Clearly not."

The whisk of a blade being drawn snagged his attention. Otero leaned close to whisper in his ear, "This is going to hurt."

The explosion shook the entire building down to the foundations. A secondary impact moments later sent a cascade of ages old detritus trickling from the ceilings. Elves were knocked off their feet. Then the fury of automatic rifle fire started.

Cursing, Otero rose to her feet. "Lock them with the humans. I'm going outside. No one gets in here. No one."

Xander watched her storm off as he was hauled to his feet and shoved along. That's when he locked eyes with Gwen for the first time since his incarceration. His heart warmed with determination.

THIRTY-FIVE

"What was that?" Moose all but screamed as the Inn rocked from the heavy impact.

Steadying himself, Willard pulled her close. "That was an explosion. Someone is attacking these clowns."

Her eyes went wide, their whites shining in the dim light. She mouthed the words explosion and attacking. Willard offered a thin smile, one of his hands moving to cradle the back of her head. Golden hair spilled between his weathered fingers. Another burst of machinegun fire lit up the night, making both jump.

Willard turned and glared at one of their captors who had slipped inside when the shooting started. "You going to see what's going on or are we that great of company?"

"Keep quiet," the man on the right shot back. His eyes flit back and forth between the prisoners and his partner.

Willard snorted, a forgotten defiance slipping back into place. "Or what? You'll kill us? Who are you people anyway?"

The clack of a weapon charging gave him pause. Face darkening, the second man took a step closer. "Humans. Always frigging humans! We should kill them now and get back out there. It sounds like they need our help."

"We got orders," the first replied.

"Miscommunication happens all the time. Besides, they're just humans."

"What's he talking about, Willard?" Moose whispered. "Why do they keep calling us humans?"

Mouth agape, he could only shake his head. They operated a quaint bed and breakfast while catering to the growing part of America interested in finding ghosts and ghouls in the dark places of the country. Featured on a few television shows, he never imagined what amounted to an all-out war erupting in the middle of the night.

Moose's teeth chattering, drew Willard's attention. He spied a golden light. It was mere inches from the gunmen and creeping closer. He took a step back, ensuring to raise his hands to appear nonthreatening. The last thing he needed was the nervous man to fire off a few rounds under the wrong impression. A heartbeat later the light touched the first gunman. Willard watched as the light, quick as lightning, flared once and funneled into the leg, disappearing entirely.

Convulsions wracking his body, the gunman dropped his weapon, using the wall for support. When he opened his eyes, golden light shined through. The second man moved away, turning his weapon on his companion.

"Stay behind me," Willard said to Moose over his shoulder.

The first gunman recovered his weapon, pointed it at his friend and fired.

***

Viviana stared at what could only be described a nightmare. Skeletons and partially decomposed remains stretched across an empty field built upon dead flowers and wilted brush. Scorched tree trunks stabbed the vermillion skies, the odd combination of black and brown on the bare trunks a reminder of the finality of all things. Carrion birds circled in dark clouds, dropping bits of flesh and bone in a macabre rain.

"What is this place?" she uttered.

From behind her, the preacher bowed his head. "Where all things go to die. It is a refuge of predators who continue devouring long after their victims have passed."

"Such places should not exist," she whispered.

"Agreed, yet that does not alter the fabric of reality. Each of us now rests in this brutal environ. The one who keeps us prisoner is within the clearing. He you must confront to save us."

Rethinking her decision, Viviana recoiled from the bone numbing chill pulsing off the scene. Unnatural, the elf had doubts about her abilities to stop, much less destroy, whatever supernatural power presiding.

"I can't defeat this." She gestured as a handful of crows swooped in to dine on a rotted body. Gore dripped from the arm as they squabbled over the juiciest bites without regard to the flopping appendage.

Her stomach roiled.

"You must. The future hinges upon your actions, elf-maiden. There is no one else."

She faced him. "What am I supposed to use to fight a … what is it, a demon?"

"It has many names."

"Right. I have nothing to use against this beast," she protested.

Dipping his head, the preacher said, "Hold out your hand."

Hesitant, Viviana did. Her heart thundered in her ears, the pounding of waves upon a broken shore. She felt the weight before her mind registered the shaft in her hand. Blurred at first, she watched the object materialize into a spear of golden light. An impossible weapon for improbable times.

"What, how?" she asked.

"There yet remain forces for good in this world, elf-maiden. Evil does not yet hold sway over all," the preacher replied. "Use this weapon on your quest."

Seven feet tall, the weapon weighed no more than a feather. Etched with ancient runes running the length, the spear radiated energy. Viviana felt it pulsing into her, imbuing her with strength she never imagined. The blade was a full foot, razor sharp and imposing. Doubt left her. With the spear in hand, she felt able to conquer the world.

Viviana gave the preacher a final, thoughtful look before stepping into the killing field. A roar emanated from the dead trees.

The challenge accepted.

The stench reached her first. An overpowering miasma of filth and decay filling her mouth with the acidic ting of bile. Pushing through the discomfort, Viviana focused on the beast ahead. Nestled in the center of the clearing, the creature burrowed among the throngs of corpses and skeletons. She doubted all these unfortunate souls met their end at the Inn, meaning the monster must have taken them from elsewhere and used this place as a nesting ground. The travesty of it disturbed her.

Tentacled appendages flailed in the false night. The crunch of jaws on bone echoed like thunder. She spied scales covering the monster's back. Not a monster, Viviana decided, but a demon. For what other creature in existence contain the combination of nightmares? Six stalks jutted from the top of its skull, each with a roving eye surveying its kingdom. A muscled arm whipped up from the ground to snatch another corpse, dragging it down into the pit.

Infuriated, Viviana planted the spear in the ground and bellowed, "DEMON!"

Vibrations rumbled far below her feet, threatening to rob her balance and cast her to the carnage. An angry whine responded. Four arms with human hands pulled the demon from the pit. A carpet of bones burrowed into its flesh and provided additional armor. She stared at the bank of eyes above an impossibly wide mouth boasting millions of razor-sharp teeth. Pieces of flesh wedged between many.

Her revulsion inspired action, for this beast deserved killing. Steeling herself for the onslaught she knew must come, Viviana charged.

Her assault caught it by surprise, for never had one been bold enough to attack. She covered the distance, fleet of foot, in heartbeats. The spear burned with power. Raw energy coursing through her veins as she became a living extension of the weapon.

Viviana leapt the final meters. The spear rose high overhead. A three prong tail whipped up from the pit to strike her in the torso and knock her off course. Hitting the ground with a thud, Viviana tucked the spear into her body and rolled through the impact. The elf maiden drew up to one knee, her right arm cast back for balance.

The demon roared.

Smell of death wafting from it, the demon doubled in size, filling the horizon. Smaller demons clung to the bones, leering and taunting her. A thousand visions promising a thousand dooms threatened her. Closing her eyes, Viviana burrowed her soul into the power of the spear, latching on to whatever fell energies created it.

It was a war capable of ripping her apart, erasing her from existence. Doubling her focus, Viviana accepted the eldritch strength and met the demon's fury with reckless abandon. They clashed in a flurry of steel, claws, and desiccated flesh. Each blow struck sawed away great chunks from the demon yet failed to reduce any of its aggressions.

Battered and bruised, they fought.

And fought.

And fought.

Viviana stood amidst a growing pile of hacked limbs and chunks of flesh. Her breathing was heavy, yet she felt none of the exhaustion that should have otherwise claimed her. Opposite the elf, the demon heaved under labored breaths. She suspected the end loomed, though for who remained to be seen. Reading herself for another round, Viviana glimpsed the unexpected. There, just beneath the jaw, was a soft patch of flesh pulsing with every heartbeat. It might prove the opportunity she needed.

Reinvigorated, Viviana attacked.

The demon roared as she charged. A tentacle lashed out, threatening to split her in two. But instead of running into the blow, Viviana ducked and slid under the appendage. Her strike was lightning quick, the tip of the spear plunging into the exposed flesh with every ounce of remaining strength in her weakened form. Unimaginable sounds ripped from the demon's throat as it became wracked with convulsions. Pustules and lesions burst, spilling viscous fluids into the ruined earth. Leaving the spear in place, Viviana crawled from beneath the demon as it drove itself down upon the spear, impaling the entirety of the weapon into its brain.

It struck the ground hard, producing seismic shocks rippling far and wide. When at last it no longer moved the demon began dissolving. Puddles spread before being absorbed into the ground. The sonic scream faded, and the first hint of sunlight broke through the oppression.

Viviana ran until she stood back beside the ghost of the preacher. "Is it done?"

He nodded. "It is. You have done the impossible."

"I guess that means you're free?"

"It does. You have saved us. We can now transition to whatever end we have earned," he replied. "Words cannot express my gratitude."

"It was my pleasure."

Supernatural strength fleeing her, Viviana suddenly slumped to her knees. "What happens now?"

"You will return to your body at the moment you left," he said. "I should warn you; the way forward will not be easy. Even now there is great conflict raging. Death may still await."

Shit, the princess! An onslaught of thoughts rushed her. Xander and whatever forces he was beholden to. The gods only knew what other factions had converged on the sleepy inn and threatened to undo all she'd striven for.

"Do you know who these forces are?" she asked.

He did and told her.

Viviana's eyes lit up, for once again the game had change. Instead of a demon in the netherworld she recognized a fallible opponent. One capable of dying like the rest of them. The spark of an idea struck, and she relayed a special request to the already fading ghost.

His return smile was almost sad as he said, "It will be done."

She closed her eyes.

THIRTY-SIX

Constantin Andros' sword ripped free of the already dissolving dark elf. He bellowed a challenge to those yet engaged. The foyer had become a charnel house of slaughter. Dark elves died by the dozen until a carpet of ashes blanketed the wooden floor. Death rode his shoulders, a willing spectator with vested interest. The Old Guard commander became one with his sword, an extension of violence honed through the aegis of time and experience. Though the prime minister's army ranked among the best of elfkind, they paled in comparison to the martial prowess of the Old Guard. He wasn't even breathing hard yet.

"That you, Constantin?"

He stiffened at the indignity as the woman's voice sang above the sounds of battle. "Who speaks to me?"

"Oh come on, you forgot me already?"

Squaring in the direction the voice taunted, Constantin leveled his sword. "Come forth and address me appropriately, not like a coward hiding in shadows."

"If I do that you'll kill me," she replied. "How about we make a deal?"

"I do not make deals," he growled.

"You will if you know what's good for you," she countered. "Let me and my people go, and we can forget this unfortunate incident ever happened."

"Not likely."

Silence settled over them. The fighting paused, both factions listening to the two elves deciding their fates. Uncomfortable by the shift, Constantin waited for a reply. He never expected the one he received.

A second voice spoke up, "Commander Andros, this is Princess Gwen. Do as she says. Please. She has myself and Xander prisoner. She's going to kill us otherwise."

"My orders are to retrieve you to your mother, Princess. They do not mention the future disposition of this force, whom I surmise belong to the prime minister, nor the fallen champion."

"What makes you believe I'm bluffing, Constantin? I don't need either of them alive. We both have orders but there's no reason this needs to continue. Let me go and you can have the brat."

He barked a laugh. "You'll give me the princess? Just like that?"

"Just like that," she confirmed.

"There's the problem, Otero." At her hiss, he chuckled. "Oh yes, I have guessed your identity. Who else but you would seek to elevate herself through a despicable moment such as this? Regardless, you know you cannot stop my team. Over half of your dark elves are dead. The others will soon follow until only you remain. You I will kill last."

He was rewarded by the bark of a pistol. Three rounds struck his armor without penetrating.

The battle renewed.

Elves continued dying. This night there could be no compromise.

Constantin smiled as he went back to work.

***

One hundred times. That's how often Daniel rethought his decision to accept Blackmere's proposition and head back to New York. One hundred times, perhaps all since arriving in the sleepy town of Nichols. It was a place where nothing exceptional happened. Where honest men and women struggled to make a living in an uncaring

261

world. Who could have suspected an event bound to determine the future of elfkind would play out right under their noses?

He groaned. "If I make it through this I swear my next book will be a comedy."

"Huh?" Nevada Slim asked.

Daniel cursed, forgetting he was on an open channel with the rest of the team. "Nothing. Stay sharp. We don't know what to expect."

Lapse of judgment notwithstanding, Daniel led the team on foot from the vehicle, where Slim waited to come to their rescue, to the Fainting Goat. The battle raged ahead. He imagined a brutal scene and prepared for the worst. Daniel was content with letting the opposing forces shoot their way out before Murphy reminded him if Xander died they would never know. Without leaving any bodies behind, the elves could come and go without anyone ever knowing they were here. He needed closure. The prospect of spending the rest of his days looking over his shoulder numbed him.

He sent Klaus back into an overwatch position, trusting the others had enough to see the job done. Nevada Slim had been adamant about joining them, but Daniel needed a getaway driver he trusted, not a dark elf bent on revenge. Instinct said leave Murphy behind. The compromised agent's integrity left much in question though and keeping him close ensured no further chicanery.

Him and his team crossed the road, converging on one of the overturned gun trucks. Daniel counted heads before poking his around the mangled frontend. Equipment and weapons scattered the ground between them and the Inn's porch—it was all that remained of the elves that had been here.

Muzzle flashes and crisp reports of small arms fire echoed from behind the building, carried on a stiff breeze blowing through. Daniel found it peculiar there were no exterior guards. Those who once formed the perimeter were either dead or pulled away to the firefight by the river. He suspected a trap and, despite being armed and prepared, was loath to tackle the ten brutes who jumped into the battle. Experience taught him zealots were the most dangerous in any fight. Why would elves be any different?

Slipping back behind cover, he told them, "Looks like we're going through the front door. I take point. Murphy bring up the rear. Thraken your job is to find Xander."

Jenny's hand shot up. "Ooh Daniel! What about me? What do I do?"

His mouth opened and closed, eyes pinched. "Jenny, you do what you do best."

"Goody!"

When she smiled ... well it was a sight he prayed to never witness again. Clearing his throat he asked, "Klaus, you still got my back?"

"You're not giving me much to do, Daniel."

He didn't have a problem with that. No action meant no problems. Unable to delay the inevitable further, Daniel rose, trained his rifle on the Inn, and stalked his way over the battlefield, trusting the others followed. He made it halfway before the door opened and a pair of elves ran out. Both burst apart before Daniel heard the shots.

Instincts kicked in. Daniel rushed the final few meters, running through the drifting ash and put his back to the relative protection of the wood siding to the right of the door. Murphy was the last to join him, eyes wide in shock.

Daniel held up a hand to halt everyone in place and listened. The Inn, for all the chaos raging around it, appeared quiet inside. He caught raised voices but little else. A supercharged energy pulsed up from the ground, slipping into his boots and through his body much as the eldritch energies of Craig-E-Claire had before Jenny performed her magic. He pressed an ear to the cold window to see if he could make out what was being said.

"Let me go and you can have the brat."

"You'll give me the princess? Just like that?"

"Just like that."

He turned to peek inside just as the room erupted in violence. The Old Guard charged into their foes with ruthless abandon. Daniel marveled at their dedication, surprised how none had yet fallen to a numerically superior foe. Furniture shattered. Glass broke. Guttural shouts rose above sporadic gunfire as the battle devolved to hand to hand. Doubting the efficacy of his plan, Daniel remained in place.

"I don't want to go into that," Thraken muttered, strings of now greasy hair sweeping across his face.

Daniel empathized but saw no other option: Finish the mission and go home. Alive. He shifted to get a better view and froze. Golden yellow light flowed up from the basement, swirling across the floor like a fine mist ankle high. Tiny fingers reached out from the haze, grasping at ankles and bootlaces. Daniel blinked, unsure what he saw. After the events from earlier in the night he found himself in a strange position where the impossible existed and reality devolved into a twisted mess.

He spied Xander on his knees at the top of a small staircase. The elf appeared beaten and bloodied. There was no easy route to him. The Old Guard thronged the main floor, now battling with a host of dark elves. A woman with a gun to Xander's head viewed the battle with clear disgust etched into her hard face. *Guess I'm not the only one with a grudge.*

"Thraken, think you can slip through this mess and get to him?" Daniel asked. "I think the princess is with Xander but can't tell from here."

A window shattered nearby, the broken body of an elf half hanging out from it.

Thraken swallowed and pointed at his chest. "Me? In there? Didn't I just say I didn't want to?"

Laying a comforting hand on the gnome's shoulder, Daniel replied, "It's not about what we want to do, but what needs to be done. You're the smallest one here and can slip detection. This is your time to shine, buddy."

Unconvinced, Thraken said, "What do I do when I get in there? I can't sneak both of them away. We'll all get killed."

"Leave that to me," Murphy interrupted.

Daniel's eyes narrowed. Until now the DESA agent proved all but useless on their mission. He wanted to think a change had come over the man after being exposed and knocked on his backside, but Daniel wouldn't put it past him to betray them all again at his earliest convenience. "What do you have in mind?"

Voice wavering, Murphy said, "Let me go in and use my authority. That should distract them enough for Thraken to slip in and do his thing."

Daniel shook his head. "Too risky. You'll be killed or captured."

"What other choice is there?"

A tugging on his trouser drew his attention to Jenny. "Got a better idea?"

She smiled and pointed at the mist. "Look! That's old power. Almost as old as me. Don't go inside yet."

He vowed to get to the bottom of who and what Jenny was before the end. Tracking her finger, Daniel watched as the mist coalesced, hardening around those it already marked. Faces twisted in agony. Muscles clenched. Bones cracked. The Old Guard, likely imbued with magic armor, drew back as one, collapsing on their squad leader. The dark elves cried out, terrified.

"Jenny what—"

Dumbstruck, he watched as hands and claws grasped the elves and started pulling them down into the aged wooden floors. Some fought back. Swords chopped down. Rifles spit bullets to no avail. A weeping laugh echoed deep within the walls of the Fainting Goat Inn.

When Jenny started clapping, he shivered.

Daniel noticed then the woman holding Xander captive jerking him to his feet and forcing him down the darkened hall and out of sight. Frowning, he punched the wooden siding. He needed to find a way up to the second floor, away from the nightmare mist. But how?

"Klaus, are you picking up anyone else outside?" he asked.

"Not yet, but from what I can tell that's going to change in a hurry," the dwarf replied.

Shit. "We need a new plan."

Giggling, Jenny opened the door and stepped inside.

"Jenny, wait!"

The door closed behind her.

Daniel, left with no other option, told the others, "Pull back. We need to see if there's a secondary entry point."

"What about her?" Murphy asked, eyes wide.

Giving the door a final look, Daniel said, "Nothing we can do about that. She's on her own. Let's move."

THIRTY-SEVEN

Willard watched in horror as the man burst apart in a puff of dust and ash instead of blood. When Moose cried out, he did the unthinkable. He sprinted at the killer, tackling the man to the ground in a heap of flying elbows and knees. Restraint snapped within him as he battled for his life, his establishment, and his love. Old techniques flowed back into forgotten muscles as Willard beat a relentless assault upon the dazed elf. Years of army training returned.

He flipped the man on his back and, snatching him by the hair, slammed his head into the floor several times. Blood spread with a fleshy thwack. Willard kept slamming until Moose's soft voice called his name weeping. Blinking as the battle rage left him, he crawled off his opponent and rolled the body over, ensuring to swipe all weapons in the process. The last thing either of them needed was to be shot in the back for being careless.

The man was unconscious, beaten into submission. It was then Willard spied the pointed tips to his ears sprouting through sweaty black hair. "Moose, look at this."

"What is it?"

He rubbed his jaw, the first lance of pain shooting through his body. "I don't know but I don't think this fella is human."

Curiosity getting the better of her, Moose leaned forward. "What have we gotten ourselves into?"

"Hell if I know, but we're not going to make it through the night if we don't do something now." Willard tucked the pistol in his belt and hurried to the closet. He returned a moment later with a shotgun in hand; spare

267

rounds jangling in his pockets while he loaded the weapon. Once awakened, that old army training refused to be put away. Slamming a round in the chamber, he hoisted the shotgun like a seasoned professional and pressed against the door while summoning his courage.

"We're not going down without a fight, Moose," he said. The words, meant to calm her, served more to bolster his fledgling courage.

A chorus of screams coming from the foyer brought a quick pause. Without knowing or seeing what was happening, Willard's knees started knocking. Sure, the Fainting Goat had a slight ghost problem, but nothing in their history suggested anything worse—until now. He settled back, unwilling to risk it until he had a better understanding of why so many were screaming. Perhaps discretion was the better part of valor after all.

***

Otero shoved Xander into the room at the end of the hall, satisfied with the fleshy thump he made impacting the wall. The princess followed at gunpoint, confident she wouldn't be harmed. The presence of the Old Guard below suggested the queen had other plans for her wayward daughter. Otero wasn't willing to cross that line, not yet.

The prime minister gave specific orders concerning royalty.

The fallen champion was a different story.

"Over there, in the corner and keep quiet," she ordered the princess.

Gwen slipped past her to snatch Xander by the shoulders and help him to the old rocking chair by the window. He groaned as he collapsed, the guttural sound in sharp contrast to creaking wood. The princess used her sleeve to dab away some of the blood on his face.

"You got what you wanted, Otero," she hissed. "What's next?"

The screams grew louder before Otero closed the door. She needed to think. To find a way free of the nightmare awakened below. Everything had gone wrong. From the Old Guard's arrival to whatever eldritch power awakened by their presence, the mission to collect Xander and the princess seemed doomed.

"Your men don't sound like they're having much fun," Gwen pressed. "Sooner or later that power is going to be finished with them, if the Old Guard doesn't kill it first, and it will be coming for you. There's nowhere to hide, Otero. No backdoor or escape route. You're trapped."

"As are you!" Otero almost screamed. Her pistol danced, landing on Gwen's face. "If I die, you die. Remember that."

"Oh, I'll remember. Don't you worry about that." Gwen's voice dropped low. "It's getting awful quiet down there. I wonder how many are left? Basil's not going to be happy with you."

"Quiet," Otero snapped. She began pacing, desperate to find some resolution to her dilemma. After watching one of her soldiers dissolve under the yellow haze she knew there was no weapon in her arsenal capable of stopping that power. Death, ever leering with mockery, lingered a stone's throw away. A wild gleam filled her eyes as a plan hatched.

"I don't need him," she said. "You're the prize. With Xander gone I can take you back to the prime minister and become the hero we all need. You will pay for your crimes against our people and elfkind will at last rise from the detritus of society to reclaim its rightful place in the world."

269

"You're mad," Gwen retorted. She folded her arms across her chest, planting her feet shoulder width apart. "It won't work."

"Mad enough to want to live," Otero countered, stepping closer. "On your feet, pretty boy. You're going to be the distraction while the princess and I slip out the back."

Spitting a mouthful of dark blood, Xander stayed sitting. "Kill me if you must. I've grown tired of your games, Otero. There is no place in your new world for me."

Stunned, she reeled back. Such lengthy periods of her life were spent hating this one man, for him to cease resisting and accept his fate robbed her of fulfilling the vengeance in her heart. Otero snatched him by the collar, dragging him to his feet before shoving him to the door and back into the hall.

Sounds of struggle and chaos dulled. She figured Constantin and his Old Guard were just about done mopping up her soldiers. Otero snorted. Basil's finest were no challenge to battle hardened veterans. If she only had such power at her disposal. Perhaps being Champion was no longer enough. Replacing Constantin at head of the Old Guard proved a far greater opportunity once Basil completed his coup.

Xander followed without struggle, though he did look back once at Gwen before hanging his head.

"Time to die, *Champion*," Otero hissed in his ear.

Gwen jerked, desperate to prevent what she knew must follow.

Xander nodded. "Yes, it is."

Before she could question his words, Xander reached into her boot sheath, pulled the combat blade free and stabbed deep into her unprotected armpit.

The blade pierced her heart.

She released him and reeled back, desperately trying to pluck the blade free. Rich blood flowed down her armor. Her skin paled. Centuries of ruthless ambition, always striving for the unobtainable, bled out on the floor of a quiet inn along a cold New York river. Inglorious. Unsatisfied.

Eyes crossed, she fixed Xander with a confused look. "But I won."

***

Crawling away as Otero dissolved to ash, Xander landed in Gwen's arms. She circled him with a warm embrace, resting her chin on his sweat soaked head. He convulsed, torment and denial freeing his emotions.

"Come on," she whispered after a few minutes. "We're not out of this yet. We need to find Viviana and get out of this damned place."

Viviana? What's she doing here? He nodded, unwilling to let go of her. "Is there a back door?"

***

Jenny slipped into the foyer unnoticed. All around her elves and dwarves fought and died. Amusing as the battle was, she found little interest in it. The triviality of elfkind did little more than get in her way more often than not. An eld creature from when the world was young, Jenny could not be contained by any mortal construct. Hers was meant to be the domination of all life. Yet instead of raw hatred so many of her kind fell to, Jenny decided on a softer life. One filled with mystery and wonder. Hiding from the animosity of violence, she strove to enjoy her days rather than despise them.

Until now.

Grasping hands stretched forth from the yellow mist. Icy fingers curling around her ankles. She giggled at the touch. "Oh you naughty thing. You should always ask a girl's permission first. Bad. Bad. Bad."

A pair of elves fell to the power blade of an Old Guard. Those few survivors were too far lost in bloodlust to abandon a losing fight. Armor and weapons cluttered the floor. Several half-devoured corpses were imprisoned in the floorboards. She viewed them dispassionately, for each soul fed the power of the inn.

Catching the grizzled Old Guard sergeant's eye, she said, "You should get your people out of here. It's not going to be safe in a moment."

The Old Guard commander stared at her. She could feel his instincts recoiling from energy pulsing off her. Anathema.

Watching him, she grinned when he barked an order and his squad disengaged to retreat into the driveway.

Jenny waited for the door to close before marching into the center of the room. The last elf died with a garbled scream, yellow mist belching from her mouth. Jenny found amusement in the creativity but little else. Hands swarmed her, circling like sharks smelling blood. She swatted one away and it dissolved with a psychic scream. Others recoiled, as if all connected.

Emboldened, Jenny kicked and skipped through the field of hands. Pressure built, threatening to tear the fabric of reality—she ignored it. Intent on defeating a worthy foe, Jenny relished unleashing her powers for the first time since dinosaurs walked the earth. The night in Roscoe paled in comparison to what she enacted now. Each hand smote gave her strength. Old temptations resurfaced, urging her to succumb and give in to her true nature. Delirious off that power, Jenny stomped an angry foot down.

The ground quaked.

The Inn moaned. A cosmic sound siphoning away through space and time.

Mist rose to envelop her. Fingers like blades stabbed into her flesh. She felt pain for the first time in memory. Jenny curled her hands into tiny fists and tipped her head back. Her scream matched the Inn's. The supernatural power enthralling the Fainting Goat fought back, unwilling to let go its hard-earned prize.

To combat this, Jenny allowed her flesh to dissolve, to return to her natural state. Focusing all thought on the enemy power, she allowed herself to be pulled down, deep into the darkness of the earth. It was here her battle would play out. Two titans seeking domination with nothing less than the fate of the world at stake.

These were the moments she lived for.

THIRTY-EIGHT

Daniel lamented losing Klaus' overwatch capability as he led his diminished team around the right side of the beleaguered inn and into a natural blind spot. Sounds of battle continued beating a woeful tune in his head. For now, that was someone else's problem. Running on dwindling adrenalin, Daniel felt outgunned and overmatched by the stronger forces duking it out around him. His once strong strike team now reduced to a disgraced field agent and gnome tracker unused to pitched firefights, had him again questioning his rash decision to join the fight.

His two best assets were sitting too far away to do anything if things went sideways, but he had been in less than favorable situations before and come out unscathed, for the most part. Rifle trained forward, Daniel crept around the corner of the inn and punched a pair of rounds into the lone guard on station. The elf burst apart as Daniel waved his team on.

"Murphy, flank right. Thraken go left. Shoot anyone on sight. We don't have any friends here," he whispered.

"I'd like to shoot something," Klaus grumbled over the headset.

Daniel smiled despite himself. Dwarves, he learned through brief interactions, had a way of getting under your skin and making you forget their natural abrasiveness.

A short time later they secured the rear of the building. None spied any sign of their enemies, though Daniel found it odd how a small john boat drifted down river with a slumped over man in dark clothes in the middle. Another unfortunate soul wrapped up in the affairs of elves.

"Now what?" Thraken asked.

Good question. Daniel looked around for an easy access point to the inn, but nothing presented itself other than a small porch on the far side promising a quick return to the middle of the firefight. The last place he wanted to be. Knowing Xander was within, perhaps already dead, fueled his inspiration. An old trellis looking far too fragile to support his weight, beckoned.

"Thraken, think that can hold you?" he asked, gesturing.

The gnome rolled his eyes. "I'm sure it will, but I don't want it to."

"None of us have much of a choice in this. Xander is inside. We need to extract him before a stray round takes him out."

"What makes you think he'll come easily?" Murphy chimed in; Daniel's gaze made him flinch.

"Just get up there," Daniel told the gnome. "Get eyes on Xander and, if you can, get him out here. Do not engage with the enemy unless there's no choice."

"I won't be around much longer if it gets that far," Thraken half-joked. "Wish me luck."

The gnome began the climb with nimble deftness. Daniel watched him move while beating back any sensation of hope threatening to spring forth. They were a long way from being in the clear. A crash to his right drew his attention. Head and rifle whipped around in time to see the last thing he expected.

Xander and Gwen were climbing out a broken window. Daniel glanced back to Thraken. The gnome had reached the second floor and was prying open an unlocked window. Too late to recall him without giving his position away, Daniel slipped across the distance to where descended.

Sometimes the sun shines on a dog's ass ...

Gwen dropped first, quickly rising to assist the wounded Xander. Once both were on the ground, she paused long enough to give him a fierce hug.

"Come on, your boat can't be far," she urged, slipping one of his arms around her shoulders to support his weight.

"It's farther than you think," Daniel called out.

Xander hung his head and started laughing. "You just don't give up, do you?"

"Not when my family is on the line," Daniel said. He stepped out of the shadows; rifle trained on Xander's chest. "You've done enough damage, Xander. Time to end this once and for all."

"I was never your enemy. Never once did I so much as raise a hand in anger against you or your wife," Xander countered. "Let me go. You'll never hear from me again."

"Nothing is that easy."

"It can be."

Daniel shook his head. Footsteps approached from behind as Murphy and Thraken collapsed on his position. "I'm done playing your game, Xander. This ends tonight. You are a threat to everyone and everything. One way or the other you're going back to your cell."

Gwen slipped between them. "Over my dead body."

"Relax, love. That phrase means little considering what happens when we die," Xander cautioned. "Daniel, did it ever occur to you that your vaunted government agency might be lying? That all you know, have been fed, is just a line used to keep you in step and me sidelined while bigger players take the field?"

Daniel paused. He knew better than to trust any government agency, but Blackmere had been more than certain Xander was the root of all evil and a plague needing to be stopped. Why he didn't put a round between the elf's eyes the moment he spotted him remained a mystery. Perhaps it stemmed from an aversion to pointless killing. He once vowed to never harm another living thing again after returning from the war. Seeing Xander reunited with the woman he loved sparked thoughts of Sara, alone and unsure of what was happening. He wondered how she would react if their roles reversed.

A primal scream from deep within the earth vibrated up through their boots, settling in the hollows of their souls like an unwanted guest.

Murphy rounded the corner but fell to his knees, vomiting.

"Time is running out. We need to leave. Now. Daniel." Xander resumed his place in front of Gwen. "We are not enemies. We never were. Sure, I tried to overthrow the king and queen, but that never should have involved you. It was a mere twist of fate that sent you to my sister's office the night the dark elves struck. This was never your war. Go home to your wife and forget us. I beg you."

"He's a dangerous man," Thraken whispered, coming to Daniel's side. The jangle of equipment announced Murphy closing in from the opposite side of the house. "Don't trust him."

"I'm not asking him to, gnome. I'm asking him to take a chance. It's the only way any of are getting out of this nightmare."

Surprised at himself, he lowered his gun barrel slightly. "What did you have in mind?"

***

"Come on, Moose."

Willard led his wife through the carnage, odd how there were no bodies amidst the piles of uniforms and gear, and out the front door. The shotgun in his hands felt good, a normal extension and casual reminder of glory days long past. They found overturned vehicles burning in their yard, scores of abandoned rifles and a host of spent shell casings.

Willard heard Moose sniffling. Their manicured inn was all but a ruin. What they'd spent their lives building brought down around them in the strangest experience of their lives.

The march of heavy boots drew his attention. Willard watched, mouth agape, as ten giants in resplendent armor filed down the road. The glow from their swords burning deep in the fading night. In their wake came a moaning wail. He and Moose turned to see the Fainting Goat Island Inn flare bright yellow and vermillion, then grow dark.

"What do we do now?" she whispered to him.

He wrapped an arm around her shoulder and squeezed. "We rebuild. I just hope the insurance company buys our—" Willard paused as an unlikely trio slipped from the back. He gripped the shotgun tighter after seeing each was armed. "Hold your ground. We don't want any trouble."

Their leader lowered his weapon and held up and empty hand. "We're not here to give any, pal."

"Who are you people? What do you want here?" Willard asked.

"That is a complicated story. I'm Daniel. It's unfortunate tonight culminated at your establishment ..."

"Lovely place," a smaller man piped.

Frowning, Daniel agreed. "Right, but our business is done. I wouldn't worry about any damages. The federal government will be more than happy to cover the cost and help you rebuild."

"You can't offer that," a man at his side muttered.

Daniel spun on the younger man. "I just did and if you open your mouth one more fucking time I'm going to knock your teeth down your throat."

Rebuked, the man fell silent.

"Sorry about that," Daniel told Willard. "We'd appreciate it if you didn't tell anyone about this. At least not for a while. Top secret operation and all."

Willard snorted. "You expect me to trust the government?"

"No, not really. I don't. But I do know no one is going to believe you," Daniel said. He keyed the headset, and said, "Slim, Klaus, the mission is over. Xander is dead."

They waited in awkward silence, one soldier recognizing another, until a dark SUV rolled into the driveway. The smell of cigar smoke filled the air.

***

A warm glow lighting Klaus' face as he appeared. "Where's Jenny?"

Daniel glanced back at the inn. "She went inside. I doubt we'll be seeing her again."

"What happened in there?" Nevada Slim asked, getting out of the truck. Daniel saw the elf's face was twisted in rage.

"I … I don't know," Daniel admitted. "Some powerful energies collided and just about everyone died."

"The inn is haunted," the woman, the innkeeper's wife most likely, chimed in.

"Of course it is," Daniel muttered. "That explains a lot."

A second car pulled up and Daniel waited for Blackmere to join them. The senior DESA agent wore a look of disdain when he got out of the front passenger side.

"Where's Xander and the princess?" he asked.

Daniel slipped a sidelong glare at Murphy before answering, "They didn't make it. A lot of strange shit went down in there and I don't know how to explain half of it."

Suspicion in his eyes, Blackmere said, "Unfortunate. I'd like to see the remains."

"Thraken, please escort Agent Blackmere to where Xander and the princess fell," Daniel asked.

The gnome bobbed his head and took off without waiting for Blackmere.

Rolling his eyes, Daniel looked to the innkeepers, commenting, "Like I said, government matters."

"I did not have my revenge," Nevada Slim snapped.

Wincing, Daniel said, "Sorry, Slim. There was nothing I could do. It happened too fast, and we were outgunned."

"You should have let me blow up the whole place." The dark elf shook his head. "At least he is dead. My father's death is avenged."

Daniel said nothing.

Blackmere returned a moment later. He looked older, wearing his age with a heavy burden. Daniel, for his part, felt nothing.

"Looks like it's all wrapped up," Blackmere began. "I'll have containment crews deployed today. You and your team did well, Daniel. Not the outcome I had hoped for, but one unavoidable given the unexpected circumstances. Tonight will send ripples through the elf clans. I don't suppose you care to inform the queen her daughter is dead when you return to North Carolina?"

"Sorry, bud. This is your show. I'm just hired help." Daniel gave a false smile. "Does this mean I can go home?"

"Head back to Newburgh. Turn in your gear and give a final report of the mission. I'll have a plane waiting for you by sundown," Blackmere confirmed. He looked at the others. "The rest of you will go through standard debriefing. Agent Murphy, you stay here with me. We have a lot to talk about."

He extended his hand which Daniel accepted.

"I hope we don't meet again," Daniel told him.

Blackmere grinned. "Remember my offer. It's on the table for as long as it needs to be."

"Oh, I remember."

THIRTY-NINE

Dragging herself from the mud and grime of the riverbank, Viviana Cal had never felt so abused. Every muscle and bone in her lithe body ached. She bled from a score of cuts. Her clothes were tattered shreds. Any dignity she once possessed was reduced through humility and the supernatural drumming she'd received. Spitting a mouthful of blood and detritus, the elf pushed up to her hands and knees and retched the contents of her stomach.

Once finished, Viviana wiped her mouth and eyes and, after blinking away the tears, took in her surroundings. Nothing felt familiar. Wherever she was, it was far from where she'd started. The inn was gone. As was the river. No mountains peppered the skyline. No dull drone of car engines racing down the interstate.

She felt primal. Free. But like all good things, Viviana knew this would never last. She was an agent of the queen of elves, incapable of avoiding her duty.

Rising on shaky legs, she sniffed the clean wild air and, gauging the direction of the rising sun, headed south. Some things just felt right. Shoeless, it was a long walk back to civilization and the inevitable conversation with Morgen on the whereabouts of her daughter. All questions she had no answers to give.

That could wait until she had a hot meal in her and the opportunity to shower with a change of clothes. The caw of a crow reminded her she had a long way to go before any feeling of normalcy returned.

***

The knock on his door came much sooner than Basil Kadis expected. Finishing the last of his scotch, he set the empty glass on the mahogany desk and bid them enter. In swept several Old Guard, armed and armored. Constantin Andros strode at their head, the ever faithful leader of the fanatically devoted. New scars adorned his weathered face.

"Constantin, how pleasant to see you again," Basil drawled.

The Old Guard fanned out in a semi-circle with Constantin in the center. "Basil Kadis, you are under arrest for your part in the conspiracy to assassinate the princess and usurp the throne. Have you anything to say before you are taken into custody?"

Basil's right eye twitched. A thousand thoughts swirled through his brain. Centuries of planning, carefully cultivating his agents and organization for a new era of elfkind. All crashed down around him. Wasted.

"What is there to say?" he asked, clicking his tongue on the roof of his mouth. "I shall present my case to the queen herself. Not one of her flunkies."

"Queen Morgen will not meet with you, Prime Minister. I'm afraid you are to be sentenced at once."

Defeated, Basil sank back into his chair and closed his eyes. His right hand quested for the hidden pistol under the desk.

***

Alone in her lofty tower, the queen of the dark elves stared out over the Raleigh skyline. Dark clouds gathered on the horizon, bringing the promise of a proper cleansing. Lines creased her face. She'd spent only a moment lamenting the loss of her daughter and the treacherous Champion of Light. A handful of tears mourning their passing before the mask settled in place. She'd spent so long locked in a role it came easy, but at a cost to her soul.

Thoughts of reunification among the clans entertained her as the stormed neared. The prime minister was removed. A formidable rival taken from the board. Nothing stood between her and total domination. But at what cost?

Elfkind stood upon a precipice. Should she push too hard it threatened to collapse. Push not enough and none of the loss and sacrifice from the last few years meant anything. Morgen pursed her lips. Perhaps it was finally time to set aside their differences and heal old wounds. A time to focus their attention on humanity and the sweeping tides with which they'd turned the world to their own.

Morgen ignored the door opening behind her followed by the quiet shuffle of feet. Her closest advisors, come to offer condolence and bring news of new developments among the clans. There would be plenty of time for business later. Tonight she chose to remember her daughter and her husband.

***

Kneeling before a gathering of nobles, senior ranking military members, and the queen, Nevada Slim felt ridiculous in a long tailcoat and tie. The only part of his ensemble making any sense was the haggard boots he refused to take off. His once oily hair was combed and treated, lending a respectable appearance leaving him feeling ill at ease. He missed the hat and the constant piece of straw dangling from the corner of his mouth like an old-fashioned cigar from a spaghetti western.

Hands trembling, Slim was forced to confront the one moment he never wanted. Today was a coronation of sorts. He looked up into the queen's stern gaze as she laid an ancient sword upon his left shoulder.

"Rise, Baron Visilias, and take your rightful place among the noble class," she said.

Cheers and scattered clapping broke out among those gathered, but Slim heard none of it. He stood in line.

Shook hands for what felt an eternity. Smiled and pretended to remember who he spoke with. All part of the grand ruse.

When at last the party broke up Slim was left standing alone with the queen. His heart trembled, for though she had lost much of her strength, she remained the most formidable persona in the clans.

Morgen offered a wry grin, holding out her arm for him to take. "Welcome, Baron. Or should I call you Nevada Slim?"

"Does it matter?" he asked.

Her laugh cut him deeply. "No. I suppose not. We have much to discuss, you and I. Come, let us have a drink and talk about the future."

Stomach in knots, he settled into a leather chair and listened.

***

Sunlight warmed their faces. Wisps of clouds peppered the deep blue equatorial sky, marred only by flights of pure white birds. The sound of waves crashing inspired calm. A sense of peace neither had felt in centuries. Lounging in the sand with rum filled coconuts beside them, Xander and Gwen held hands.

"Have I told you how much I love you?" Xander asked, eyes closed. He smiled as she squeezed his hand.

"You don't need to. I thought about you every day we were apart," she replied. "I knew we'd be together again."

He lacked her faith but wisely chose to keep that to himself. "We wouldn't be if not for Daniel. He didn't have to let us go."

"Must have been his sense of fantasy romanticism," Gwen replied. She leaned her head back and closed her eyes. "You do plan on keeping your word, right? No going after him or his family?"

He pushed his sunglasses up to his forehead and stared at her. Golden hair framed her bare shoulders, giving her the appearance of a goddess. "I never had any intentions of going after him. That's a story his government concocted to get him to play."

She smiled. "Good. I think I like him after all. Maybe he'll put us in his next book."

"Yeah, maybe."

Gwen sighed. "You know my mother will discover the truth eventually. This won't last forever."

"Quiet, my love. Let the future handle itself. For now, we have today."

EPILOGUE

Abner Grumman crept through the darkness with unusual caution. Caves were far from his preference, but he was a man who did as needs must. Slight of stature and lacking in looks, Abner made up those deficiencies by developing a cunning largely unmatched by the rest of his kind. Goblins, after all, weren't known for vast intellect.

The runt of his brood, Abner fought and clawed his way through life until it got him to this point. A determined survivor, he avoided honest society and became a thing of the past, a relic hunter. Reasoning anything was possible after watching far too many action and adventure movies, the goblin grew more resolute. A fortune awaited. He merely needed to find it.

Which led him to now, him in a forgotten cave in the middle of North Carolina, crawling through the muck and spiderwebs in search of an ancient weapon capable of negating magic and imbuing the owner with unparalleled martial prowess. Abner grew giddy with excitement as his foraging took him deeper underground until he came upon a rotted door.

Palms slick, Abner pushed the door open and waited. Elves were notorious for their schemes and traps and getting killed this close to the prize would only prove insulting. He reached down for a small rock at his feet and rolled it into the center of the chamber—nothing. Still not satisfied, Abner untied the scarf from his neck and waved it in the doorway. Again, nothing. Emboldened, the goblin swallowed his diminishing panic and stepped in with eyes squeezed shut.

A heartbeat passed. Then another. He was still alive!

Abner opened his eyes, taking in the musky room. Lacking decoration or style, the room was barren save for growing lichen and moss covering three walls. The steady drip of ground water beat a steady rhythm. Abner ignored it all. His gaze focused on the object of his desire.

Centered in the room on an obsidian pedestal was the fabled Sword of Grimspire. The how and why of it arriving in North America was a muddled tale filled with conflicting accounts. None of that mattered. Here, buried deep in the clay rich soil, was Abner Grumman's opportunity to become the man his mother never imagined him capable of becoming. A smirk etched in his flesh, he curled stained fingers around the sword and lifted it high.

"I'll show them. I'll show them all," he barked.

"Put me down or I'll slice your throat out."

Abner squawked and dropped the sword. The ground vibrated when it struck. Taking a step closer, he peered down at the ancient blade, certain he misheard. Swords can't talk. Can they? "Impossible."

"Nothing is impossible, but if you touch me again I will kill you," the sword replied.

Partly terrified and partly thrilled with the opportunity to put his claim to life in the angry demeanor of the sword, Abner knew life was about to turn in his favor.

Besides, what could possibly go wrong with possessing a sword vowing to kill you?

THE END

DESA and the Elves will return in:
From Whence It Came
Dec 2023

Pick up a sword and join the team!
Evil never rests and neither can we.

Warfighter Books

Signup for our newsletter today and follow us on social media for updates, new releases and more!

Newsletter:
https://www.subscribepage.com/warfighterbooks

Facebook: https://www.facebook.com/WarfighterBooks
Twitter: https://twitter.com/ChristianWFreed
Instagram: www.instagram.com/christianwarrenfreed/

Check out these other great reads by
Christian Warren Freed

It is a troubled time, for the old gods are returning and they want the universe back...

Under the rigid guidance of the Conclave, the seven hundred known worlds carve out a new empire with the compassion and wisdom the gods once offered. But a terrible secret, known only to the most powerful, threatens to undo three millennia of progress. The gods are not dead at all. They merely sleep. And they are being hunted.

Senior Inquisitor Tolde Breed is sent to the planet Crimeat to investigate the escape of one of the deadliest beings in the history of the universe: Amongeratix, one of the fabled THREE, sons of the god-king. Tolde arrives on a world where heresy breeds insurrection and war is only a matter of time. Aided by Sister Abigail of the Order of Blood Witches, and a company of Prekhauten Guards, Tolde hurries to find Amongeratix and return him to Conclave custody before he can restart his reign of terror.

What he doesn't know is that the Three are already operating on Crimeat.

CHRISTIAN WARREN FREED

COWARD'S TRUTH

A NOVEL OF THE HEART ETERNAL

Welcome to Ghendis Ghadanisban.
City of god-kings.
City in turmoil.

The god-king is dead! Whispers of murder spread through the city known as the Heart Eternal. His death allows an ancient evil Razazel to return and resume its quest to dominate all life. As if that isn't enough, warring factions threaten the jewel of the desert. The only way to prevent this is by a group of reluctant heroes to escort a young boy filled with the dying god's essence to the ancient mountain of Rhorremere so the god-king can be reborn. It is a quest bound to claim lives, for evil never stops.

Far off in the mountains, a squad of stranded space marines sells their services in the hopes of being rescued. Their search brings them in conflict with too many enemies. Forced to join the quest, it is a decision that may prove their ultimate doom.

Fate and destiny clash as agents of good and evil set forth to stake their claim.

Welcome, friends, to the Heart Eternal.

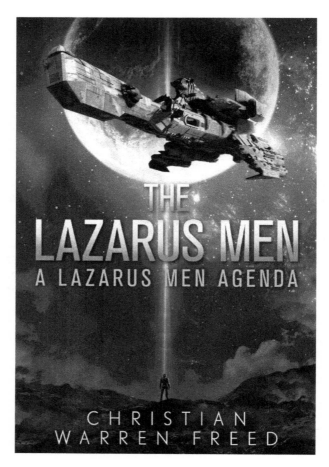

THE
LAZARUS MEN
A LAZARUS MEN AGENDA

CHRISTIAN
WARREN FREED

Welcome to the world of the Lazarus Men.

A thrilling sci-fi noir adventure combining the best mystery of the Maltese Falcon with the adventure of Total Recall and suspense of James Bond.

It is the 23rd century. Humankind has spread across the galaxy. The Earth Alliance rules weakly and is desperate for power. Hidden in the shadows are the Lazarus Men: a secret organization ruled with an iron fist by the enigmatic Mr. Shine. His agents are the worst humanity has to offer and they are everywhere.

Gerald LaPlant's life changes forever the day he accidentally witnesses a murder and discovers an alien artifact in his pocket. Forced to flee, he is chased across the stars by desperate men who want what he has and are willing to stop at nothing to get it. Along the way Gerald meets a host of villains and heroes, each with hidden agendas. If Gerald has any hope of surviving, he must rely on his wits and avoiding the one thing that could get him killed more than the rest: trust.

For he has the key to the galaxy's greatest treasure. Half want him dead. Half need him alive.

It's a race against time to see which wins.

AUTHOR BIO

Christian W. Freed was born in Buffalo, N.Y. more years ago than he would like to remember. After spending more than 20 years in the active-duty US Army he has turned his talents to writing. Since retiring, he has gone on to publish over 25 military fantasy and science fiction novels, as well as his memoirs from his time in Iraq and Afghanistan, a children's book, and a pair of how to books focused on indie authors and the decision making process for writing a book and what happens after it is published.

His first published book (Hammers in the Wind) has been the

#1 free book on Kindle 4 times and he holds a fancy certificate from the L Ron Hubbard Writers of the Future Contest. Ok, so it was for 4th place in one quarter, but it's still recognition from the largest fiction writing contest in the world. And no, he's not a scientologist.

Passionate about history, he combines his knowledge of the past with modern military tactics to create an engaging, quasi-realistic world for the readers. He graduated from Campbell University with a degree in history and a Masters of Arts degree in Digital Communications from the University of North Carolina at Chapel Hill.

He currently lives outside of Raleigh, N.C. and devotes his time to writing, his family, and their two Bernese Mountain Dogs. If you drive by you might just find him on the porch with a cigar in one hand and a pen in the other.